The Vendetta Tree

A Commissario Beppe Stancato Novel – Number 5

Richard Walmsley

Other titles by the author

The Puglia series
Dancing to the Pizzica (2012)
The Demise of Judge Grassi (2013)
Leonardo's Trouble with Molecules (2014)

Short stories
Long Shorts (2015)

The Commissario Stancato novels – set in Abruzzo
The Case of the Sleeping Beauty (2015)
A Close Encounter with Mushrooms (2016)
The Vanishing Physicist (2017)
Death Is Buried (2020)
The Vendetta Tree (2022)

The Curse of Collemaga (2019)
A free-standing novel set in Abruzzo

Puglia with the Gloves Off – Salento
A travelogue (2019)

*'Che un uomo può sorridere e sorridere ed
essere un furfante…'*
(Amleto)

'That a man can smile and smile and be a villain…'
(Hamlet)

**This novel is dedicated to our shared and
precious European culture and heritage.**

*This story is suitable to be read by anyone over the age of
thirteen – with parental approval where appropriate.*
RW - author

Prologo

Olive trees all over Italy tend to be a gregarious race, standing nobly in serried ranks like guardians of the land. But this particular olive tree stood in a bare stretch of countryside all by itself. The Gran Sasso mountains rose up majestically behind it – a snow-capped backdrop to this seemingly uninhabited expanse of nature. The olive tree was as tall as a two-storey building, old, centuries old maybe. It was gnarled and tough like an elderly *contadino*[1] whose arms spread out in all directions in defiance of the elements.

Commissario Beppe Stancato stood staring at the tree for the first time. He even walked the extra hundred or so metres right up to it, deciding that he might draw strength and inspiration by running his hand over its rough bark - a gesture of respect to its venerable old age.

It was all too easy to imagine the dead man whose body had been found on the end of a rope, dangling from one of the higher branches. Touching the trunk, Beppe could only feel its stolid resistance to the passing of time and to the arbitrary violence of mankind - already quite disturbing enough. Yet, its tree-spirit was moved by the nanosecond-long contact with this stranger.

---

[1] A peasant farmer : a granger

Beppe sighed as he walked back to where his two companions were waiting for him. Inexplicably, he found himself thinking about his own father. He vowed to himself that, as soon as this case was solved – if indeed there really *was* a case to be solved – he, Sonia and their two children would make the long journey down south to visit his family in Calabria again. It was high time he made up for his neglect of his family in faraway Catanzaro. His mother had almost given up phoning him in recent weeks. His infinitely patient father merely suffered his son's absence in silence – never uttering a reproachful word.

Facing eastwards now, Beppe could see other olive orchards, peopled by hundreds of smaller, cultivated olive trees – deliberately planted less than a century ago. Beppe prayed that the disease blighting olive trees in Puglia never reached the unspoilt *Abruzzese* countryside, stretching away into the blue distance.

The disease had a name - Xylella! The very word struck a discordant note - a malign spirit rising up from the crucible of an alien, pre-historic witch's brew.

'There, Beppe. Do you feel better after that?' asked his toxicologist friend, Bruno Esposito. Unsubstantiated reports that strange growths in some local olive groves had been spotted in the region where the hanged man had been found had prompted Bruno to accompany his friend on this tentative, preliminary investigation. The news about the decimation of olive trees in Puglia had spread northwards to other regions whose livelihood depended on olive oil.

The *commissario's* junior colleague and friend, *Agente* Pippo Cafarelli, was smiling to himself at the teasing familiarity with which Bruno's words had been delivered. The *commissario* put an arm round the shoulders of each man as the three of them headed back through the olive groves to the farmland and the scattered houses visible on the outskirts of the village of Picciano.

'Where on earth can we begin, *ragazzi?*' he asked under his breath.

'We can't do much, *capo,* until we have the results of the autopsy on the dead man,' said Pippo. 'We are presuming it was a suicide... aren't we?'

The shadow of doubt in his voice was apparent.

Beppe Stancato was silently shaking his head.

'*I* don't believe it *was* a suicide,' he stated quietly.

'And what makes you jump to *that* conclusion, Beppe?' asked Bruno Esposito tersely.

Beppe could hardly admit that it had been the tree which had put the notion into his head in a single flash of clarity. It was the sort of thing that, if it got into the local papers, would spread rumours like wildfire. He could imagine the headlines in *Il Centro,* Pescara's local newspaper:

'*Commissario discovered conversing with olive trees! Is our famous detective losing his marbles?*'

He wondered how Don Emanuele, the Archbishop of Pescara, would react to such a piece of news. Did talking to trees fall into the category of spiritual communication? Beppe might put the question to Don Emanuele next time they were in each other's company.

Beppe simply stated the obvious deduction which had sprung to mind only minutes previously.

'Who would bother to climb up on to one of the highest branches of that tree if all they wanted to do was to put an end to it all?' asked Beppe. 'Any of the lower branches would have done the job just as effectively. No, it feels more like a cached warning – or an act of brutal revenge.'

Bruno Esposito sighed.

'If it is any consolation to you, Beppe, that was precisely what I was thinking too.'

Pippo Cafarelli was nodding to himself.

'*Sono d'accordo con voi due,*[2] he finally added in a subdued voice. 'If it *was* a suicide, then why wasn't the ladder still there?'

4

'*Appunto, Agente* Cafarelli,' added Beppe.

Yes, there was undoubtedly a case to be solved.

1: *Groping in the dark…*

Commissario Beppe Stancato had a problem which he and his team had rarely had to face before in any of his more notable cases. Who *was* the victim whose lifeless body had, with some difficulty, been removed reverentially from the higher branches of the olive tree only the day before with the help of the *Vigili del Fuoco?*[3]

The *Questore,* Mariastella Martellini, had received a quietly spoken, anonymous phone call from an educated man who had stated it was his 'moral duty' to report that a body had been found just outside Picciano – hanging from an old olive tree. A suspicious death, the caller had insinuated.

'You should send someone to take a look,' the voice had stipulated. The caller had gone on to mention something about Xylella-infected plants being deliberately placed in a nearby orchard.

The elderly-sounding male had hung up – as if he dared not stay on the line any longer for fear of the call being traced. Mariastella Martellini had kept the recording of the call to play back afterwards.

The *Questore* had contacted an officer in Collecorvini – the nearest town to Picciano - which had a small two-man police

---

[3] The fire-brigade

station. In point of fact, Mariastella noted, the station was run by one male and one female officer.

The disgruntled male officer had been dispatched by 'that new woman *Questore* in Pescara', whom he had never met, to investigate the claim. He had spent most of the day trying to identify, from the scant information he could winkle out of the inhabitants of Picciano, where the ancient olive tree was situated.

It had been late afternoon before he had contacted Mariastella Martellini with details as to where the offending olive tree – with body - was situated. She had consulted her *commissario* and both she and Beppe had decided that he should take a trip to this remote village on the River Fino – taking Pescara's resident toxicologist with him, plus a uniformed and armed *Agente* Cafarelli for good measure.

The 'victim', who was only in his late thirties or early forties, had been transported to Pescara for the inevitable autopsy the day before Beppe, Pippo and Bruno's visit to the scene of the incident. The only person Beppe had spoken to over the phone was the officer from Collecorvini – who had told him that he, the *commissario,* would be wasting his time.

'It's just a simple suicide,' he stated with the authority of one who has already made up his mind that he should take the easy way out to forestall another fruitless day spent in this insignificant village.

As soon as Beppe and his team of two had returned to the village centre of Picciano after walking back from the olive tree, they had headed for the only bar in the main street. It was aptly named *L'Olivo Nero,*[4] Beppe thought.

The sight of three strangers - one of whom was wearing a police uniform – entering the bar was the sign for the couple of male clients standing at the bar to down their drinks in one gulp and leave the bar with a hasty wave of a hand and a muttered *'A dopo, Adelina!'*[5] in the direction of the young woman who ran the bar.

She gave her new clients a neutral, professional smile as she asked:

'Che cosa desiderate, signori?'

The three men ordered simple espresso coffees, which were produced with professional efficiency and placed on the bar with a flourish. She did not attempt to make polite conversation, nor did she query their presence in this out-of-the-way *comune.* She excused herself with the words:

'I need to see to my son's lunch. *Scusatemi un attimo*[6]*,'* as she disappeared out through a doorway behind the bar leading to her living quarters.

Beppe and his companions sat down at a table.

---

[4] The Black Olive Tree
[5] See you later, Adelina.
[6] Excuse me for a moment

'Not very forthcoming in this village, are they Beppe?' stated the toxicologist, grinning.

'I have the sensation they know why we are here and are instinctively closing ranks,' replied the *Commissario*. 'For reasons known only to them.'

'Why don't I disappear outside in a minute or so's time, *capo?*' suggested Pippo Cafarelli. 'The absence of a uniform might make the lady open up a bit.'

'Or, more likely, it will worry her even more because she will be wondering what you're up to,' suggested the toxicologist, Bruno Esposito, gleefully.

But Beppe nodded in agreement with his colleague.

'Buona idea, Pippo. We can try and see if that helps.'

Pippo got up and went out of the bar closing the door loudly. The result was that Adelina ran back out into the bar holding a four-year-old boy in the crook of one arm, fearful lest the three strangers had gone off without paying.

Instead, she was faced with the two men dressed in civvies – one of whom was looking at her with a disconcertingly steady stare.

'Do you own this bar, *signora?* Asked the one with the fixed stare. His voice was kind but his eye contact remained unblinkingly concentrated.

'Sì, signore. It belongs to my husband – and myself.'

'My name is *Commissario* Stancato, from Pescara. We are here because there have been reports of a man found dangling from a rope out in the countryside. I suspect you must be aware of the incident?'

The owner of the bar nodded. She seemed to be clutching the boy more tightly to her right breast. A wary expression stole across her face.

'*Sì, commissario,* of course.'

'I presume you must know who the man was? This is a very small place…'

'I don't know who the poor man was. I understood he wasn't from this village…'

Her voice trailed off.

'You have a lovely son, *signora*… Adelina. If you hear anything a little more concrete about the man's identity, perhaps you would let us know next time we are in your bar.'

The bar owner was more shocked at being addressed by her first name by this stranger, whose eyes seemed to be boring into her inner mind. The promise of returning to her bar had been delivered so gently. But he had somehow managed to make it sound like a veiled threat. This unusual *commissario* had a way of making her feel it was incumbent upon her alone to tell him what she knew.

The other man smiled at her and nodded as if to confirm her impression of this policeman. 'You can't fool *him,*' his smile seemed to imply.

'You *do* have a beautiful son, *signora,*' Bruno Esposito added as he placed a five euro note on the counter with a gesture which indicated he wasn't expecting the small change.

Beppe and Bruno turned round to leave the bar. Bruno's hand was already on the door handle when Adelina's voice spoke from behind them.

'You should try the house near that olive tree, *signori.* It's hidden from sight by the olive grove...'

Adelina's eyes were plainly appealing to the *commissario:* 'But you didn't hear that from me.'

Beppe smiled and nodded at her in acknowledgement that the message had been received. She had heard about this policeman's formidable reputation. She prayed that her momentary lapse of discretion would not lead to sinister consequences for her and her family as a result of her unpremeditated revelation to help this detective on his way.

* * *

At first sight, there appeared to be nobody at home. The three men had made the return journey on foot to find the house near the olive tree – despite the distant rumbles of thunder high

11

up in the mountains. The two-storey country farm house was well concealed behind a row of trees. Only a dusty vehicle track led them between a narrow gap in the trees.

What Beppe had been expecting to see – although he conceded that it was pure speculation – was not there.

'If this was where the victim lived,' he said quietly to his two companions, 'there is no *lutto*[7] sign in the windows.'

The only hint that there might be someone at home was the presence of a beat-up black Peugeot sitting nose forward in the space in front of the main entrance door.

Bruno and Pippo did a tour round the house to see if there were any signs of life. They returned to where the *Commissario* was standing, shaking their heads to indicate they had found no hint of there being a living soul inside the gloomy house.

'Somebody must be inside, *capo,*' said Pippo. 'I can smell something cooking.'

His chief was looking thoughtful, as if his mind was elsewhere.

'Like to share your thoughts with us, Beppe?' asked Bruno pointedly.

'I'm puzzled about that man we met as we were leaving Adelina's bar.'

---

[7] In mourning (a sign, always displayed in black lettering, in the windows of the house of a deceased person.)

'You mean that tall guy you didn't want to talk to?' asked Bruno. 'When you nudged me in the ribs to get me doing the conversation bit? Yes, Beppe. I got the message! Why didn't you want to talk to him? He seemed a normal kind of person – as if he was happily in charge of his life...'

'Because there was something about his face which was familiar. He looked Calabrian and as soon as he began speaking, I knew I was right.'

'Ah, so you didn't want to open your mouth in case you gave the game away – that *you* hail from Calabria too!'

'I was just put on my guard. He stared at me for a split second as if *he* recognised *me*. Whether he had seen me on the local TV station or whether it went further back in time before I arrived in Pescara...'

Agente Pippo Cafarelli concurred with his chief.

'He spotted me further down the street and he actually stopped in his tracks for a fleeting second. I felt he was wondering what an unfamiliar *sbirro*[8] was doing in his village.'

'Well, he looked a pleasant enough bloke to me,' repeated Bruno. 'And he did have an engaging smile.'

'A smile can often conceal the inner workings of a man's mind, Bruno. But you did have the presence of mind to be vague about our true reason for being here. *Bravo,* Bruno!'

---

[8] A cop

'Well, I know I accept everybody I meet at face value, Beppe. But I would not go so far as to tell a stranger what I was really doing in this town…'

'Yeah, telling him you were looking for signs of *Xylella* was a good idea.'

'Well, he almost laughed at that notion, Beppe.'

'Yes, but while he was still smiling, he was looking down the street at Pippo. His eyes were sending out a different message. *Why do you need a policeman with you if you're looking for diseased olive trees?*'

Bruno sighed.

'I bow to your greater wisdom, *amico mio.*'

Beppe went up to the door of the farmhouse and knocked with his bare knuckles. Nobody came to answer the door. A violent clap of thunder – much closer than up till that moment – drowned out any hope of hearing noises inside the seemingly deserted house.

'One more try, *signori,*' said Beppe. 'We'll all walk away from the house together.'

It felt as if they were playing that children's game *Che ore sono, Signor Lupo?*[9] The trick was to choose exactly the right moment to swivel round.

_____

[9] What's the time Mr Wolf?

'Aspettate! Aspettate, ragazzi![10] When I say 'now', Pippo look at the downstairs windows, Bruno the upstairs… NOW!'

What Pippo actually saw was the front door open a crack and the figure of a young woman in a nightdress peering momentarily at their departing figures before the door was swiftly closed again.

That was the moment when the heavens opened with a flash of lightening and a simultaneous explosion of sound which seemed to shake the firmament.

'There was a greenhouse in the garden behind the farmhouse,' shouted Pippo over the noise of falling rain.

The three men ran back and, soaking wet, took cover from the torrent descending from the skies above, which threatened to shatter their fragile shelter within seconds.

While Beppe and his colleague, Pippo, were looking simply wet, the chief toxicologist's attention seemed to have been caught by some plants sitting at the back of the spacious greenhouse.

'Hey, Beppe! Come and have a look at these. You'll never guess what I have found!'

Beppe and Pippo looked at the plants which seemed to have had the power of transforming Bruno Esposito's face from

---

[10] Wait lads

15

its habitual state of suppressed humour to one of deep concentration.

'They look like potted plants to me – with nice little white flowers attached,' said the *Commissario*. 'The kind that Sonia would leave out on our balcony.'

'So, what are they, *Signor* Bruno?' asked Pippo.

Bruno was looking ever more serious.

'Well, what they appear to be is ornamental coffee plants. They are typical of the kind of plant imported into Italy from all over the world – especially from Latin America.'

Bruno's revelation, which was obviously intended to be deeply significant, was met with a polite silence.

'*E allora?*' asked Beppe finally.

'There is a school of thought gaining ground, *signori,* that such plants as these are responsible for importing the *Xylella* bacteria into Italy. The bacterium is all too common in Latin America.'

'But what are they doing in this greenhouse?' asked Beppe.

'That, I would suggest to you *Commissario,* is a matter that you might want to investigate,' replied Bruno with a return to his usual mildly bantering tone. 'I shall take one of these plants away with me. I hope you've got something in the car to wrap it up in? Like an evidence bag, for example?'

The rain had been reduced to a drizzle as the storm had passed on heading eastwards towards the Adriatic Sea.

'Should we have another go at getting the woman to open the door to us, *capo?*' asked Pippo.

'No, I don't think it will help. She'll clam up, that's all. I think I shall come back tomorrow in the company of my secret weapon! But I shall have to clear it with our lady *Questore* first,' replied the *Commissario.*

Neither Pippo Cafarelli nor Bruno Esposito expected to be enlightened by Beppe. They were not disappointed.

'Besides which, we may have the results of the autopsy by tomorrow, which might give us a bit more to go on,' concluded Beppe.

2:   *The reluctant occupant…*

'Let me get this straight, *caro commissario,*' the lady *Questore,* Mariastella Martellini, was asking Beppe. 'You wish me to give permission for your Sonia to come out of maternity leave so that you can take her back with you to Picciano tomorrow?'

'Yes, Mariastella. She is dying to interrupt the pleasant monotony of being a housebound mother, and, as she says, do something professionally useful. And we have a young lady, who might turn out to be the victim's spouse, who is too petrified even to open the door to us. It needs the feminine touch, I feel.'

'Will Sonia be in uniform? I imagine so.'

'That is what Sonia would like, Mariastella, but I have the feeling that a uniform might scare the young lady out of her wits. It might defeat our objective if she sees a police uniform.

'I cannot see any reason why she should not go to Picciano with you, Beppe. After all, Sonia is still officially *Agente* Leardi, isn't she! Let's say 'yes' and see what happens. But you should stay with her at all times, *commissario.* That much you must faithfully promise me.'

'*Grazie, Signora Questore.* I promise – even faithfully. Sonia will be thrilled. It will be almost her first day off child-minding in five years. And Veronica and Lorenzo's grandparents can't wait to spend time alone with them. Veronica goes to her elementary school in Atri until lunchtime. She bosses the other children around most of the time. She says she's going to be a policewoman when she grows up.'

'I hope your Veronica doesn't see 'bossing people about' as synonymous with a policewoman's role, Beppe.'

Beppe graced her observation with a spontaneous laugh before pressing ahead with the matter in hand.

'I don't suppose we have the autopsy report through yet, do we, Mariastella?'

'I'll chase them up and let you know via a text message. Is there anything else I ought to know, Beppe?' asked the lady *Questore* pointedly.

The *commissario* thought he ought to mention their encounter with the 'smiling Calabrian' earlier that day. He thought about it for all of three seconds before replying to his chief.

'No, that's about as far as we got today, Mariastella.' After all, he was not sure that this chance encounter had any relevance to the case of the hanging man – even if his instinct was telling him that there might well be a connection.

The *Questore,* however, let out a mock sigh. She had noticed the pause before her *commissario* had answered her question.

'Ah – so there *is* something you are not telling me, my dear *commissario,*' she said as she hung up before he could attempt to deny the charge.

* * *

An innocent-looking couple walked into the bar *L'Olivo Nero* at about half past nine. They were holding hands and chatting together. Adelina did not recognise the *commissario* from Pescara who had been there the previous day. She approached the table where they had sat down near the window where the sunlight was pouring in through the curtained windows.

It was only when she returned with coffee and *brioches* on a tray that she recognised him. She almost tipped the contents on the floor.

'*Commissario!*' she said in a stifled whisper. A look of something approaching terror crossed her face.

'This is my wife, Sonia, mother of our two children, Adelina.'

The words were intended to put the bar owner at her ease.

Adelina managed a fleeting smile, immediately replaced by the look of panic which still showed in her eyes.

'I didn't expect you back...so soon,' she added nervously.

Instead of his fixed stare, Beppe smiled at the bar owner to reassure her.

'I wonder if we could have two glasses of water, Adelina?' asked Sonia.

Adelina nodded. Another fugitive smile, which still looked more like a grimace.

The *commissario's* mind was busy at work. He was thinking about the smiling Calabrian who had walked into the bar the day before as Beppe and his companions had walked down the road towards the house of darkness. He had been right to identify this man as a source of danger.

'She's been threatened,' he said to himself.

Before leaving the bar, Sonia and Beppe had approached the counter to pay for their breakfast.

'Don't worry, Adelina,' said Beppe almost inaudibly. 'We shan't involve you at all.'

Far from looking reassured, Adelina was looking at this police officer with her mouth open in shock. Her previous impression that this *commissario* was a mind-reader was confirmed. She managed a forced smile in Sonia's direction as the couple turned to leave the bar.

'Alla prossima, Adelina,*'[11]* said Sonia kindly.

---

[11] Until next time

'What was all *that* about, *commissario?*' asked Sonia as soon as they were outside. 'Have you been putting the fear of God into that poor woman, Beppe?

'Not me, *amore.*'

Beppe told her about the smiling Calabrian.

'Keep an eye out for him, Sonia – and be careful what you say to him. I simply do not trust him. Generally speaking, when a Calabrian makes an appearance in a place outside the confines of Calabria, it spells trouble.'

Sonia hooked her arm under Beppe's.

'I trust that this does not apply to you, *mio caro!*'[12]

The couple continued towards the far end of the village which led towards the house and the plain where the Olive Tree stood in isolation. Beppe took Sonia on a brief detour and simply pointed at the tree. Sonia shuddered once, causing Beppe to put a protective arm round her shoulder.

'I can almost *feel* that tree – even at this distance. It's a sad tree!' said Sonia, aware that her words sounded naïve.

'*Forza,* Sonia! Let's get on with the task in hand,' replied Beppe – omitting to tell her how he had put his arm round the self-same tree just one day previously.

* * *

---

[12] 'My dear.' Beppe is from Calabria - see 'The Case of the Sleeping Beauty'

Beppe and Sonia approached the gloomy house, almost entirely concealed from the outside world by the bushes and fruit trees which surrounded it.

Beppe knocked once on the front door. He was puzzled that, by putting slight pressure on the panel, it gave way. The door wasn't even locked. To his astonishment, the door was immediately opened from the other side.

The expression on the young woman's face turned in an instant from neutral to shocked alarm. Beppe's immediate impression was that she had been expecting someone else. Thus, the unlocked door.

This impression was confirmed by the panicky glances that she kept throwing over the shoulders of her visitors.

It was Sonia who attempted to take control of the situation before it got out of hand. The nameless young woman, who could not be more than twenty-seven or twenty-eight years old, looked petrified by the dilemma that the presence of these strangers provoked.

'Please don't be frightened of us. We only want to help you. We are so sorry to have startled you. I can see you were expecting someone else.'

'It's not just someone. It's HIM. Please go away – and don't let him see you.'

Her voice was pleasant even though shaky from the tension within her.

'Quickly,' said Beppe fiercely. 'What's your name, *signorina?* We're from the police and we want to help you.'

She began to close the door in their faces. Beppe was not quick enough to put his foot in the diminishing space to prevent the door being shut in their faces. It would, he reflected an instant later, have only made matters worse.

'Giorgia!' said a voice from behind the closed door.

Beppe looked at Sonia and Sonia looked at Beppe. They nodded – having cottoned on to the significance of the girl having imparted her first name to them.

There was no time to comment on their thoughts. A jeep – or some such large vehicle – could be heard approaching the house. Beppe grabbed Sonia by the arm and they ran towards the bushes and crouched down behind their cover, attempting not to breathe too loudly.

Sonia was trying not to giggle – a nervous reaction, she realised. She had not been expecting this level of excitement on her first day back at work.

Beppe did not appear to share her amusement. He risked a quick look through the bushes as a brand-new dark blue SUV pulled up beside the old black Peugeot. He caught a fleeting glimpse of the figure which got out of the car. He was carrying two shopping bags as he disappeared through the door of the house. Beppe let out an angry expletive under his breath. His premonition had been correct.

'It's *him!*' he whispered fiercely into Sonia's ear, unintentionally repeating the words that the young woman, Giorgia, had uttered a few brief moments beforehand. Beppe and Sonia moved stealthily away to where they would be better concealed. As Beppe had predicted to himself, the 'visitor' did not stay more than five minutes before they heard the car reversing away from the house and driving away again at speed. Nevertheless, they waited a few minutes longer to make sure that it did not return unexpectedly.

The couple emerged from the shadows and walked back towards the house.

'You do the talking, *amore.* She may open the door again if it's your voice she hears.'

It took Sonia a good five minutes of tapping on the door and then on the window whilst calling out the woman's name repeatedly.

'Giorgia. Please open the door. We won't stay long, I promise. Just a quick word with you and we'll leave you in peace.'

The figure who opened the door was, Beppe noted, an attractive woman despite the shabby, loose-fitting clothes she was wearing. The look of fear on her face stretched her face muscles unnaturally.

'How often does he bring you your shopping. Giorgia?' Sonia asked her quietly. 'My name is Sonia.'

'Two or three times a week. And then he comes and sees me at night time too…'

Her voice trailed off but her tensed features changed to an expression of profound distaste.

'He looks after me,' she added darkly.

'Can't you just drive off and leave the house, Giorgia?' asked Beppe quietly.

Giorgia shook her head. She looked as if she was about to cry.

'The car won't start, *signore*. He has done something to it. He doesn't want me to go anywhere…' Her voice trailed off.

'Until the fuss has died down a bit, you mean, Giorgia?'

Beppe had spoken the words in a clear, gentle voice. She just looked at this man with her mouth half open. But no words came out.

Beppe looked at Sonia and gave her an imperceptible nod.

'I'm going to write down my phone number for you, Giorgia. You can phone me whenever you want. Tomorrow, the day after…even at night time, if you need to.'

Giorgia took the slip of paper and instinctively tucked it down between her breasts. She looked as if she wanted to speak, but she didn't make it. Beppe gestured to Sonia that they should leave.

'We can help you, Giorgia,' was all she said.

The young woman watched the figures depart on foot, holding hands. She was frowning thoughtfully as she closed the door.

* * *

'What now, *commissario?*' asked Sonia.

'I'm not sure. We have already achieved what we came here to do...'

'You mean what happened just now actually represents an achievement, Beppe?'

'Oh yes, I do. We know now that Giorgia is the wife, or partner, of the hanging man. And we also know that the smiling Calabrian is involved in his death...'

'That is a bit of a leap of faith, isn't it?' Sonia felt impelled to suggest, despite her secret belief that Beppe was right.

'No, I think we both understand that it's true. But we shall need a bit more corroboration before we can justify taking positive action.'

'So, where to now, *capo?*'

'I'd like to take a look round the village,' said Beppe. 'Don't forget, there is *someone* – probably an older man – who thought it his duty to phone our *Questore,* and inform us of a murder. I would say it was a safe bet to assume that this individual is living here in Picciano, but doesn't want to be identified.'

'I had forgotten just how deviously your mind works, Beppe. Of course, you are right.'

'I also want to know if there is a taxi service in this village.'

Sonia was used to her partner's seemingly erratic thought processes. But, on this occasion, she needed time to absorb the workings of his mind.

'You mean taxi-drivers inevitably know about people's movements?' she asked.

'Something like that, *amore*. Just think about what we have discovered already. A young woman, who lives a few metres away from the Olive Tree where a man was found hanging, is scared out of her wits by some enigmatic Calabrian. Giorgia is being exploited – almost certainly sexually – by this man and being held a virtual prisoner in her own home. I know it's conjecture for now, but…well, you saw for yourself.'

Sonia stopped in her tracks as they walked up the main street of Picciano and hugged her husband lovingly.

'I'm so happy to be working alongside you, again, *amore*. It's an education. I'd forgotten what it was like.'

Beppe reluctantly disengaged himself from her embrace. His mobile phone had alerted him to the arrival of a text message.

He looked at the screen. 'It's from Mariastella,' he said. 'Maybe what she has to tell us will shed more light on the situation.'

Beppe read the message from the *Questore*. He had a self-satisfied expression on his face. He held up the phone so that Sonia could take in its content.

The man was already dead before he was strung up on the tree. Actual cause of death still not clear. Fourth finger of left hand cut off – after death! Reason? Buon proseguimento![13] *Beppe, Sonia. MSM*

There was a clear photo of the victim's face – taken by the medical team.

'Now, he has a face at least – if not a name,' said Beppe.

'And one missing finger!' added Sonia. 'How do you explain *that, commissario?*'

'I'm quite sure you've managed to work out the reason for that, *amore.*' was all Beppe deigned to add.

'I presume that it is no coincidence that it was his ring finger, Beppe?'

'*Appunto,* Sonia!'[14]

* * *

---

[13] Enjoy the rest of your day!
[14] Precisely

The little township had not taken much time to walk around. They finished their tour by standing on the ancient bridge and looking down on the River Fino as it flowed steadily by, as it must have done from time immemorial.

'Only human beings succeed so unfailingly in complicating life on this planet,' said a pensive *commissario*.

'If they didn't, then we would be out of a job,' Sonia felt compelled to add.

3: A tale of two old men…

'So, what now, *amore?*' asked Sonia, breaking into Beppe's seeming state of hypnosis as he peered at the clear waters flowing passively under the bridge.

'Did you notice a little side street off the main square, Sonia? It had a hand-painted wooden sign pointing down the *viale.* It had the word *Archivio*[15] written on it. Strange, I thought, to find a document library in such an insignificant little town.'

'Those places are usually locked up with a notice outside saying *'Open only on major saints' days'* – or else the curator is on a permanent lunch break.'

'Nevertheless, I'm curious, Sonia. Let's go and have a look anyway.'

They walked down the alley, which was so narrow that they almost had to walk single file. To their astonishment, they found the door of the pokey little premises wide open. A wooden plaque confirmed that they had reached the archival office. Beppe knocked on the door hardly expecting to see anyone inside.

'Avanti, signori,' said a male voice from somewhere inside the timbered room.

'Con permesso, signore?'[16]

---

[15] A little street : alley   Archivio – archive (document library)
[16] With permission ie 'Can we come in?'

An elderly man wearing a pair of ancient gilt-framed spectacles stood up from the desk where he was sitting behind a pile of reference books.

'I'm over here, *commissario,*' he said simply. 'Ah, I see you have not come alone. Excellent!'

'How did you...?' began Sonia.

'...know he was a policeman?' the man said completing Sonia's sentence for her. 'Call it intuition, *signora.*'

The elderly man was grinning happily at the sense of mystery he had conjured up out of thin air.

'*Commissario Stancato sono, signore.* You have probably seen me on the local TV station – TV Tavo – *vero?*'[17]

'Ah, there is no fooling *you,* is there *Commissario!*' said the man. Even standing up, he was still several centimetres shorter than Sonia.

'May I introduce myself, *signori.* My name is Leonardo Scafa – self-appointed archivist in this town. And this lovely lady? I presume she is your partner – whether in crime or not?'

Both Beppe and Sonia smiled at his unusual turn of phrase – so perceptive and yet witty.

Formal introductions and clarifications were made.

'So, I am going to be interrogated by *two* officers of the law, am I? What an unexpected honour!'

---

[17] True? Is that right?

'What did you mean, *Signor* Scafa, when you said 'self-appointed?' asked Sonia.

'Just that, *Signora* Sonia. I was in charge of Picciano's little primary school for all my professional life. When I retired, I set myself up as this seemingly insignificant community's archivist. You'd be astonished at how much history there is behind such an innocent-looking *comune*. Besides which, I could not bear the thought of being inactive for the rest of my life. This is my own house…'

'I can see that I made the right move in coming to see you, *Signor* Leonardo.'

'You may drop the title, *commissario*. You two have enlivened my solitary day by paying me a visit.'

'Can you also intuit the reason why we decided to venture down this little alley?' asked Beppe.

The archivist put on a pensive face – as if he had been asked for the answer to a complex puzzle. There was a twinkle in his eyes behind the spectacles, which Sonia noticed, were merely perched on the bridge of his nose without any other support except a scarlet cord round his neck.

'Ah, *commissario* – that is a very searching question. But maybe – I am bound to conjecture here – you were hoping I could shed some light on a certain centuries-old olive tree not far from here?'

'*Signor* Scafa – Leonardo – I honestly had no precise idea why I wanted to see you. But now you mention olive trees, there is one particular tree that I am quite curious about.'

'Coffee?'

The question, fired at Sonia and Beppe at point blank range, seemed out of context. He was on the point of replying: 'No, an olive tree.' Only after a few seconds, did Sonia and Beppe realise they were being offered hospitality.

'It will only be coffee made in a moka pot, I'm afraid. But it is the only way I ever drink coffee – and it will come with home-made biscuits.'

Sonia looked at Beppe and nodded. A refusal to sample the archivist's coffee and biscuits would have been churlish.

'*Grazie, signore.* A real traditional coffee in these surroundings would be most welcome,' said Beppe.

To their astonishment, Leonardo Scafa picked up a centuries-old telephone receiver, whose horn-like shape was dangling from a hook. He operated a handle which he spun round twice. A bell could be heard tinkling on the floor above.

Sonia failed to stifle a prolonged giggle, which did not appear to offend their host.

'Maria Rosa, we have two guests,' was all Leonardo Scafa needed to say. 'My sister!' explained the archivist with a smile.

'Now about that olive tree. Oh please, sit down, won't you? Those two chairs are antiques but quite solid, I believe.'

Beppe and Sonia were squashed together at the desk so tightly that they felt as if they would be drinking from the same cup.

'For centuries, it has been known locally as The Vendetta Tree,' began Leonardo Scafa. 'I have a photo of it on my computer. I am guessing that this is the tree you are interested in, *commissario?'* he said swivelling the laptop round so Sonia and Beppe could see the screen.

Beppe nodded. Like Sonia, he was beginning to want to smile at the situation they found themselves in. The distant past seemed to have merged with the present.

'The tree is at least three hundred years old – maybe four. When it was born – yes just like a child – it was a long way outside the confines of the village. Now, Picciano has spread out into the countryside and almost reaches the plain where the olive tree stands now. Murderers and witches were regularly hung from its branches – often still alive… I'm sorry, *signora,* I did not mean to upset you.'

The old archivist realised he had been speaking with some relish and he noticed Sonia's face had turned pale.

The sequence of events rapidly returned to comedy, when their session was interrupted by the arrival of an old lady clumping one step at a time down some hidden stairway. She was minute in stature – even shorter than her brother. She was balancing a tray in her hands which she placed precariously on the edge of the table. Beppe and Sonia looked in amazement at the ancient moka coffee pot which looked for all world like an upside-down teapot.

'It's an antique Neapolitan coffee percolator, *signori,'* explained Leonardo Scafa with a smile. 'And this is my sister, Maria Rosa.'

The word 'antique' seemed to apply equally to the sister who, nevertheless, managed a smile revealing several missing teeth before she disappeared upwards, leaving only the coffee pot and a plate of biscuits sufficient to feed a small army as a souvenir of her visit.

But the coffee was excellent and Beppe and Sonia politely ate one biscuit each – complimenting Leonardo on both coffee and biscuits.

'I could go on at great length, *signori,* but let me tell you about one story concerning the history of our olive tree, so you can see how it has shaped the history of Picciano. Once upon a time,' he began with an almost cheeky grin on his face, 'there was a man and his young wife who lived in a house not far from the Vendetta Tree. They had a whole orchard of olive trees which bore fruit every autumn and produced bottle after bottle of high-quality olive oil. The couple lived happily together, hoping to have children who would carry on the family tradition. Then one day, a man from another land arrived on the scene. But he was a villain. He had his eye on the man's pretty wife – but above all on their olive trees, which were much more fruitful than his own. One night, this bad villain decided to act. He beguiled the pretty wife with tales of devotion and future prosperity for both of them. But he went behind her back and brutally murdered the husband – leaving the terrified widow facing a life of slavery and subservience…'

Sonia was looking horrified again. She found this macabre piece of history too much to bear. She looked at her watch and nudged Beppe surreptitiously.

'We need to go and pick up the children from school, Beppe,' she hinted.

Beppe understood. He stood up and smiled at Leonardo Scafa. He had a kindly expression on his face which Sonia had rarely seen him bestow on a stranger whom he had known for such a brief time.

'I thank you for your time, Leonardo. I will come back and see you again very soon, I promise. And thank your sister too,' he added with his hand outstretched.

The two shook hands warmly. Sonia's handshake had been rather more peremptory than friendly. She had found the archivist's story disturbing for reasons which she could not quite identify.

'You should go and see the parish priest now, *commissario*. I am sorry to have upset you, *signora*. I truly did not intend to. It was a pleasure meeting you both,' were Leonardo Scafa's closing words.

'That was a bit of a waste of time, wasn't it, *commissario?*' said Sonia almost aggressively as she linked her arm tightly under Beppe's. 'He is morbidly involved with this village's past. I don't think he was even aware of the present.'

'I disagree with you, *amore,*' replied Beppe quietly. 'Just think about it. He wasn't talking about Picciano's past. Didn't you cotton on to what he was really telling us?'

After a thoughtful silence, Sonia gasped.

'*O mio Dio!* I've been out of touch for far too long, Beppe,' she said as the truth dawned in a flash of clarity.

* * *

'Bar or church first?' asked Sonia, hoping it would be the former. 'Why don't I go to the bar and talk to Adelina while *you* go and see the parish priest?'

'Because, *amore,* I need you by my side. Besides which, I promised our *Questore* that I would not let you out of my sight.'

Sonia sighed. The church, dedicated to Santa Agnese di Assisi, was just off the main square. The door looked as if it might be locked. Sonia was doing her best to steer Beppe in the direction of the main square. Just as they turned their backs on the pretty little stone church, which looked as if it had been there since the dawn of civilisation, well before the village had sprung up all around it, the church bell began to toll.

'It's a sign!' said Beppe, looking triumphantly at Sonia.

'I see you have grown conveniently superstitious just as I am dying for something strong to drink!' said Sonia, resigned to her fate.

They pushed open the church door and spotted the elderly parish priest tugging manfully on the bell rope.

'Must be time for the Angelus, I suppose,' said Beppe who never wore a watch. 'It must be nearly midday.'

The priest grinned at them and managed to shrug his shoulders to excuse himself for being otherwise occupied as he yanked the bell rope downwards almost to his knees. He managed to ring the first three of the obligatory triple chimes and then decided to give up on the remaining twelve, which were supposed to mark the hour.

'That will have to do for today,' the priest said to Beppe and Sonia with obvious relief at the interruption they had provided.

Beppe was certain he had heard that voice before – but when? And where?

'You came to see *me*, I guess, rather than the building. I don't suppose you want to get married, do you? I get the feeling you are already in that happy state…?'

The three sentences had been delivered with an angelic smile on his wrinkled face. Beppe suddenly remembered where he had heard that voice – only a couple of days previously.

'You are the one who phoned the *Questore* in Pescara the other day to report the man who had been found hanging from the olive tree. I'm right, aren't I, father? I am *Commissario* Stancato, from the Pescara police. And this is *Agente* Sonia Leardi. And yes, you are right and very perceptive. We are happily married in the eyes of God - and the World,' stated Beppe.

The parish priest led them to the presbytery without bothering to confirm or deny that it was he who had made the phone call. He sat them down at the dining table, just as three plates of salad, *prosciutto cotto,* a carafe of red wine and a loaf of bread appeared in front of them as if by magic, carried dexterously by a young woman in her twenties.

'My niece, Agnese – just like the church!' explained Don Pietro. 'She's a waitress in the local *agriturismo*.[18]'

Agnese smiled at the visitors and disappeared, with the words: 'Sorry, I'm already late for work, *signori. Buon appetito.'*

---

[18] Agriturismo – a farmhouse restaurant serving up home-produced food

They talked for over an hour. The conversation ranged across a variety of subjects – including the Archbishop of Pescara, Don Emanuele.

'What an inspiring spiritual leader he is!' declared Don Pietro. 'I try to emulate him as far as my limited spirituality will allow.'

This simple parish priest, who was one of those whose life had been devoted entirely to his vocation, finished up with the words:

'Most of what I know about the situation here in Picciano is sealed under my vow of the secrecy of the confessional. What I could say otherwise would be pure conjecture. But, Sonia, I know of your husband's reputation from the Archbishop. I am sure you will quickly fathom out what is going on in this village, without any help from me.'

'I think we have already worked out more or less what is going on in Picciano, father – *and* who is responsible. But as yet, we have no evidence upon which to act. *Pazienza!* We shall get there in time, I hope.'

'Is there anything else I can help you with while we are together?' asked Don Pietro.

'Yes, father. I would like to ask you for your assistance in unveiling what is really going on in Picciano.'

'It would be my pleasure, *commissario*. What do you have in mind?' asked the priest.

41

'I would like to hold a funeral service in your church, in honour of the hanging man - if you have no objections, that is.'

A look of puzzlement crossed the priest's face.

'You mean a *real* funeral, *commissario?*'

Beppe nodded. The priest's astonishment gave way to enlightenment. He grinned and said:

'Your husband has a very devious mind, Sonia. But I'm sure you are already aware of that.'

Officer Sonia Leardi nodded in agreement whilst still inwardly reeling from the words Beppe had just uttered.

'Nothing like a funeral to bring the skeletons out of the cupboard, is there?' said the priest with a wry smile. 'Would you like to set a date right now, *commissario?*'

'No, father, the post mortem has still to be completed. I shall come back and see you again presently. By the way, father, can you tell me how people get about in this village? I mean, is there a taxi service by any chance?'

Don Pietro looked momentarily stunned by the unexpected banality of the question.

'Ah, *commissario,* I see what you are driving at. No there is no taxi service in Picciano. But lots of people use a taxi-driver from Collecorvini – including myself whenever I need to go to Pescara. His name is... let me think. Yes, Gregorio Massaferri.'

Beppe was looking smugly at Sonia. 'I was hoping that was the taxi-driver you had in mind. I became acquainted with him during a previous investigation.[19] Thank you, Don Pietro – for your company, your hospitality – but above all for your courage.'

'Be very wary, *commissario*. There are dark forces at work in this small community. Please feel free to take refuge here in the presbytery if ever you feel threatened.'

Beppe and Sonia took their leave of this unusual priest and walked back to where they had parked their car.

'I think we should go home now, Sonia. Don't you?'

Sonia nodded in silent agreement. Her first step in becoming involved in policework after so many years' absence had reminded her poignantly how easily the shabby forces of evil can hide beneath the familiar face of daily life. She placed her left hand on Beppe's thigh and left it there until they had reached the safety of their home in Atri – where she could resume her uncomplicated role as the mother of Lorenzo and Veronica.

'Thank you, *amore,* for taking me with you today. I had forgotten what it was like working with you. Today has brought it all back to me very forcibly.'

Beppe simply kissed her and gave her a prolonged hug before they went into the house.

---

[19] The Vanishing Physicist

'*Grazie a te,* Sonia. Your being with me gave me the impetus I needed to get this investigation started.'

4:   *La pazienza del ragno…* *(The patience of the spider)*

'Why aren't you wearing a uniform, *mamma?* You don't look like a *poliziotto.* I thought you were going to help *papà* today.'

'That isn't a nice way to greet your mother, Veronica. And your mother is a *poliziotta,*' scolded her grandmother – correcting her grammar into the bargain.

'They both really missed you today, Sonia. They have never seen you in your uniform. I think they were looking forward to it,' explained Irene, Sonia's mother.

Sonia took one stern look at her daughter and turned round and went upstairs to their part of the house without a word.

'Now look what you've done, Vero![20] You've upset your mother,' said Irene, Sonia's mother, in a kindlier voice.

Both Veronica and Lorenzo looked as if they were about to cry.

'Come here, you two kids,' said Beppe coming to the rescue. 'Let me tell you what amazing things your *mamma* has done today.'

He led them out into the garden and crouched down to be on their level. He talked to them, telling them in simple terms what had happened during the day.

---

[20] Vero – short for Veronica

45

'So you see, *tesoro,*[21] he told Veronica, 'your mum did something really important when she managed to get the lady in the sinister house, who was too scared even to open the door, to tell us what her name was. A police uniform would have frightened Giorgia too much. That's why *mamma* didn't put her uniform on. But I would never have learnt the lady's name if your mum hadn't been with me.'

'But *mamma* is angry with me now,' said a very penitent daughter.

'I don't think she's angry with you, Vero. Just look behind you.'

Sonia had put her uniform on for the first time in years. It transformed her mother into a heroine in Veronica's eyes. Both children ran towards Sonia with open arms and got the hug they had secretly wanted. Neither of them spotted that she was wearing bedroom slippers.

'Sei stupenda, mamma!' cried her daughter.

Lorenzo simply stood with his mouth open in amazement. Then the five-year-old stood to attention and performed a military style salute.

The four went back into the house, laughing.

* * *

---

[21] Treasure – a term of endearment

It was much later, after they had finally managed to settle two over-excited children down to sleep, that Beppe and Sonia lay in bed analysing the morning's events. Beppe had had to tell Veronica and Lorenzo all over again about their exploits. Suspecting that Veronica would spend the next school day giving her own version of the story to her classmates – as well as to her teacher - Beppe had had to give a carefully vetted version of the story to Veronica and Lorenzo. But he was mindful to avoid the kind of outlandishly fictitious tales that he usually spun when making excuses to his doting mother for having 'neglected' her for weeks on end – as she always claimed was the case. Veronica would have been smart enough to see through his flights of fantasy and would not have hesitated to pour scorn on them.

Lying together, Beppe and Sonia talked at length about the implications of what had happened that day.

'There is something bothering me,' concluded Beppe just as they were about to fall asleep. 'Something in Picciano which wasn't there – simply because I wasn't looking out for the obvious…'

That was as far as he got before sleep took over in that magic moment of oblivion, which they so often experienced within seconds of each other. Happily for Sonia, she was not woken up in the early hours when Beppe suddenly sat up in bed and exclaimed out loud:

'That's it! The *frantoio!*[22] Where was the olive press?'

Sonia woke up to find her husband moving about just before the sun had risen – as he always did when he had had some revelation during the night and was impatient to put the thought into immediate action.

Over a hurried breakfast, the decision was made that Sonia would once again accompany Beppe on his trip back to Picciano – without her uniform on. Their children's desire to see their mother dressed up as a policewoman seemed to have been satiated. It was Sonia herself who asked Beppe what she should wear.

'Normal clothes again,' he had stipulated without hesitation. 'We need to find out a lot more about the situation in that village before we alert anyone that there is an official crime investigation in progress. *Pazienza, amore!'*

Veronica and Lorenzo resigned themselves happily enough to being kept in order by their grandparents for another day. Sonia's father, Roberto, offered to accompany the children to and from school – a less stressful experience than *nonna* Irene provided, considered Veronica privately.

'I feel safer when I know that *mamma* is with you, *papà,'* stated Veronica to everyone's surprise just before they set off for school. Beppe never ceased to be in awe of these

---

[22] Olive press. Good oil is always pressed and labelled by well-established, local family run plants

sudden revelations which disclosed what his daughter was thinking in the secret places of her expanding seven-year-old mind.

Sonia gave Veronica a reassuring hug with the words: 'We won't be taking any risks today, *amore mio* – will we Beppe?'

'Absolutely not,' he replied confidently. The days' events were destined to make him revise his predictions to some extent.

His vision of a day's covert investigation was overturned by a phone call from the *Questore,* Mariastella Martellini, just as they were preparing to leave Atri and head for Picciano.

'I just needed to inform you of one important development, Beppe. I have just authorised your friend the toxicologist, Bruno Esposito, to take a small team with him to Picciano later on this afternoon. He tells me that the little coffee plant that he took away with him for analysis was riddled with the *Xylella* bacteria. I understand that you discovered several such plants in a greenhouse belonging to the house where some young woman lives…'

'Bruno must wait for me before he goes anywhere near that house, Mariastella. That young woman may well turn out to be the wife of the murdered man. She's already traumatised enough.'

'Don't worry, Beppe. Bruno understands the delicacy of the situation. But the removal of those plants could hardly wait, I am sure you would agree. He will liaise with you at three o'clock. He suggested meeting you at some bar called…'

'It's alright, Mariastella. I know which bar it is. It's practically the only one in the village,' Beppe reassured her. 'Is there anything else, *Dotoressa?*'

'Yes, *Commissario* – since we are being so formal. I wouldn't mind an update on your progress…shall we say tomorrow afternoon? Here at the *Questura?*'

'I take it that is an order?' Beppe asked as casually as he could.

'*Commissario,* I don't give you orders – unless I am really obliged to, that is!' she said laughing, as she hung up without waiting for a reply. Sonia, who had been listening with one ear to the phone call, was smiling broadly.

'Our *Questore* really has got you sussed out, hasn't she, *amore?*'

Beppe merely grunted as they got into the car and headed – so Sonia was informed – for Picciano via Collecorvini - in order to renew an acquaintance with a taxi-driver called Gregorio Mazzaferri.

'You never know, Sonia. He might just be able to help us.'

* * *

As they drew up in front of the taxi-driver's house, Beppe was relieved to notice that the ancient FIAT Tipo, which Gregorio used to ferry his customers about, was parked outside in the road. But it was the taxi-driver's wife who opened the door to them. She eyed the couple up and down suspiciously.

'Good morning, *signora*. I don't suppose you recognise me. We met once a few years ago.'

'He can't take you anywhere today, *signori*. That car has an electrical fault which needs fixing.'

It sounded like an excuse which she trotted out whenever her husband did not feel like getting out of bed.

'I am *Commissario* Stancato from the Pescara police – and this is Officer Leardi. I just want a word with your husband, *signora,*' said Beppe showing the lady his ID document.

The revelation of the identity of her visitors brought on an attack of pure panic.

'It wasn't my husband's fault,' she began in a rush to get all the words out. 'He just drove off without thinking because he was late for his next customer. He will go back and pay for the petrol as soon as he gets up. It was just a mistake, *commissario. Siamo gente onesta!*'[23]

It was Sonia who poured oil on troubled waters.

---

[23] We are honest people

'We are not here because of that incident, *signora*. We need your husband's help with another matter altogether. Rest assured. He is not in any trouble as far as we are concerned.'

The taxi-driver's wife made no move either to invite them in nor to fetch her husband. Beppe put on his disconcerting stare.

After at least fifteen seconds, she appeared to cotton on to what was expected of her.

'I'll see if he's around, officers.'

'We will wait for him inside,' said Beppe stepping uninvited over the threshold followed by a determined-looking Sonia. She was getting back into the swing of police work again, she felt.

To their surprise, the taxi-driver's wife did not go upstairs to rouse her husband, but went out of the back door into the garden courtyard.

'She's heading for the chicken pen, Beppe,' said Sonia in amusement. 'Maybe her husband is collecting eggs?'

'Or more likely he's hiding there believing we are here to arrest him for driving away from his local petrol station without paying,' chuckled Beppe.

A very wary-looking taxi-driver emerged suspiciously from the coop and was led back to the kitchen by his wife. It looked as if he was getting a telling off for leaving her to cover up for his misdemeanours.

Unlike his wife, Gregorio Massaferri instantly recognised the *commissario* from Pescara. His face broke into a smile of relief.

Ah, è Lei, commissario! A pleasure to see you again after such a long time.'

The taxi-driver's relief was short-lived. His face clouded over again as he realised that the presence of two police officers in his kitchen might spell some more serious trouble than the problem he had inadvertently brought upon himself. The fear that some government official must eventually cotton on to the fact that ninety percent of his customers paid him in cash was a constant threat.

'Don't look so anxious, *Signor* Massaferri. We were wondering if you could help us identify someone. That's all. May I ask you if you ever pick up fares from Picciano in the course of your travels?'

'Oh yes, *commissario*. Far more frequently than in Collecorvini, simply because the bus service which goes to and from Picciano only runs twice a day.'

In his relief, Gregorio Massaferri's desire to help knew no bounds.

'I want you to take a look at this photo, Gregorio. Can you identify this man?'

The *commissario* handed him the photo taken by the medical team. He was holding his breath and noticed that his heartbeat had increased marginally despite himself.

'Oh yes, *commissario,*' replied the taxi-driver without a second's hesitation. 'He was a regular – always off somewhere. I took him to the airport or the station about nine or ten times a year. Maybe more.'

'Do you remember his name, Gregorio? It is most important.'

Names seemed to cause him more problems than faces. His features screwed up in the effort required to recall the information. Beppe wanted to shake him.

'CAPRIOLO! That's it! No, that's the animal, isn't it?'[24] he said, embarrassed by his own illiteracy.

'Come on, Gregorio,' said Sonia encouragingly. She sensed that her partner-in-crime's impatience might fatally undermine the taxi-driver's self-confidence.

'CAPRIOTTI! That's it!' proclaimed Gregorio, triumphantly.

'And do you remember his first name, by any chance?' asked Beppe in a kindlier voice.

Once again, the taxi-driver's face went into minor contortions.

---

[24] A roe deer

'I think I remember his wife calling him Daniele, *commissario.'*

'Ah, his wife. You mean that rather tall, skinny blond woman, I suppose?' Beppe shot the words at him.

Gregorio Massaferri's reaction was in total contrast to his previous performance.

No, 'spiace, commissario.[25] You've got that wrong. She's a very attractive young brunette – only about one metre sixty tall, I would reckon.'

Beppe gave the astonished taxi-driver a hug which almost produced an outburst of pent-up tears. The taxi-driver's wife poured the coffee straight into the saucer. She let out a little shriek, thinking her husband was being assaulted.

'Come on, Gregorio. We will take you down to the petrol station and sort out your problem. I'll back you up all the way.'

Gregorio Massaferri was beaming as he handed back the photo of the hanging man to this now-friendly police officer.

'Mille grazie, commissario.'

Gregorio thought he should add something positive to make up for his earlier attempts at identifying the man in the photo.

'Mind you, *commissario.* I have never seen my passenger looking quite so pale...'

---

[25] 'Spiace = Mi dispiace – I'm sorry

'That could be because he is dead, Gregorio – I am sorry to have to tell you. Come on, let's go,' said Beppe.

The taxi-driver's wife had to leave two cups of coffee and a plate of biscuits untouched on the table. She was looking quite put out.

5: A close encounter with the Smiling Man...

The presence of the *commissario* was rendered quite superfluous when the owner of the petrol station greeted Gregorio Massaferri like an old friend.

'I knew you'd be back today, *Signor* Massaferri. I know my faithful customers – and which ones are honest.'

The taxi-driver looked embarrassed as he shook Beppe by the hand. He had deprived himself of sleep and lost face into the bargain.

Beppe and Sonia got into their car and headed back towards Picciano, leaving the disconsolate taxi-driver to find his own way home.

'The walk will do you good, Gregorio,' had been Beppe's parting shot – delivered with a disarming smile. The *commissario* considered he had already done his good deed for the day.

'That was a bit mean of you,' Sonia chided him. 'We have to pass in front of his house on our way to Picciano.'

Beppe simply put his foot down and sped off.

'He can walk off his embarrassment all on his own. We don't want another stop outside his house. His wife will offer us coffee and biscuits all over again. It would be so impolite to refuse, wouldn't it!'

Sonia sighed. He was right, of course.

It was Sonia, in the passenger seat, who spotted the painted wooden arrow which was pointing up a partially surfaced farm track on the left as they passed the official signpost just outside Picciano.

'Didn't you say you were wondering where the *frantoio* was, *amore?* Well, we've just driven past it.'

Beppe braked the car suddenly and reversed it back along the country road at close on the speed he had been doing going forward until he had drawn level with the track which went uphill to the oil press.'

'*Brava, amore!* Without you I would have missed it altogether.'

'I still don't quite understand why it is so important to you, Beppe,' said Sonia.

'Neither do I, Sonia. Just a feeling I have…'

Sonia knew all too well that her husband's 'feelings' about an ongoing case were never to be ignored.

After a half-kilometre climb in second gear, they reached a spacious, unsurfaced parking area big enough for over fifty cars. Apart from two or three other vehicles, probably belonging to the owners, their car was the only one there.

The ground floor of the traditional country farmhouse had been converted into a shop. The spacious first floor was obviously where the family lived, Beppe assumed. They could make out a modern factory area behind the house where the olives would be pressed, bottled and labelled.

Beppe and Sonia were greeted by a young man in his twenties who looked unduly pleased to see them.

They must be struggling to survive, Beppe surmised – or else it was still too early in the day.

The shop display was limited to clear glass bottles filled with olive oil for sale, a table with open bottles on it with fresh pieces of bread in a basket, ready for visitors to dip into little bowls of oil. But there was also an appetising display of cold meats in a refrigerated display case.

'The products are all sourced on a *chilometro-zero* basis from around Picciano,' announced the young man enthusiastically. There was, however, a note of desperation in his voice, Beppe intuited. He looked at Sonia. Her eyes told him that she had the same impression.

'I get the feeling…' began Beppe. 'Sorry, what should I call you?'

'Di Sabatino – Tommaso.'

'The same name as the olive oil,' noted Sonia, looking at the labels on the bottles of oil on sale.

'Yes,' replied the lad. 'My dad's been pressing olives all of his adult life. We ran a sort of cooperative society on behalf of all the local growers…'

'Past tense?' interjected the *commissario*.

The lad seemed to be torn between anger and tears.

'Maybe your father should be present too?' suggested Beppe.

'Why? Who are you? What concern is all this to you, *signori?*' asked the lad, looking from Beppe to Sonia.

'If I tell you, will you go and fetch your father for me?'

'Maybe,' said Tommaso, battling between discretion and curiosity.

'I am *Commissario* Stancato, from the Pescara police. And this is *Agente* Leardi, my colleague. But it is imperative that you keep this to yourselves for now.'

The lad nodded, in awe of this man who was staring straight into his inner mind, it seemed.

'I'll go and fetch my dad,' he whispered.

The father appeared, looking unshaven and a little haggard, some fifteen minutes later. He looked reluctantly at the man claiming to be a chief inspector of police. In the end the father shook the proffered hand, muttering 'Davide Di Sabatino'.

'What do you want with us, *commissario?* We have enough troubles in life without being investigated by the local police because of some bagatelle.'

He was evidently on the defensive.

'Let me tell you what we have discovered so far, *Signor* Di Sabatino. That will save you the painful task of putting your troubles into words.'

'May we talk outside in the open, please *commissario?*'

'Significant?' thought Beppe.

'Of course, we can. We quite understand... May I call you Davide? It's so much easier, *vero?*' suggested Beppe kindly.

The owner of the *frantoio* merely nodded. He looked too anxious to care about how this policeman chose to address him.

The group of four traipsed in single file out into the open.

By the time Beppe had finished recounting what they knew – or had surmised - the father and son were looking astounded at this softly spoken police officer.

'You seem to have grasped our situation admirably, *commissario,*' observed the father.

A look of fear had returned to his face.

'But you are a Calabrian too, aren't you *commissario?* Judging by your accent,' said the *frantoista.* 'How do we know you're not...?'

It was Sonia who replied.

'Do not be afraid, *Signor* Di Sabatino. I am from Abruzzo – and the *commissario* happens to be my husband. All you need to do is phone the *Questore* in Pescara to put your mind at rest. Here is my badge and…'

Beppe fished out his ID badge and showed it to the man and his son, before adding:

'But I must impress on you both that our presence in Picciano is, at the moment, to be considered totally unofficial. Not a word to a single soul – *capito?*'

It was Tommaso who first heard the sound of two horses coming into the compound. He took one look at the riders. He had turned white with a quasi-numinous look of fear on his now pallid face.

'*O mio Dio!* È LUI!'[26] he gasped in terrified disbelief at the sudden appearance of the man they had just been talking about.

Beppe would not have instantly recognised the smiling Calabrian, since he was wearing a riding helmet strapped to his chin. He was accompanied by a dark-skinned girl of sixteen or seventeen whose jet-black hair cascaded down from beneath her riding helmet. Her olive complexion betrayed her southern origins. She looked broody and beautiful.

Beppe reacted instinctively. The words 'It's HIM' had galvanised the *commissario* into immediate action.

---

[26] Oh my God. It's HIM

'Whatever happens, whatever you hear me saying in the next few minutes,' he whispered fiercely to the little group, 'don't look surprised. Sonia – photos,' he ordered enigmatically.

Sonia had her smart phone out and ready within seconds as Beppe turned round and walked directly towards the riders with a broad smile on his face – followed closely by Sonia. The face of the Calabrian was, on this occasion unsmiling. He had not expected to see strangers in this place.

What Sonia had not been expecting was that the words which issued from her husband's mouth were spoken in a perfect Bolognese accent. The timbre of his voice had altered too. She had almost forgotten about Beppe's renowned skill at mimicking regional accents. He appeared to have acquired some knowledge of the Bolognese dialect into the bargain.

'Mo s'l'è bel, cal caval!'[27] exclaimed Beppe standing directly in front of the advancing horse, which the rider reined in at the last moment.

The Calabrian was looking threatening as he instinctively removed his helmet in order to express his anger at this apparent invasion of his privacy. He was too late to react to the clicks of the smart-phone camera pointing in his direction.

Sonia smiled at him and waved a hand in greeting as she moved to one side and took a photo of the girl on the other horse.

---

[27] 'Quanto è bello, questo cavallo!' – What a beautiful horse!

The manner in which the man dismounted and walked aggressively towards Beppe would have intimidated anyone else. 'What a handsome couple you make!" said Beppe reverting to normal Italian but retaining a perfect Bolognese accent. 'I assume this must be your daughter, *signore?*'

The man was smiling again but the look in his eyes was cold and appraising as he walked up to Beppe and stood in front of him with less than a metre of space between them.

'I think we have met before,' said the Smiling Man. 'Maybe two days ago in front of the *Olivo Nero* bar in the village. You were with another man. I remember your face. You never said a word on that occasion. That struck me as strange. And now you have the nerve to take a photo of me – and, yes, my teenage daughter. I take exception to your invasiveness.'

Beppe had difficulty keeping up the casual act but he was not about to fall into the trap of appearing to be cowed by this man, who stood a good twenty centimetres taller than him.

'Oh, I apologise, *signore*. We are just holidaymakers from up north. We want to capture the atmosphere of this place. You are obviously an important member of the community here. But, are you certain it was me you saw?'

'The man you were with came out with some outlandish tale about olive trees being infected with Xylella. What have you to say to that, *Signor…?*

'Balboni,' replied Beppe on the spur of the moment, quoting the only other Bolognese surname that came to mind - apart from the lady *Questore's*.

'Ah yes, *signore*. I do remember now,' said Beppe, forcing himself to adopt an apologetic tone. 'But I had only just met that man, you see. In the bar. His comment took me by surprise as well. Do you live in Picciano yourself? You would know about infected olive trees, I suppose…'

'Yes, I have an estate here – with about one hundred olive trees on it. I run a riding school in the village. Perhaps you and your partner would like to visit me in my home? It is the very big house on the hillside above the river. You can't miss it. I shall expect you soon. I assume you must be on holiday for a few more days. It would be my pleasure to entertain you and your partner,' said the Smiling Man in a voice of cool appraisal.

'Cocmel ban,' said Beppe with his most engaging grin, as the Calabrian remounted his horse preparing to ride off – business apparently forgotten. Beppe seemed to remember from his conversations with his boss, Mariastella Martellini, that the dialect expression he had come out with meant something like 'over my dead body'.

Sonia was talking quietly to the daughter who had dismounted from her horse. Her father had called out to her to hurry up. But she turned to her horse and whispered some secretive words. The horse made no sign of wishing to follow the departing mount or its rider.

'I am supposed to give this envelope to that man over there,' said the girl pointing towards the owner of the *frantoio*.

'I can do that for you,' said Sonia kindly. 'You can trust me, *signorina* – I'm a policewoman, you see.'

Sonia doubted that her revelation had been taken in by this girl. But she rapidly changed the subject, just to be on the safe side.

'*Come si chiama, signorina?*'[28] Sonia wasn't sure why she had used the polite third person question form. Probably because the girl looked physically older than the manner in which she spoke.

'*Barone*,' replied the girl.

'I meant *your* name,' smiled Sonia. 'Not your beautiful horse.'

The girl blushed and giggled at the misunderstanding.

'My name is Aurora,'[29] she said but my dad doesn't like me telling anybody what my full name is. But you are *simpatica, signora…*'

The smiling man's daughter seemed suddenly to be aware that her father had ridden off out of sight. She looked

---

[28] Come si chiama? Sonia uses the polite form of the verb rather than 'Come ti chiami?' The girl assumes Sonia is asking for the horse's name.
[29] Aurora – Dawn, in English

anxious. She remounted her horse and rode off with a wave of the hand in Sonia's direction. Her smile had vanished.

* * *

Beppe and Sonia – who had tucked the heavy envelope under her left shoulder – walked towards Davide and Tommaso Di Sabatino.

'That was a brilliant performance, *commissario!* I had forgotten how inventive you can be!' said Sonia.

'Grazie, amore,' Beppe replied simply.

'But, you know, that girl has something not quite right with her. She gave the impression of being…detached from reality.'

'Well, Sonia, I guess even a mafioso is subject to creating offspring who might suffer from some mild disability.'

Sonia looked at Beppe and realised he had had the same thought as she had.

'I do not envy her being brought up by that man!' whispered Sonia.

Further discussion came to an end as they reached the father and son. They were both staring at Beppe with a mixture of awe and trepidation on their faces.

'You are a marked man now, *commissario.* I have never met anybody in this village who has stood up to him as you did just now,' said Davide, the father.

'You will have to be very wary if you are intending to accept his invitation, *commissario, Agente* Leardi. The more he smiles, the more likely you are to come to some harm,' warned Tommaso. 'We know of too many people who have suffered at his hands. Notably the man who took his own life by hanging himself...'

'If I accept his invitation, it will be in the company of half the police force in Pescara, *signori.* Don't worry! And as we are being frank with you, I must tell you that Daniele Capriotti was murdered before he was hitched up onto that tree with a rope round his neck.'

'And the young woman in the house near the Vendetta Tree? She must be...?' asked Sonia.

'His widow, yes...' said the *frantoista. 'La povera!'* [30]

Neither father nor son had registered great surprise at Beppe's frank revelation.

'It is amazing what you have found out already,' said Tommaso.

'At the moment, I simply want to rattle that man's cage a bit. I do not want him to know that we are already on to his game. So... *acqua in bocca,* [31] *signori!'*

---

[30] Poor thing

Davide Di Sabatino and his son both nodded. They had got the message.

'That is why I took you out of the shop just now, *commissario*. The girl who deals with the customers is from the village – not family.'

Sonia suddenly remembered she had an envelope tucked under her shoulder which she was supposed to deliver to the father.

'I don't suppose this contains any good news for you, *Signore*. That man's daughter was supposed to give it to you in person.'

'As usual. He always farms out the unpleasant tasks to other people – even to his own daughter, it seems,' said the *frantoista* in disgust. 'He has a couple of thugs whom he keeps hidden in that huge house to do his dirty work for him. I don't suppose that he was personally responsible for killing Daniele Capriotti,' concluded the father bitterly.

'What is in that envelope, *signore?* Do you know?'

'Oh yes, *commissario*. It will contain a document which, if I sign it, will reduce me to being a mere franchisee of my own olive business. He will be able to sell every litre of our beautiful olive oil to whoever he likes. Presumably to the mafia in Calabria. I dare not say the name…'

'Then I will say it for you, Davide. *La 'ndrangheta.'*[32]

---

[31] Lit: Water in the mouth = 'Mum's the word'

69

Both the father and the son gave a start on hearing the name of the Calabrian mafia said out loud. If it was said at all, people usually spoke in a muffled whisper.

'We shall hang on to this document for you. If he asks you if you have signed it yet, make up some story – such as you had to hand it over to your lawyer before you sign it. He won't do you any harm until you have signed it!' said Beppe cheerfully.

'Coraggio, signori,' added Sonia. 'We are working on your side now. One day in the not too-distant future, we are going to catch this man and put him away for years.'

Davide Di Sabatino made a sign with his head to his son, who trotted off back to the shop. He returned clutching a bottle of olive oil.

'It's not much, I know. Not even as a bribe! But please accept it as a token of our gratitude that you took the trouble to come and see us, *commissario*. You have given us a glimmer of hope.'

Hands were shaken all round.

'I don't suppose you know the Calabrian's name? It is the one thing we haven't found out yet.'

'No, I'm sorry, *commissario*. He has never divulged his name to anyone. He does all his shopping in Collecorvini. He

---

[32] The word is of Greek origin – meaning 'heroism' and 'virtue' – no comment!

doesn't even send his daughter to school – because he will have to supply an official document if he does.'

Beppe was not surprised.

'But he did let slip one day that he came from Catanzaro – if that is any help?' Davide Di Sabatino added. 'But don't I detect a slight Calabrian accent when you speak, *commissario?* Is that why you managed to put on that perfect Bolognese accent? You didn't want *him* to realise…'

'Another thing to keep under your hat, *Signor* Di Sabatino,' said Beppe with a stern expression on his face.

Sonia looked obliquely at Beppe with the first hint of real fear in her eyes. Catanzaro was Beppe's home town – where his parents and his married sister and her children still lived. His 'escape' from Calabria to the relative safety of Pescara all those years ago had come full circle.[33]

'It was bound to happen sooner or later, *amore,*' he said as they walked back towards their car. Sonia was clutching Beppe's arm tightly.

'*Che Dio ci aiuti!*'[34] was all she said to herself as they got into the car and headed towards the village centre.

---

[33] See 'The Case of the Sleeping Beauty'
[34] May God help us!

6: *Agente Leardi breaks the deadlock…*

The silence which pervaded the inside of the car on the short journey to Picciano was broken by the sound of Beppe's mobile phone ringing.

'Can you see who that is, *amore?*' asked Beppe, glad of the excuse to break the tension in the air. Sonia extracted the phone from Beppe's pocket and looked at the screen.

'It's Mariastella,' said Sonia, touching the green icon without waiting for Beppe's say-so.

'Buongiorno, Signora Questore. Io sono Sonia. Beppe is driving at the moment…'

'It's a pleasure to hear your voice again after such a long time, Sonia. May I give *you* the update?'

'With pleasure, Mariastella,' replied Sonia, looking sideways at Beppe with an eyebrow raised. Beppe was driving purposefully along the main street looking out for a parking spot and did not seem to register Sonia's querying glance.

'The man found hanging from the tree was killed by a bullet from a small calibre revolver in the back of his head – mafia style. There was evidence of his hands having been tied behind his back. We didn't spot the bullet hole straight away because his healthy head of hair concealed the point of entry. He had been 'cleaned up' by whoever killed him before hanging him up on the tree…'

Sonia had been shocked into silence.

'Are you still there, Sonia?' asked the *Questore* anxiously.

'*Sissignora. Mi scusi…*'

'Are you alright, Sonia? You sound very shocked.'

'I'm fine, Mariastella. We have had a very busy morning, that's all,' she replied.

The lady *Questore* understood instantly that something had happened to disturb Sonia's equilibrium.

'Would you be able to accompany Beppe to Pescara tomorrow morning, Sonia? As you know, I am meeting Beppe for an update. It would be more meaningful if you were there too.'

'*Grazie,* Mariastella. It will be a pleasure,' replied Sonia.

Beppe, who had parked the car, smiled at Sonia and placed a reassuring hand on her thigh. By the look on his face, it was apparent to Sonia that she was not the only one who sought reassurance.

The couple got out of the car and walked up towards the street towards the *Olivo Nero.*

'We both need that strong drink today, Sonia,' he said calmly. There was no need for them to discuss the implications of the revelation that the Smiling Man had his roots in Catanzaro.

* * *

Adelina's face had briefly lit up as Beppe and Sonia entered the bar. But the guarded look of fear soon re-established itself. She placed the coffees and two glasses of grappa on their table and made as if to walk back towards the bar.

'Are you expecting a visit from someone?' asked Beppe gently, looking at Adelina straight in the eye.

The bar owner shrugged her shoulders.

'*Non si sa mai, signori.*[35] He turns up when he feels like it.'

'Please sit down for a minute, Adelina. There is something that we have to tell you. It won't take a minute.'

It was Sonia who had spoken to Adelina, in a firm but reassuring voice.

When Adelina had sat down, perched on the very edge of the chair, Sonia began talking in a confidential voice, leaning forward towards the woman so that her voice was little more than a whisper.

'We have just met the man who you are so scared of. We know who he is. You are right to be afraid, Adelina. He comes from the same town as the *commissario* grew up in. For now, he believes we are just visitors to this town. The *commissario* – my husband – tricked him into thinking he is from Bologna...'

---

[35] One never knows

Was that just the hint of amusement in her eyes that Beppe picked up as Adelina shot Beppe a rapid glance?

'If he should come in while we are here, just act as if you know nothing, Adelina.'

It was Beppe who had spoken.

'He will find out soon enough who I am. Protect yourself by feigning ignorance, Adelina. Does our friend have a name?' Beppe asked as casually as he could.

'He likes being called Don Giulio,[36]' said Adelina. 'He has never revealed his family name to anyone.'

For obvious reasons, concluded Beppe.

'How long has he been living here, Adelina?' interjected Sonia.

'About six months, *signori.* It seems like an eternity.'

'*Grazie mille,* Adelina. You are very courageous. Let's hope you will not need to be in this situation for much longer,' said Beppe in the stage whisper in which the brief conversation had taken place.

'Now, Adelina, it's nearly lunchtime. Do you think you could bring us something to eat and drink, please?'

It was Sonia who had made the request in a normal voice. Customers were beginning to arrive and Adelina had shot to her feet as soon as she had heard the door opening.

---

[36] 'Don' is a title applied to priests and mafia bosses alike.

'*Subito, signori!*' said Adelina, managing a smile for the first time as she addressed her 'normal' customers.

While they were awaiting their food, Beppe got Sonia to send the photos she had taken back at the *frantoio* to *his* phone.

'Let's send the photos of the Smiling Man to Pippo. He should be able to identify who this 'Don Giulio' really is.'

It was Sonia who sent two of the clearer pictures she had taken to their colleague, Officer Cafarelli – with the injunction that it was '*urgentissimo*'. *Assume he is from Catanzaro,* Sonia had added.

Beppe phoned his colleague, the toxicologist, in the hope of moving forward the planned operation to remove the Xylella-ridden plants from the greenhouse as soon as possible.

'We have got as far as Collecorvini, Beppe. It was a bit too early to arrive in Picciano, so me and the two lads decided to stop for lunch here in the supermarket cafeteria.'

Beppe grunted. Other people's need to have lunch irked the *commissario* no end when he had become involved in an investigation.

'Make it a quick one then,' said Beppe tersely. 'We'll meet you down the main road from the *Olivo Nero.*'

'*Pazienza, amico mio!*' replied an unruffled Bruno Esposito. He knew his friend the *commissario* all too well. 'The planet will still be revolving round the sun by the time we reach you. *Buon appetito* to you too, Beppe!'

'Do you by any chance have a spare bio-suit with you in the van, Bruno?'

It was Sonia who had put the question to the chief toxicologist. She and Beppe had discussed over lunch how they would both be best employed during the removal of the infected plants in the greenhouse. Beppe had considered it might be a good idea to extend their search to the olive groves belonging to the late Daniele Capriotti.

'You should be there to reassure Giorgia. She will, I imagine, be terrified if she sees men walking round her property with bio-suits on. She might imagine the Aliens have landed.'

'But I shall need a disguise just in case the Smiling Man decides to pay a visit while we are there, *vero,* Beppe?'

'*Brava,* Sonia. You might want to try talking to Giorgia again. There's still a lot we don't understand and she will be a vital witness if ever we get that far...' stated Beppe, who inevitably had begun to grasp just how hazardous their investigation was likely to become.

'And what will *you* be doing?' Sonia asked with a feeling of foreboding that he would be on his own – the one aspect of any investigation which she feared most. 'You have to remember you promised not to take on the role of the lone hero again!'

Beppe smiled.

'Have no worries on that score, *amore*. I promise that the only person I shall confront will be the parish priest, Don Pietro. I have a very special funeral to arrange.'

Sonia knew better than to ask for details – at least until they were back home and the children had been lulled into a state of slumber. Even then, there would be no guarantee of enlightenment until Beppe himself had come to terms with his own extravagant schemes.

* * *

'You don't happen to have a spare cassock that would fit me, do you, Don Pietro?' the *commissario* asked the parish priest after they had discussed the mundane issues involved with arranging a funeral. Don Pietro was a good fifteen centimetres shorter than Beppe.

'Oh, I am sure there must be an old cassock or two belonging to one of my predecessors, *commissario*. I'll see what I can unearth. Are you intending to impersonate a member of the priesthood, by any chance? Isn't that a crime?'

The old priest was obviously highly amused by this notion.

'Well, yes, *padre,* I guess you have a point. But the only alternative would be for you to impersonate a member of the police force!'

The parish priest laughed gleefully at the suggestion.

'I would most certainly be a retired policeman – and one who had shrunk to well below the minimum height required for the job, *commissario* – as much as I would like the change from being a priest,' Don Pietro replied with feeling. 'But why…?

'I have not worked out the details of the service as yet, Don Pietro. But the ceremony is certain to put the cat among the pigeons!'[37]

'I think you may be right there, *commissario*…'

* * *

On looking out of her kitchen window, Giorgia Scarpa was terrified to see three men in extra-terrestrial space suits walking into the greenhouse. In the same instant, she heard someone knocking on her door and calling out her name.

'Giorgia… Georgia… It's Sonia, the police officer. You remember me, don't you? Please don't be scared. Open the door and let me in PLEASE! I need to talk to you. There is nothing to be anxious about…'

---

[37] Scatenare un putiferio / finimondo (polite): Fare un casino (colloquial) For those of you who are linguistically curious.

Giorgia overcame her state of petrification and managed to let her visitor in as Sonia detached the face-gear from the bio-suit.

'Giorgia, thank you. If that man arrives, just act as if you are trying to get rid of me. We know who he is now because we talked to Davide Di Sabatino, the *frantoista,* just an hour ago. My colleagues outside are removing those plants from the greenhouse. They may be infected.'

'I wasn't sure what they were, Sonia. I put them in the greenhouse myself after my husband...'

Giorgia had begun to talk normally, Sonia noticed with relief, until she had reminded herself of her loss.

The tears began to flow – probably for the first time in company since the trauma of her husband's death, Sonia understood. She hugged the weeping girl until the wailing became mere sobs.

What had shocked Sonia most was the realisation that Giorgia appeared to be unaware of the fact that her husband had been murdered. Sonia debated with herself and decided it would be better to break the news to this young woman without delay. That way she would understand that her husband had not taken his own life, which is what had driven her to her present state of despair.

'Giorgia…I think you should know one thing. Daniele did not desert you. He was murdered by that man and his cronies.'

Giorgia burst into a fresh flood of tears. But Sonia detected a note of secret relief amidst the tears, as she consoled her again with a protracted hug, rocking her gently from side to side.

They began talking. Sonia had just got round to telling Giorgia about their encounter with 'The Smiling Man' earlier on, when Bruno Esposito arrived at the door. They had finished their exploration of the olive groves and were ready to leave.

'Try to be brave for just a little longer, Giorgia. We don't want HIM to know we are onto what he is doing just yet. But soon we shall take you away and put you in a safe hiding place.'

'But where *is* he, Sonia?' sobbed Giorgia.

The sensitive Sonia realised just in time that Giorgia was referring to her husband.

'He is still with the medical team. My husband, the *commissario,* is going to organise a special funeral for Daniele. He is not going to rest until this Don Giulio is behind bars, Giorgia.'

The next thing Sonia knew was that she was being hugged warmly by this troubled soul.

'*Meno male che ci sei tu!*[38] Sonia,' said Giorgia with renewed tears of relief.

* * *

In the end, it was Beppe who returned well before the four 'bio-suits' walked back up the road to where their van and Beppe's car were parked.

A good disguise, thought Beppe. Except for the fact, he noted, that even with those shapeless medical garments on, it was always possible to distinguish the manner in which a woman's gait is so different to that of a man.

Sonia looked very glad to have removed the cumbersome suit as Beppe got out of his car and walked towards the forensic team.

'No Smiling Man, as you feared, Beppe,' said Bruno. 'We've bagged the remaining plants – including one which was still hidden under one of the olive trees in the orchard. I shall have to check it out in case we need to treat the trees nearby. Sonia will tell you her side of the story on your way home, I am sure…'

'*Grazie infinite, ragazzi,*' said Beppe to Bruno and his team as they shook un-gloved hands all round.

---

[38] Just as well you are here for me

'*Andiamo a casa,*[39] Beppe,' said Sonia decisively, as they got into the car. Beppe did not need persuading. They had left Picciano several kilometres behind them before Sonia related what had happened in Giorgia's house.

'I'm glad I went along with the men, Beppe. I did manage to get Giorgia to confide in me – although she is still very reluctant to go into details. She is a traumatised soul. We need to get her out of the whole environment as soon as we can persuade her to leave.'

'So, what *did* she tell you, Sonia?'

Sonia told him in detail.

'Most of the time was taken up shedding tears. I think she has been too shocked to react to Daniele's death to find the time to grieve properly – and she never really had anyone to turn to.'

'*Brava,* Sonia!'

'Incidently, Beppe. I did ask her if her husband wore a distinctive ring on his finger. She told me it was the wedding ring his father had worn. The inside of the ring was engraved with the father's name. I simply prayed she would not ask me there and then if she could have the ring back…'

'You mean, she did not ask you that question, Sonia?'

Sonia shook her head. She did not see the puzzled look which had briefly crossed Beppe's face.

---

[39] Let's go home

Beppe pulled into the forecourt of a rural petrol station and hugged her.

'I could not have achieved any of this if you had not accompanied me over these last two days, *amore*. You do know that don't you?'

'Why the past tense, *commissario?*' was the terse reply.

'Because, from now on, I think you should stay safe – for the sake of our children.'

'I am coming with you to Pescara tomorrow for our meeting with Mariastella…'

'You do not need to feel obliged to…'

'On *her* invitation!' stated Sonia in a voice which clearly indicated that the decision was out of Beppe's hands.

7:   *Mariastella Martellini lays down the law...*

'I'm glad you are here today, Sonia. Quite apart from the pleasure of seeing you back in Via Pesaro,[40] your presence will guarantee I get the full version of the story!'

These words were spoken by the *Questore* accompanied by a playful glint in her eyes as she looked challengingly at her second-in-command.

The *commissario* let out a profound sigh, betraying what he was feeling inside. Mariastella was taken aback by this unaccustomed reaction to their customary banter.

'I assure you, Mariastella, I have no desire to conceal any aspect of this investigation from you,' said Beppe solemnly.

Before heading for the *Questore's* upstairs office, Beppe had been greeted by an anxious Pippo Cafarelli.

'I have found out the identity of the Smiling Man, as you refer to him. You're not going to like this, *commissario...*'

'I think I already know roughly what you are about to tell me, Pippo. So, out with it!'

'His name is Giulio Spanò. He belongs to one of the *'ndrangheta* clans which operate in and around your home town...Catanzaro. I am sure you must have come across that name in the past...'

---

[40] The street in Pescara where the Questura is situated.

Pippo's voice petered out as he saw the look on Beppe's face.

Beppe felt a spasm of dread on learning the identity of the Smiling Man. His escape from Calabria all those years ago had come full circle.

'Thank you, Pippo. It is just as I feared.'

Pippo looked sympathetically at his friend and chief.

'You will have to be very cautious and watchful from now on, Beppe,' said Pippo quietly. Pippo could sympathise with Beppe. He too had escaped from the Pugliese mob in Foggia well before Beppe's arrival in Pescara. He too had had to face up to his worst fears being realised during the course of a previous investigation shared with Beppe. He had protected his chief's identity by pretending *he* was the *commissario*. Pippo had been shot in the knee for his pains by a member of the Pugliese mafia. He still walked with a slight limp as a result of the encounter.[41]

'It's not *me* I am worried about, Pippo,' was all Beppe had added before heading upstairs to re-join Sonia who was waiting for him outside Mariastella Martellini's office.

* * *

---

[41] See 'A Close Encounter with Mushrooms'

The lady *Questore* listened without comment to every word which Sonia and Beppe uttered – each one of the pair of them taking over the narrative from the other when one of them paused - not knowing which element of the account should be revealed next.

When, finally, they had brought Mariastella up to date, she applauded them as if the first act of a theatrical play had been performed before her very eyes.

'I can see why you two decided to get married,' she said solemnly. 'You really are a team in every sense of the word.'

The warmth and sincerity with which their *Questore* had uttered these words succeeded in washing away the negative atmosphere created by this new threat to the fundamental honesty and decency for which their country was renowned.

'Thank you, Mariastella,' said Sonia. ''You have just confirmed why we are together and why we chose this path in life.'

Two unobtrusive tears, engendered by their rapport, had appeared in the corners of Mariastella Martellini's eyes. She shook her head as if to suppress them before she resumed the conversation.

'From now on, we must assume that your identity will soon become known to this Giulio Spanò. You will have to be three times more vigilant than usual. For the sake of your family, Sonia, I think you should stay away from the field of battle over the next few weeks – or however long it takes. And you, Beppe, will take no further action unless you are in the company of as many of your fellow officers as we can spare. I hope that it is eminently clear, *mio caro commissario!'*

Sonia looked relieved. Beppe had something else to say.

'My concern is not principally for myself – or even our little family in Atri. As soon as my identity is revealed, it will only be a matter of time before the Spanò family in Catanzaro will have me in their sights. I am more afraid that it will be my parents, my sister and her kids who will be at risk…'

The *Questore,* from Bologna, was less aware of the way that the *'ndrangheta* worked than Beppe was. It was she who turned a shade paler as the enormity of the potential risks which this investigation might involve became apparent.

'Would you rather I handed over the whole investigation to the *Carabinieri,* Beppe? I would quite understand…'

Sonia and Beppe, still surreptitiously holding hands below the level of Mariastella's desk, shook their heads in perfect unison.

'No way, *capo!'* said Beppe. 'There are too many innocent lives at stake in that small town. We can't stop now.'

'So, Beppe, what will your next move be?' asked Mariastella.

'I want to hold a very public funeral in Picciano for the tragic victim of this affair – Daniele Capriotti.'

'And for the sake of his wife, Giorgia – who is going to need police protection very soon, I fear,' added Sonia.

'And how, precisely, do you intend to have this funeral conducted, Beppe. Knowing you, it won't be the normal kind of ceremony!'

'I fear not, *capo*. To begin with, it will be me disguised as a priest who will be giving the oration.'

'Then I shall most certainly be at the ceremony,' stated the lady *Questore*. 'I cannot possibly sanction such a crazy plan as this unless I am present too. I hope that meets with your approval, *commissario!*'

Sonia smiled.

'I am sure my husband will have no objections, Mariastella.'

Beppe inclined his head in submission.

'I was hoping you would add weight to the occasion by your presence, *Signora Questore.*'

The meeting was closed amicably – even affectionately. There was a buzz in the air which had been absent beforehand. Mariastella Martellini had intimated that she would 'intervene' by using her authority to alert the local constabulary in Catanzaro that extra protection might be needed in the near future for a family with the unusual surname of Stancato.

'I thank you Mariastella. That would put my mind at rest. May I suggest you wait until after the funeral? First, I would like to explain what is happening to my father.'

'Of course, Beppe,' replied the lady *Questore*. 'Now, will you both go back to Atri and spend time with your two beautiful children – who I shall look forward to meeting again. They must have grown up a lot since I last saw them.'

Veronica and Lorenzo displayed more than their usual joy at seeing their *mamma* and *papà* entering the kitchen, where they were chewing their after-school *merenda*[42] in subdued silence.

'I think you should stop being a *poliziotta* for now, *mamma,*' Veronica said to Sonia. 'I think Lorenzo needs you back home to look after him as only you know how.'

Sonia was marvelling at how Veronica's powers of self-expression had developed – almost overnight, it seemed. It was a stark reminder to her that grandparents are no permanent substitute for their own mother and father.

'And what about you, *tesoro mio?*' Sonia asked almost fearfully.

'*Anch'io, mamma!*'[43] replied Veronica. '*Va da se,*[44] as granddad Roberto keeps on repeating.'

---

[42] snack
[43] Me too
[44] That goes without saying

Sonia looked at Beppe almost apologetically – as if to say that her priorities were about to revert to motherhood.

Beppe merely smiled and hugged her briefly.

'*Grazie, amore mio.* I couldn't have got this far without you.'

In the intimacy of their own bed, they talked about what paths this investigation was likely to take. Sonia had gleaned scant information as to how complex Beppe's vision was of the part the funeral of Daniele Capriotti would play.

But there was one detail of his plan which the *commissario* had failed to reveal – even to Sonia. He wanted the full impact of his *mise en scène* to remain his own personal secret until the moment of revelation was upon them. It might well backfire completely, he admitted. It was the recollection of a remarkable sermon he had witnessed when he was no more than seven years old which had furnished him with the idea. It had been the first – and only - time in his childhood he had been truly bowled over, by an extraordinary monk.

8: *The Smiling Man is not amused...*

He was sitting round a table in the dining room. His two squat, dark-skinned vassals had not been invited to sit down – they never were. They were looking obsequiously at their boss's scowling face. They knew that look too well. They were not intending to query the reasons for his discontent by even a raised eyebrow. It was more than their lives were worth. His words, when he finally spoke, emerged in the form of an angry, muted monologue.

Outside, in the grounds of his estate, Aurora was sitting astride her horse. She waved in her father's direction. For a few brief seconds, a softer look stole over his features as he smiled and returned her wave. It was all over in less than five seconds.

'*C'è qualcosa che non va!*[45] I've got something inside that's eating away at my guts. There's a man walking around this village – and a woman with him. He's got a northern accent. But he isn't what he seems to be. I know it.'

'Well, *capo...*' began one of his henchmen.

'Shut your mouth, *Antò!*[46] I'll ask for your opinion when I want it. I've seen him twice in the village. Yesterday - it was up at the *frantoio*. He took a photo of me on the horse... and his woman spoke to Aurora. They're up to something. And I've

---

[45] There's something wrong
[46] Short for Antonio.

seen a uniformed *sbirro* lurking around too – one who doesn't belong here. Not one of those two goons from Collecorvini...'

There was a protracted silence.

'Well, don't just stand there! Say something. *Cazzo!*[47] Why do you think I keep you two here rather than sending you back to Catanzaro where you belong.'

The Smiling Man had raised his voice suddenly.

'We'll find out what's going on, Don Giulio. We know what to do.'

'Go and scare those peasants out of their wits, *ragazzi!* And don't come back here until you've got something. Start off with those morons up at the *frantoio*. That couple must have said something to them. The man was speaking with a Bolognese accent. And then do the rounds in the village – that priest, for example... NOW!' shouted the Smiling Man standing up angrily. Go and do what I pay you for! You might have hung that decoration up on the olive tree, but you haven't done anything else since then!'

His two henchmen scuttled out of the room and disappeared into the courtyard. They got into a battered-looking FIAT Tipo and drove out through the open wrought iron gates.

They headed out of Picciano on the road towards Collecorvini.

---

[47] F - - k

'Where are you going. Antò? We've just driven past the *frantoio!'*

'I dunno, Mimo.[48] I was thinking we should just leg it down to Catanzaro – and go into hiding in the hills. I know a place…'

'But I've left all my stuff behind. We can't just go off like that. HE will be on to us straight away. And that means big trouble for us, Antò.'

'Yeah – but if the cops have got wind of what is going on here, they'll be onto HIM in no time at all. And guess who's going to get it in the neck! Not HIM but US! We are the ones who helped bump off that guy! He's gonna shop us if he gets into a tight corner, Mimo!'

'Turn round and go back to the *frantoio,* Antò. Let's go through the motions today. Then if the cops start poking round, we'll get out when he's got something else to worry about.'

'I just wanna go home, Mimo. I don't trust HIM…'

'Let's do it my way – just for now! OK?'

---

[48] Mimo – short for Domenico'

9: The Commissario prepares for action…

As soon as he had contacted Mariastella and told her what he needed, Beppe headed for their local coffin-makers. The two middle-aged craftsmen looked at him in total disbelief and asked to see his official police ID badge again.

'You want us to do WHAT, *commissario?*'

'You heard me properly the first time, *signori!* And if you utter a single word to anybody – including your respective sainted grandmothers – I shall personally come back and measure you up for *your* two coffins! *Siamo chiari?*[49]

The coffin-makers appeared suitably impressed by the severity of the expression on the *commissario's* face.

'I promise to come back in a week or so's time and explain everything,' Beppe concluded in a friendlier tone of voice. 'Then you will be able to tell the story to the whole of your family – and the rest of Atri[50] too, if you so wish.'

'We cannot wait to have our curiosity satisfied, *commissario*. We'll have the job done for you by Monday morning. It just so happens that nobody in Atri seems to be needing our services at the moment.'

'Some might say that is a happy situation, *Signor* D'Angelo!' stated Beppe with a smile.

* * *

---

[49] Is that clear? Lit: Are we clear?
[50] Atri – the town where Beppe and family share Sonia's parents' home.

Without leaving Atri, Beppe's second port of call was the local printers' workshop where, among many other items, the family-run business produced those posters that appear all over Southern Italian towns announcing the departure of a loved one.

Eyebrows were once again raised high – although the shock was less severe than at the coffin-makers'. Beppe, with Sonia's help, had decided upon the wording of the poster the previous evening.

The more senior printer – the father or uncle, Beppe supposed – was equally as surprised by the text of the poster-to-be as by the photo of the deceased which the *commissario* had presented them with.

'May I point out that it is customary, *commissario,* to supply us with a photo of the deceased taken while they are still alive. I don't mean to state the obvious to you…'

'I see I shall have to take you into my confidence, *signori.* This photo is the only one we have of this young man. He was brutally murdered, but his death was passed off as a suicide. Do you begin to see that these posters will have a very different role to play than the traditional posters you are in the habit of dealing with?'

The two men had turned pale but the older partner looked intrigued rather than upset.

'I assume this poster will *not* appear in Atri, *commissario?*'

'Correct, *Signor* Manfredi. You need have no concerns on that score.'

'And I am sure you are about to warn us as to the need for discretion. Have no fear! Our lips are sealed – *vero, Gianni?*' he added pointedly to his young partner.

'Please make this a priority, *signori*. I shall need them as soon as possible – today, preferably.'

The printer nodded, adding only:

'And how many copies will you need?'

'Fifty,' replied Beppe with no hesitation. 'That should be enough.'

'You can come by early tomorrow morning and collect them, *commissario*. The ink needs to dry out properly. Is that soon enough for you?'

* * *

On returning home, Sonia informed Beppe that she had received a call from Giorgia Scarpa, followed almost immediately by a call from Don Pietro, the parish priest of Picciano.

'It seems that the Smiling Man has sent out the troops - a couple of ugly-looking thugs – to find out if anyone in the town has come across a stranger who speaks with a Bolognese accent. These two hoodlums were doing their best to sound threatening. It seems that the Smiling Man has become somewhat nervous about this mysterious figure from Bologna – not to mention his wife. Have we come across anybody fitting this description, *amore?'*

Beppe smiled at Sonia's words, stifling the sense of anxiety that he felt in the pit of his stomach.

'Good! We've caught his attention. He's feeling threatened and he cannot quite identify the source of his unease. But we must take immediate steps to remove Giorgia out of harm's way. I need to go back to Picciano immediately simply to reassure…'

'NOT on your own, Beppe Stancato! You do remember what Mariastella told you, don't you? Your life could be in danger if HE recognises you.'

Beppe could visualise the consequences of disobeying either Sonia or his chief, the lady *Questore*. For the first time in his career, he realised that he required the authority and the support of other interested parties before putting his crazy schemes into practice.

'I must be getting old,' he muttered to himself with a degree of self-awareness he would have hitherto dismissed.

* * *

Beppe had spent the rest of the day taking the all too familiar drive down to the police headquarters in Pescara. The *Questore,* Mariastella Martellini, was smiling at her second-in-command over her desk. She was looking relieved – as if the main obstacle to her secret misgivings about her *commissario* had finally been removed.

'It is good to see you here, Beppe. Tell me how we can all help you with the next step in your fight against the mafia.'

Thirty minutes later, she was looking less relieved – but fully aware of all the implications involved in the workings of her colleague's devious mind.

'I will be present at this mock funeral next Wednesday – in the company of as many of our officers as I can spare. I appreciate you do not want to go into the details of how you intend to conduct this theatrical performance, Beppe. But I am intrigued to know how you intend to deal with the actual burial of the victim, Daniele Capriotti. We must be respectful of the dead!'

'That is why I have come today…*Signora Questore*…Mariastella,' said Beppe. He had noted the brief look of hurt on his chief's face when he had used her formal title. 'I have been severely castigated by Sonia at the mere suggestion that I intended to return alone to Picciano…'

'Sonia is right, Beppe. It is too risky. Tomorrow is Friday. Why don't I get two of our team to meet you tomorrow morning at the *frantoio,* let's say – armed and uniformed. Would you go along with that?'

'*Ti ringrazio,*[51] Mariastella. And one of the things I wish to do tomorrow, will be to reassure the victim's wife, Giorgia Scarpa, that we are going to give her our protection from that mafioso, Giulio Spanò. I want to talk to her about the real funeral too. She will have an important part to play in the mock funeral on Wednesday. That has got to be entirely convincing if my scheme is to work...'

'I could insist that you put me in the picture now, Beppe,' stated the lady *Questore.*

'What? And spoil all your fun?' replied Beppe with a tantalising grin. 'Who do you intend to send to Picciano tomorrow, may I enquire, Mariastella?'

'You may enquire, *commissario!* But I would rather keep you in suspense,' she replied, taking malicious pleasure in her quiet revenge.

Beppe bowed respectfully at his *capo's* astute retort as he stood up ready to take his leave with good grace.

'Not Officer Luigi Rocco,' he said. 'He is too conspicuous. We should leave him for the 'funeral' on Wednesday – and the inevitable aftermath.'

---

[51] I thank you

'Let it be a surprise for you tomorrow, Beppe!' was all she said.

For only the second time in their acquaintance did Beppe feel the necessity to approach his chief and give her a hug. She seemed to be expecting the gesture.

'*Grazie,* Mariastella!' he said. 'You are the best!'

When he had finally left her office, Mariastella Martellini found herself wiping an emotional tear away from the corner of her eye. She sighed – wondering what machinations her maverick second-in-command was reserving for her the following week.

'It had better be worth it, Beppe Stancato!' she threatened out loud to the empty office.

* * *

Beppe arrived at the *frantoio* before his 'escorts'. On the back seat of his car a large package containing fifty funeral posters took up most of the space. In the boot, he had acquired tubs of glue and the brushes needed to attach the posters to various walls and bill-boards in the little town of Picciano – and, he intended, in and around the neighbouring town of Collecorvini. He had decided that he and whichever officers turned up from Pescara would invade the two-man police station in Collecorvini to enlist their help in spreading the word about the 'funeral' to as wide a public as possible. He would rely on the wording of the poster to arouse the curiosity of the local population. He wanted the little church to be full the following Wednesday.

Beppe looked at his watch. His escort was due to arrive. A police car was driven enthusiastically up the track leading to the olive press. Two smiling young police women jumped out of the car looking almightily pleased with themselves. Beppe's heart almost sank. It was the two 'Cs' as they had been nicknamed; Cristina Cardinale and Emma Campione.

But Beppe felt his mood lifting as the two young women approached him brimming with devoted enthusiasm. Mariastella had, as ever, made the correct decision.

'It's great to see you girls!' stated the *commissario,* shaking the two hands which they proffered simultaneously as if vying with each other to see whose hand their favourite *commissario* would shake first. Beppe resolved the 'dilemma' by shaking both hands held out to him simultaneously – one in his right and the other in his left hand; a gesture which provoked a peel of delighted laughter from them both.

'Now, this is what we are going to do this morning – and probably this afternoon in Collecorvini. It depends how long we have to spend in this village. We've got to do the rounds and put up as many of these posters as possible – with the help of various people.'

The 'Two Cs' took one look at the poster and their mouths dropped open – the smiles temporarily wiped off their faces.

Officer Cristina Cardinale began to read the wording out loud for the benefit of her colleague:

*A much-loved husband and citizen of Picciano will be respected during a memorial service to be held in the Church of Santa Agnese di Assisi on Wednesday 5th May. Daniele Capriotti had his life brutally taken from him by a member of the **n'drangheta,** who left his body hanging from the Vendetta Tree. Please attend the service in support of his widow, Giorgia Scarpa. The memorial service will be conducted by your parish priest – Father Pietro – with the assistance of Commissario Stancato from the Questura in Pescara.*

ALL ARE WELCOME

'We'll take the police car, *ragazze.* I'll leave mine here. Yours has a bigger boot for all these posters and glue-pots.'

There followed a tour of Picciano by the three officers, which took in the individuals with whom Beppe had already made contact on his previous visits – notably the *parroco,*[52] Don Pietro, and the archivist and his diminutive sister. They were dragooned into service. It was Don Pietro who displayed the

---

[52] Parish priest

greater enthusiasm – promising to recruit helpers from amongst his more aware parishioners. He took fifteen posters and a tub of paste.

'Take some extra ones, Don Pietro – just in case you need to replace any posters that get torn down overnight – as I suspect will be the case.'

'That should be enough to make sure nobody in the village misses the news,' said the priest with a note of triumph in his voice. 'We are so indebted to you, *commissario*. The vast majority of the people here are close to despair over what is happening in this town. God bless you, and your colleagues, for taking our plight seriously.'

'Let's wait and see how great the impact is after next Wednesday, Don Pietro,' was Beppe's cautious reply as they left him at the door of the *canonica*,[53] still smiling broadly.

'I hope he won't suffer as a result of his courage,' said *Agente* Emma Campione as if to herself.

'The Smiling Man will have too many other things to worry about to take it out on the parish priest,' said Beppe. 'In any case, if they take our advice and put up the posters after dark, they should remain anonymous.'

The *frantoista,* Davide Di Sabatino, and his son had been quietly delighted to support the *commissario.*

---

[53] presbytery

'We will put up as many posters as possible in the shop and at the roadside too. We've got an advertising space on the public bill-board in town too.'

'We hope you will attend the funeral service next week too, *Signor* Di Sabatino,' interjected *Agente* Cardinale with a suitably coquettish expression on her face.

'We wouldn't miss it *per tutto l'oro del mondo, signorina!*[54] You and your colleagues will be saving our lives and our livelihood – quite literally.'

Beppe Stancato wanted to caution the *frantoista* against premature optimism – but thought better of it.

* * *

'Now, the most important visit of all, *ragazze*. We are going to visit a young lady called Giorgia Scarpa. She is the wife of the murdered man. I am glad you two are with me because a couple of smiling female faces will reassure her.'

Officers Campione and Cardinale were making as if to get back into the car.

'On foot, ladies,' Beppe added. 'Her house is very near – and I don't want to alarm her with the sight of a police car arriving.'

---

[54] For all the gold in the world

Beppe was quite taken aback by the transformation which manifested itself as soon as they reached the house hidden behind the trees. Giorgia was getting into her car and looked as if she was about to go out. There was a brief second of something between fear and defiance on her face when she turned round to face the unexpected callers. She smiled as soon as she recognised Beppe's face and the negative expression vanished.

'I thought your car wasn't working, Giorgia.'

'In the end, I called out my mechanic. *That man* had only taken away the battery,' she said with a measure of disdain in her voice. 'I'm going out to get my own shopping from the supermarket in Collecorvini.'

'The fact is, Giorgia, we were coming to offer you a place of refuge out of reach of *Signor* Giulio Spanò.'

'*La ringrazio, commissario.* But I am staying. I am going to face up to that man whatever the risks involved. He murdered my husband, officers – and if he didn't do it in person, it was he who gave the orders. It is *he* who is stealing our business from us by way of threats – and murder.'

Beppe looked at this newly defiant woman and smiled.

'In that case, *Signora* Giorgia, I am about to ask you to help me catch him out. If you can spare me a couple of minutes of your time, I will explain to you precisely the part I would like you to play…'

Officers Campione and Cardinale were disappointed to be excluded from the party as an intrigued Giorgia led Beppe back into her house.

'I need you two to stand guard outside,' he said smoothly. He did not intend that *anyone* should know the details of his scheme except those who were directly involved with the deception.

'I'm sorry, *ragazze.* If it is of any consolation to you, I even refused to let Mariastella Martellini into the secret.'

'Then you had better be intending to invite *us* to this piece of theatre, *commissario!'* threatened *Agente* Emma Campione.

* * *

Beppe emerged through the front door in the company of Giorgia Scarpa after only ten minutes. They had covered a lot of ground.

'How in heaven's name did you come up with such an idea as that, *commissario?'* asked Giorgia.

'I hope you don't feel daunted by it, Giorgia.'

'It's quite brilliant, *commissario.'*

'Not a word to anybody, mind!' said Beppe unnecessarily.

By way of reply, Giorgia merely gave him a contemptuous look as she got into her car, ready to drive off.

'Ok, *ragazze,*' said Beppe turning to his two waiting officers. 'We're finished in Picciano for today. Let's head back to the *frantoio* so I can pick up my car. And then we'll head for Collecorvini.'

The two police officers were walking up the main street towards the police car, one on each side of their *commissario.* Suddenly, the one thing which Beppe had prayed would never happen, *did* happen. As the group approached the *Olivo Nero*, he recognised the figure of the Smiling Man stepping out from the bar. He appeared to be talking to someone inside the bar – almost certainly Adelina – jabbing an aggressive finger in her direction.

Beppe cursed under his breath. He had no time to dream up some subtle strategy.

'Listen, *ragazze,* and don't ask questions. Make a scene NOW and arrest me - for whatever reason comes into your heads. And make sure that man up ahead can hear what you are saying… and call me Balboni!'

It was Officer Emma Campione who reacted first – her acting skills coming to the rescue. As the Smiling Man recognised Beppe from their previous encounter, he was taken aback by the two police women who seemed to be pinning the man's hands behind his back as they attached a pair of handcuffs to his wrists.

'Balboni! We are arresting you for indecent assault. You should be ashamed of yourself at your age!' shouted Officer Campione.

'And stand still while I put these cuffs on you, Balboni,' shouted Cristina Cardinale, quickly catching on to the sudden turn of events.

One extra twist of the *commissario's* resisting right arm brought a cry of pain from their prisoner, which barely needed to be simulated.

To Cristina and Emma's astonishment, their captive began swearing in a dialect that was totally unknown to them. The shock was so great that they nearly let go of him – only brought back to reality by the fact that Beppe made a supreme effort to escape.

'You just come quietly, Balboni!' shouted Emma Campione, 'or we shall charge you for resisting arrest as well.'

The couple ushered their prisoner up the hill towards the parked police car, exaggerating their efforts as they pushed past the Smiling Man.

'You're a witness to this!' Beppe shouted at the mafioso – in his best Bolognese accent.

Giulio Spanò was smiling with his mouth, but his sharp eyes held a quizzical look – yet again expressing his suspicions that some kind of scene was being acted out for his benefit for motives which were not at all transparent.

'*In bocca al lupo, Balboni!*' he called out sarcastically as the 'prisoner' was shoved unceremoniously into the back seat of the police car.

* * *

None of the three people in the police car said a word until they were on the road leading to the *frantoio*. *Agente* Cardinale was driving whilst her companion was in the back with their captive.

'Alright, officers. If you would be so kind as to remove these handcuffs now, I would be most grateful.'

The two girls finally broke the tension by bursting out in uncontrollable mirth, as Officer Campione struggled to free their *commissario*.

'That was the most entertaining thing that has happened to us since we started our career as police officers,' said Cristina Cardinale as they pulled up outside the *frantoio*.

Beppe had forced himself to maintain his most severe facial expression. He was not intending to allow the girls to gloat.

'I would like to know, *Agente* Campione, 'what you were thinking when you decided – without due reflexion – to accuse me of indecent assault. You could have gone for pickpocketing!'

It was hard to resist the gales of laughter which ensued without Beppe breaking into a smile. In the end he simply said:

'You were both superb, *ragazze.* You saved the day! Now, we had better get going in case that man decides to follow us.'

'Excuse me, *commissario,* but why don't we save time by driving you to Collecorvini and drop you off afterwards?' suggested Cristina.

Beppe smiled.

'Brava, Cristina. *Grazie di cuore* to both of you. *Andiamo!'*[55]

* * *

The senior male police officer in Collecorvini showed a deep reluctance to do anything – except complain. He obviously believed that a policeman's life was quite acceptable only when nobody was committing a crime.

'I told you it was a simple suicide, *commissario.* Why all this fuss about holding a memorial service?'

'Because he was murdered, *Agente* Conte. By a member of the *'ndrangheta* working an olive oil scam only twelve kilometres from your police station. You had better get used to the idea because you are going to be involved personally from

---

[55] Lit: Thanks from the heart. Let's go.

the moment you attend the funeral next Wednesday. You might even have to be prepared to face the mafia. Now, I want you to get me the local mayor on the phone. I need to speak to him.'

Agente Conte looked as if he wished his retirement age had already been reached as he grudgingly did what this imposing senior officer had instructed him to do. His colleague - with officers Campione and Cardinale in tow - had been glad to have something useful to do. Sticking funeral posters up in the company of these two enthusiastic young officers, who explained exactly what had been going on in a village which came under their jurisdiction, reminded her why she had become a policewoman all those years ago.

Officers Campione and Cardinale eventually made their way back to police headquarters in Pescara. They ran into Officer Pippo Cafarelli.

'I bet you didn't know that our *commissario* can do regional accents to perfection, did you Pippo?'

Officer Cafarelli smiled and replied:

'Oh, he's been playing that old trick again, has he?'

Pippo was inevitably dragooned into relating the previous incidents in which their *commissario* had displayed his unusual linguistic talent.

* * *

Back home with Sonia and family, later on that afternoon, Beppe had only to arrange transport for a coffin to be delivered to the church of Picciano the following week.

'Am I allowed to attend this funeral service of yours next Wednesday, *Commissario?*' Sonia asked in a tone of voice which implied she intended to come anyway.

'Absolutely, yes, *amore mio.* You will have to wear your uniform though.'

'Can we come too?' asked Veronica. 'I've never been to a funeral before.'

'School comes first, *tesoro,*' was the only reply she got.

Veronica had already begun to master the art of getting her own way. She decided she would bide her time and wear down parental resistance bit at a time. She was intelligent enough to understand that this 'funeral' would fall into the category of a spectacular show. It was worth a try, she reckoned. As a last resort, she could always burst into a fit of tears and claim she was afraid of being left alone on the planet with her strict grandmother. That was bound to work!

Beppe still had one difficult task to fulfil before bedtime. He was not looking forward to it. He needed to contact his father. This would inevitably mean having to convince his mother that it was not because he was unwilling to talk to her – but simply that he had TWO parents that he loved. Sonia had volunteered to be present when the phone call was made. She was an expert in handling Beppe's overly doting mother. Sonia was almost the only person in the world who called her mother-in-law by her first name – Imelda; some saint from Bologna who lived in the 14th century.

'So what have you to say to your father that you cannot say to me, Giuseppe? He is watching a film on Rai 1. I can give him a message on your behalf. It must be at least three weeks since you phoned me. I know you think you can do without your mother…'

'No, *mamma*. I am only forty-nine years old. Of course, I still need you…' replied Beppe desperately.

It was Sonia who calmed the ruffled feathers and distracted Imelda enough to persuade her to put her husband on the line. The process took a further fifteen minutes off their lives.

It was a relief for Beppe to hear his beloved father's voice – inevitably calm and full of simple wisdom.

'So what you mean, Beppe, is that we should think about moving out of Catanzaro for a time in case the Spanò clan decide to take it out on us. Have I understood you correctly?'

'*Sì, papà.* I'm so deeply sorry to involve you in all this. You should probably warn Valentina[56] too. She only lives a short distance from Catanzaro. A bit too close for comfort, I'm afraid…'

---

[56] Beppe's younger sister

'*Non è colpa tua, Beppe.*[57] It's entirely the fault of the mafia – and the inability of those in power to get a grip on organised crime. This kind of problem was always bound to catch up with us at some stage. Leave it with me. I'll phone you as soon as I have something worked out. I have family up north. They will help us. But they will need a bit of notice.'

'*Grazie, papà.* I knew you would understand.'

As Beppe put the receiver down, he heard a sort of keening noise like a wounded seagull. Obviously, his mother had caught the gist of the conversation.

'*Povera mamma!*' he whispered to Sonia. 'Her familiar world is about to be overturned.'

---

[57] It's not your fault

10:   *The Smiling Man unmasked...*

The citizens of Picciano had divided themselves into two distinct categories; those who had seen the posters and come to the conclusion that their salvation might be close to hand. They were driven by an overwhelming curiosity to be present at the church service. The other category tended to be older people for whom the word **'ndrangheta** on the poster had awakened their worst fears of midnight reprisals. The latter remained indoors all morning – and prayed that their absence would be taken into consideration by 'that man'.

The sight of the two hoodlums employed by Don Giulio, as they knew him, tearing down the posters, which had magically returned the following morning, was enough to alert the population that something life-changing was in the wind.

The Collecorvini contingent which arrived at the church of Santa Agnese di Assisi, headed by the mayor, were all dressed in black. The mayor had obviously misunderstood what he had been told by that *commissario* from Pescara. He had been led to believe that they were attending a real funeral rather than a 'memorial service'. They were few in number, however. The mention in bold type of the mafia clan from Calabria had deterred the rest of the population. They all prayed for the citizens of their neighbouring community – but, naturally, one did not wish to get involved if one was not directly affected.

One had to think of one's family. The two uniformed police officers from Collecorvini were present in the church of Sant' Agnese – one willingly so and the other not.

Beppe was content. The church was more than three quarters full. He had abandoned the idea of wearing a cassock. The need for pretence had long gone. He had committed himself and his colleagues to going through with this elaborate charade.

The coffin had been placed in the nave of the church on a high pedestal. That was odd, thought the congregation. Only the more perceptive members of the congregation silently wondered why there appeared to be no lid on the coffin. A solid-looking wooden step-ladder had been placed by the side of the coffin.

A row of uniformed police officers from Pescara – men and women – were sitting at the back of the church, looking solemn. The *Questore,* Mariastella Martellini was sitting very upright, observing every person who crept almost furtively into the church.

Only those members of the congregation who swivelled their heads round from time to time were puzzled to see two young children, amidst the ranks of police officers, looking expectantly at all those around them. A sister and her little brother obviously. Curious, they thought.

A uniformed *commissario* was standing at the foot of the pulpit staring at the entrance to the church door. He was waiting for his intended adversary to arrive. Beppe was not unduly worried by his non-appearance. Giorgia Scarpa would have text-messaged him by now had she had any indication that she had been unable to persuade the Smiling Man to enter the church.

'Come on Giulio,' she said coaxingly. 'Let's go and find out what this policeman is up to.'

She had linked her arm under his and was urging him to enter the church.

'If you don't go into the church, it will look as if you really have got something to hide. You know how everyone in this town respects you. You've simply got to show your face, *amore.*'

Giorgia was cringing at the sound of the words she was obliged to utter in order make Beppe's great hoax a reality. She simply could not let him down. She was equally sure this would be the last time that she would be forced to pretend she was ignorant about his role in the annihilation of her husband.

The church door was flung wide open violently. Everybody instinctively turned round to see who had just come in. A subdued groan spread out like a wave across the congregation. The most feared man in the town had just entered, leading the wife of the deceased man by the hand. Davide Di Sabatino, the *frantoista,* looked fearfully at his wife. Had they placed too much hope and faith in that *commissario?* A uniformed policewoman in her thirties had boldly stood up as the Smiling Man entered the church – making sure that she was seen by the mafioso before he and Giorgia sat down near the back of the church. Don Giulio Spanò was smiling insolently back at the lady *Questore* – quite indifferent or unaware as to her rank.

The parish priest made the sign of the cross and in a frail voice that only grew stronger as he got into his stride, began to speak.

Bless you all for having the courage – and maybe also the curiosity – to be present today. I must make it clear that, properly speaking, this is a memorial service. We have not as yet been able to send Daniele Capriotti to his final destination, thus giving some peace to his beloved wife, Giorgia – whom we all know and love so well. She has shown us all how brave she is by being present today – despite the threat to herself.

Don Pietro managed to look pointedly at the Smiling Man and maintain his expression of deep disapproval for ten long seconds.

May God and The Virgin Mary be present with us all, over the next few weeks. In the name of the Father, and of the Son, and of the Holy Spirit. Now I shall pass you over to a man who has fearlessly taken up our cause to rid us all of the evil in our midst.

Don Pietro descended the steps of the pulpit amidst a deep silence. Nobody in the congregation moved nor uttered a word.

The figure who took his place was familiar to most of the congregation from the local TV station, Tele-Tavo. There was a collective gasp of astonishment which spread round the nave like a sudden breath of wind. This was certainly going to be no commonplace memorial service.

The only individual who reacted differently to the *commissario's* appearance was the Smiling Man. If he had had a smirk on his face during the priest's brief address, any vestige of it disappeared in a trice. The man standing with all the marks of authority in his bearing was none other than that idiot from Bologna. It must be his *sosia,*[58] he thought. He had to be mistaken. He was shaken to the core and felt rising anger as the light dawned – and the man began speaking in what was clearly a Calabrian accent. He felt the first hint of fear mixed in with fury that he had been duped.

Good morning to you all. I am Commissario Stancato from the Pescara police force. I would like to add my thanks to you all for coming to this church today. If you came here simply out of curiosity, then I intend to satisfy that curiosity in full.

I first came here more than a week ago in the company of one of my colleagues and the chief Forensics Officer from

---

[58] A double : a look-alike

Pescara. We had received an anonymous phone call from someone in this town. He wished to draw attention, not only to the discovery of some Xylella-infected plants discovered in one of your precious olive groves but also the death of an unknown man found hanging from The Vendetta Tree just outside your little town.

May I state now to any who might have believed that this was a suicide that we quickly discovered that the man, whose memory we are honouring today, was brutally murdered with a bullet in the back of his head – a mafia-style assassination.

Beppe had to wait until the angry reaction of the shocked citizens of Picciano had died down. A certain police officer from Collecorvini was, Beppe noticed, sitting very stiffly in his chair – looking shaken for the first time.

I do not wish to dwell on such painful truths with Giorgia Scarpa present amongst us. Her courage and powers of recovery have been remarkable. She is a very brave woman.

Beppe's flow of words was interrupted by a brief round of respectful hand-clapping.

Finally, I wish to say one thing. The real funeral of Daniele Capriotti will take place here in the next few days, with the victim's family present. In that open coffin is NOT the body of Daniele. Not the body of any victim of a crime. Unusually, anybody looking into this coffin will see, not the victim, but his KILLER.

Beppe had raised his voice dramatically on pronouncing the final word. He had to stop himself from uttering the words: *In the name of the Father...* whilst making the sign of the cross. 'Don't get too carried away, *Commissario!*' he told himself.

Giorgia was ready to play her part. She stood up and made as if to walk up the aisle towards the coffin. The Smiling Man's hand shot out to restrain her.

'LET HER GO, DON GIULIO!' intoned Beppe in stentorian tones.

The congregation, now completely agog with curiosity and the sense of mystery which had been generated by the *commissario's* words, watched the figure of Giorgia Scarpa climbing up the steps of the ladder and peering into the open coffin. Her hand went to cover her mouth. She stepped down and headed to the back of the church. Only a few older members of the congregation thought she was crying. The majority – self-evidently the mafioso too – could plainly see that she was suppressing the desire to laugh.

Giorgia walked right past the Smiling Man, not even deigning to look in his direction. She headed for the row of policemen and sat down next to Sonia Leardi. Lorenzo moved over to share his big sister's seat. The three of them were smiling at Giorgia as if she had just been reunited with her family.

Exactly as Beppe Stancato had foreseen, the Smiling Man – who was no longer smiling at all – headed angrily up the aisle. He mounted the steps and took one look inside the coffin. He was consumed by an inner rage.

What he saw was his own face reflected in a mirror set into the base of the coffin.

11: Aftermath...

Without bothering to step down from the coffin, Giulio Spanò directed his attention to the man who had remained standing in the pulpit. The mafioso had an ugly leer on his face. Beppe had to force himself to remain calm. He stared fixedly at his adversary, devoid of all expression. After only ten seconds, the Smiling Man broke eye contact, aware that a hundred people were studying him closely. He made as if to step down from the coffin. Beppe treated him to a mock bow and an exaggerated, circular hand gesture inviting the man to take his leave. It was the equivalent of throwing down the gauntlet.

Don Giulio's head was lowered. His face betrayed his wrath at having been duped on three occasions by this police officer. He was already turning over in his mind ways of avenging his public humiliation.

He did not once glance at the row of police officers, where Giorgia Scarpa was sitting looking at her hands tightly folded on her lap. He headed for the church door which he wrenched open. He shot a glare over his shoulder at the pulpit, but there was nobody there.

The Smiling Man stormed out. He was brought up short by the sight of a huge police officer, the size of a mountain bear, flanked by three other uniformed *sbirri*, who were blocking his path. Their weapons remained inside their holsters. Don Giulio found this far more disconcerting – even humiliating. It was as if they did not regard him as dangerous enough to warrant removing their pistols from their belts.

The mafioso made as if to sidestep the three officers. He was instantly confronted by the mountain bear, who had moved with an alacrity which was astonishing for someone of his size.

'The *commissario* requested that we should treat you with respect, *Signor Spanò.*'

It was *Agente* Pippo Cafarelli who had spoken these words quietly.

'But if you would rather we handcuffed you in front of all the people who are about to leave the church and frogmarch you to a police car, then please feel free to resist arrest. It would give us all so much more satisfaction to see you shackled.'

The Smiling Man had never experienced such an attitude from the *sbirri* at any stage of his chequered career as a mobster. He felt he was losing control.

'The *commissario* will be with us soon, Don Giulio. *Abbia un po' di pazienza!*' added the third officer – a woman - one of the two whom he had seen 'arresting' their own *commissario* in the main street just outside the bar, noted the mafioso with the sensation that his humiliation had just been compounded.

Their 'prisoner' held out his wrists, in an attempt to mock their passivity.

'Handcuff me, officers. Then I can shout out loud to every member of this town how I have been wrongfully arrested.'

'Nobody will believe you, *Signor* Spanò.'

It was the 'mountain bear' – *Agente* Luigi Rocco [59] – who had growled these words at him.

Revenge! Revenge! He could feel it swelling inside his body.

On the outside, he was smiling at the three police officers. Inside, he was confused. It was as if these cops had already worked out how easy it was going to be to incriminate him. He made a supreme effort to control the inner turmoil. Revenge would have to wait for a day or two.

* * *

Beppe and the *Questore,* Mariastella Martellini, emerged from the church side by side, followed closely by Sonia and Giorgia Scarpa who was holding Veronica and Lorenzo by the hand. She seemed very much at ease chatting to Beppe's children. Beppe kissed Sonia as the group, including Giorgia, headed towards the main street where Sonia's car was parked. They were heading back to Atri. Beppe had insisted that Giorgia

---

[59] See previous novels. He had been likened to one of Abruzzo's mountain bears by his colleagues, out of respect for his imposing stature.

needed protecting from a thwarted and unpredictable mafioso. She had shown only token resistance to the idea.

The *commissario* then walked towards the three officers who had formed a wall around the Smiling Man – should he decide to attempt to evade them again. Mariastella Martellini was already heading towards their captive, eying him up and down as if taking stock of what a *real* mafioso looked like. It was, despite her having been a *vice questore* in Bologna, the first time in her career she had met a member of the *'ndrangheta* face-to-face. She was secretly relieved to have Beppe standing by her side. It was, however, the *Questore* herself who uttered the words:

'Giulio Spanò, you are under arrest for intimidation of the public, criminal coercion and suspected murder. I shall leave my second in command, *Commissario* Stancato, to go into the procedures of your arrest. But, be clear about one thing, your nefarious attempts at money-laundering and seeking to acquire all rights of producing olive oil in this community are a thing of the past. You should concentrate on thinking how you will undertake your defence as to the brutal murder of one, Daniele Capriotti. I wish you luck in attempting such an impossible task. *Commissario?'* concluded Mariastella, inviting Beppe to continue the assault on the Smiling Man – in his own inimitable fashion – based on the tenuous scenario which they had sketched out over the telephone the previous day.

'Are you certain this is going to work, Beppe?' Mariastella had asked.

'Not at all, Mariastella,' Beppe had replied. 'But it's worth the shot."

'That is so reassuring, *mio caro commissario!*' she had added with ironic gravity.

The expression on Don Giulio Spanò's face hardened as he watched 'that *commissario*' walking towards him.

'Where are you taking my business partner, Giorgia Scarpa?'

He spat the words out in anger. Beppe stared at him coolly before replying.

'Somewhere far enough away from you, so you will not be able to threaten her again, *Signor* Spanò. And kindly disabuse your undoubtedly intelligent mind of any notion that you are still in charge of the town of Picciano. That much my officers and I *have* achieved. You will remain in police custody tonight. Tomorrow, we are taking you back to your house in Picciano where the *Guardia di Finanza* will take all the documents away - all the illegal contracts you have made with the local olive oil producers – including the ones which you made Giorgia sign under duress. Your business status in this town is null and void. *Siamo molto chiari su questo punto!*' [60]

---

[60] Let's be quite clear on this point

'Aren't you going to charge me with murder, *commissario?* After all that display of showmanship back there? Was that just a bit of theatre put on for your audience's benefit?' sneered the Smiling Man, feeling more and more sure of himself.

'What we *know* is not the same as what we can prove, Don Giulio. But that will only be a matter of time. One day, you will slip up. Your sort always do, in my experience.'

Beppe had managed to instil a note of disdain into his words, which the mafioso instantly reacted to. It was a calculated risk on Beppe's part; he was hoping that the mafioso would be off his guard and reveal something of the workings of his mind in a situation where he would be likely to retaliate.

'Far from not being from Bologna as you attempted to persuade me, I detect a Calabrian accent, do I not, *commissario?'*

Beppe felt a hidden surge of satisfaction. The Smiling Man was about to surrender to his instinctive sadism – in front of four witnesses.

'Yes, Don Giulio. I compliment you on your ability to state the obvious – but I have not been at any pains to hide the fact from you. I come from Catanzaro – as, I believe, do *your* family.'

The fleeting look of hatred on the mafioso's face was instantly under control again. He smiled at Beppe but his eyes were like grey steel blades.

'Then I shall look forward to the pleasure of meeting your family when I am forced by your actions to return home.'

Beppe had been expecting to hear this thinly veiled threat. His face gave nothing away of the underlying anxiety he felt concerning his family's safety. He was feeling guilty about involving his family, albeit indirectly. But it was much safer to know what ground he was standing on, Beppe reckoned. He stared back at the mafioso with a wicked grin on his face.

'That is the sort of public declaration, Don Giulio, that your lawyer – had one been present – would have been at pains to prevent you from uttering.'

The look of inner fury had returned. The Smiling Man had been wrong-footed yet again.

'Take him away, *ragazzi.* You know what to do with him,' said the *commissario,* waving a dismissive hand. By that time, all of the officers who had attended the funeral were standing round the space occupied by himself, the *Questore,* Officers Luigi Rocca, Pippo Cafarelli and Emma Campione – and Don Giulio Spanò.

'I and my officers will be present at your house tomorrow, *Signor Spanò,* along with a team of senior *Guardia di Finanza* officers accompanied by our *Questore.'*

'How do you like your coffee, *Signora* Questore?' asked the Smiling Man with the attempt at an insolent smirk back on his face.

'Made by a proper *barista,* out of preference, *signore,'* replied Mariastella Martellini cuttingly. She nodded briefly at the three officers who had been assigned the task of escorting their prisoner to the police station in Collecorvini.

* * *

Don Giulio Spanò was totally unaware of the intricate planning which had gone into the preparation of round one of this, the initial stage of his arrest.

After the Smiling Man had been removed, the rest of the officers with Beppe and company present, had headed for the *Olivo Nero,* where their *commissiario's* trick with the mirror was being discussed enthusiastically.

Adelina looked reassured as she spotted Beppe amongst the crowd of police officers. Her surprise turned to unmitigated joy when Beppe informed her that Don Giulio Spanò had just been arrested. She set about the task of serving drinks with a radiant smile.

'No more than one beer for each man present, Adelina. And the same applies to the lady police officers too!'

After the brief celebration, the main body of officers left the bar together, leaving only their *Questore* and her second-in-command sitting at the table. They soon fell into deep conversation.

'Are you certain you want to play out this strategy in the manner you have outlined, Beppe? I have come to respect and almost trust your more extravagant machinations, but this one seems an unnecessary step too far. I would like to be a trifle more convinced before I agree to letting that man escape.'

'I am quite happy to abide by your judgement, Mariastella,' Beppe had said – surprising himself more than his *capo*. 'It's just that we need more corroboration that he did indeed murder Daniele Capriotti. If we go through with this scheme of mine, Spanò will feel even more sure of himself. He is far more likely to slip up if he thinks he has the upper hand. And there is no risk involved. Pippo, Emma and Luigi are quite willing to go through with the plan I outlined – even if they won't get any sleep tonight. We can convict him for evading police custody. And then, there is the added benefit that we will be able to ease out the older officer in the Collecorvini station…'

'Oh, I'm sure he will jump at the prospect of retirement six months earlier than planned, Beppe.'

Mariastella Martellini paused thoughtfully for all of ten seconds.

'Ok, Beppe. Let's do it. Leave the Collecorvini officer to me. As you say, there is little risk of Spanò escaping. But we cannot allow your family in Catanzaro to be in danger by giving that man too much freedom.'

'My family should be out of Catanzaro by now – or at least ready to disappear up north,' Beppe said with an assurance that he did not feel. He knew – or suspected – that his mother might dig her heels in over uprooting herself from the town in Calabria where she had spent more than seventy years of her life. He would phone her later on that evening from home.

'May we take a walk, *commissario?*' suggested the lady *Questore* in a mock flirtatious voice. 'I need to know where Giulio Spanò's house is for tomorrow morning when I arrive with the *Guardia di Finanza* officers.

'*Con vero piacere,* [61]*Signora Questore.*'

* * *

The Smiling Man had no reason to look cheerful. He had been locked in one of only two cells in Collecorvini's police station by the male officer. The place smelt stale and disused and the bedding felt damp and stank of old perspiration. He was going to take steps to ensure that he would not spend the whole night there.

---

[61] With great pleasure

The officer nominally in charge had looked petrified at the thought of being left alone in the vicinity of this imposing-looking gangster – who had apparently brutally murdered a young man in Picciano and left his body hanging from that ancient olive tree. Don Giulio was determined to take advantage of this older officer's 'respect' for his status. He could make out the sound of raised voices – presumably the male officer arguing with his female counterpart.

It was, however, the younger female officer who brought him water and a salami sandwich, which she passed through a space in the bars.

'Grazie mille, Agente…?'

'Evangelista,' said the woman sharply. She was also nervous in his presence observed the mafioso – but was covering it up better than her colleague.

'A reassuring name, *cara signora.'* said Don Giulio unctuously. 'And your surname… may I ask?'

'That *is* my surname, *signore,'* replied the lady officer, in a tone of voice which indicated that the exchange of pleasantries was over as far as she was concerned,

'Buon appetito,' she said gritting her teeth. She could not remember a time when they had actually had to 'host' a real criminal at their outpost of a police station. It was a novel and rather disturbing experience, she reckoned. She left without another glance in the Smiling Man's direction, firmly shutting

the dividing door which led from the cells to the front office. It was a pity it did not have a lock, she thought for the first time in her career.

Much later on, as it was beginning to get dark outside, Don Giulio heard voices raised again. As far as he could make out, the male officer was trying to get shot of his female counterpart, who seemed to be arguing that she should stay with him.

'Va' a casa, Flavia. Non c'è nessun pericolo!' [62] he was saying repeatedly.

'Interesting!' said the mafioso to himself. Maybe his plan to evade captivity was going to be easier than he had thought.

Nevertheless, he had to wait several hours before he was alerted by the opening dividing door to the presence of the older officer, who was now standing outside his cell.

'Buona sera, Agente…?' began the Smiling Man in the most affable voice which he could muster. He was smiling again, hoping he was looking friendly enough from an observer's point of view.

'Agente Leone Carota, Signor Spanò.'

He had supplied his name without having to be cajoled. The mafioso's forced leer almost turned to a real smile; anyone less resembling a 'lion' than this man was difficult to imagine.

---

[62] Go home. There's no danger.

'Ah, Agente Leone,' began Don Giulio in a soothingly quiet voice. 'I am so sorry to be the cause of your not being able to return home to your family tonight.'

Officer Leone Carota merely shrugged his shoulders as if to imply that it was nobody's fault in particular.

'I'm used to it, Signor Spanò. It's just part of the job.'

'May I ask how long it is before you can retire and be yourself for the rest of your life?' enquired Don Giulio smoothly.

'Only a few months away, *signore.*'

'You must be looking forward to having all that free time with your family, Signor Leone. I imagine you must have young grand-children…' ventured the Smiling Man.

Agente Leone Carota was feeling weak inside. It was as if this terrifying man could read his thoughts. He had been instructed by that imposing young woman, who apparently held the rank of *Questore,* to lead their prisoner on until he showed his true hand. It was all happening without him saying a thing.

'*Sì Signor* Spanò. I have three grandchildren, but…'

'I too have a beautiful teenage daughter, *agente,* and it is her birthday today. She must be heart-broken that I seem to have forgotten all about her…'

'Leave it with me, *Signor* Spanò. I'll see what I can do. But,' began *Agente* Carota fearfully, 'I shall be taking an enormous risk if I…'

Non si preoccupi, Agente Leone.[63] I shall see to it personally that you will not lose out,' said the Smiling Man in the most unctuous tone of voice he could manage.

'Wait until midnight, *Signor* Spanò.'

Officer Leone Carota headed off into the outer office.

'Don't forget my mobile phone, *agente!*'

Leone Carota simply waved a dismissive hand over his shoulder as he went into the front office, appalled by the ease and the cynical self-assurance of the man who had just attempted to bribe him.

* * *

Midnight. Don Giulio Spanò could hear the main door opening. That lily-livered[64] *sbirro* had been in five minutes beforehand and unlocked the cell door – obviously petrified that he, Don Giulio would jump out of the cell and overpower him. The mafioso had smiled disarmingly, noticing with sly amusement that Officer Leone had actually unbuckled the holster cover of his revolver.

'Buona notte, Agente Leone. *E sogni d'oro!'* [65]

Don Giulio had dropped all pretence of kindness in his voice. He delivered the words with studied cruelty.

---

[63] Don't worry : Don't be concerned

[64] Codardo : vigliacco (is the nearest Italian can get to this Shakespearian creation!)

[65] Sweet dreams. Lit: Dreams of gold

The policeman had not even looked in his direction as he scuttled back out into the main reception area.

Don Giulio counted up to one hundred and headed out into the main office. He smiled as he picked up his mobile phone from the desk where it had been left. He was tempted to use it immediately and summon his two stupid henchmen into picking him up. No, he would wait until he was outside! It had all been so easy. He had a couple of angry moments when he found that the main door would not open. No panic; there was a simple push-bar to operate the latch.

He stepped outside and breathed in the fresh night air. His first thought was to phone his 'woman' and tell her to send his two stooges to come and pick him up. He had even selected the number and was on the point of pressing the key. His eyes had taken a few seconds to adjust to the night. That was the moment when he spotted *Agente* Luigi Rocco flanked by the same three officers who had ambushed him outside the church that morning.

12: The story of the second funeral...

'I'll take care of that for you, *signore.*'

It was Pippo Cafarelli who had reached him first and nimbly taken the mobile phone out of the mafioso's hand.

Don Giulio Spanò was seething inside with suppressed rage. Yet again, he realised belatedly, he had been taken for a ride by that *bastardo* of a *commissario.*

'I would advise you from now on not to underestimate our *capo, Signor* Spanò. You will just be digging a deeper hole for yourself...'

'Deeper than the one you are already in,' piped up Officer Emma Campione. 'We can now charge you with attempting to escape from custody to add to all the other charges you are facing.'

The Smiling Man was grinding his teeth in silence. That *stronzo* had gone one step too far. He assumed that the idiot police officer who had let him escape was in on this set-up.

The gruff voice of *Agente* Luigi Rocco was growling at him to hold out his wrists. The cuffs were the final straw. He had never in his life felt these bands of steel constraining his freedom of movement until this cursed moment.

'We are taking you to a nice comfortable cell in the *Questura* in Pescara, Don Giulio. It's got a toilet and clean bedding waiting for you,' added Officer Emma Campione.

The team had been under orders to lay on the sarcasm as much as they liked.

'I want him wound up to the point where he will explode with anger,' Beppe had stipulated. The three officers were happy to oblige.

Don Giulio fumed in the back seat of the police car where he was hemmed in by the bulk of the mountain bear. Pippo Cafarelli and Emma Campione, who was driving back to Pescara at top speed, kept up a patter of casual conversation about life in general, fully aware how their nonchalance would strike at their prisoner's self-esteem.

The Smiling Man was full of dark thoughts of vengeance which persisted well beyond the night spent in his cell.

'Get some sleep, Don Giulio,' was Officer Campione's parting shot. 'You'll need your wits about you when you are interviewed by the *Guardia di Finanza* tomorrow. There's a *commandante* from Rome coming down specially to meet you,' she added as the cell door was being shut in his face.

Luigi Rocco made one phone call to Beppe to tell him that their little mission had been accomplished.

'The three of you should take a break tomorrow, Luigi. You deserve it.'

'No, *capo,* we won't desert you until that man is permanently behind bars,' Luigi Rocco stated quietly. 'I am speaking for all three of us, *capo.'*

'Well, I admit I could do with your help. Thank you, Luigi. *A domani...* '[66]

* * *

'Tomorrow' saw the *commissario* dressed in his uniform and out of the house barely had dawn broken, with Giorgia Scarpa in tow. She was looking very solemn. She had her little suitcase already packed.

Only Sonia was awake enough to see them both off with a sleepy embrace.

'Say 'ciao' to your wonderful kids from me, Sonia,' whispered Giorgia with an inexplicable lump in her throat.

'You are welcome to come back any time you want, Giorgia – without notice.'

'Let me see how I feel tonight, Sonia,' she had replied thoughtfully. 'I don't feel afraid of 'that man' at the moment, but when it comes to night time, I might not feel so brave...'

'He won't have time to worry about you, Giorgia,' added Beppe. 'He is going to be a prisoner in his own house – until it is confiscated by the state, that is.'

Giorgia and Sonia parted with a prolonged hug, before Beppe started up the engine, rudely breaking the quasi-pastoral peace of the surrounding countryside.

---

[66] See you tomorrow

'Will you be back this evening, *amore?*' asked Sonia, with a hint of dread in her voice.

'Absolutely, yes, Sonia. Remind me to phone my mother tonight…please! I keep putting it off!'

Beppe and Giorgia had a discreet funeral to attend before Mariastella Martellini was due to arrive at Picciano in the company of the officers from the *Guardia di Finanza*. The Smiling Man would be driven back to Picciano from Pescara at the same time by Luigi Rocco, Pippo Cafarelli and Cristina Cardinale, who would be substituting her friend and colleague, Emma Campione – on Cristina's own insistence.

'I want a share of the action, too,' she had protested.

Lorenzo and Veronica had spent most of the previous evening until bedtime in the company of their guest, Giorgia Scarpa – who had hardly had a moment's peace and been given a guided tour of the whole house, including the ground floor occupied by Sonia's parents, who had taken the unexpected house-guest under their roof with smiling hospitality – and more cups of coffee.

'Can we call you *Zia Giorgia?*' [67] Lorenzo had asked at least half a dozen times during the course of the day.

'I prefer just Giorgia, *ragazzi,*' she had said firmly.

---

[67] Auntie

Veronica wanted to call their guest 'Just Giorgia', but resisted the temptation to be facetious when she saw tears welling in the corner of their house-guest's eyes.

Inside, had sprung to mind the devastating thought that she, Giorgia, would never be able to share her life with children like Veronica and Lorenzo, sired by the man she had loved.

The car journey was shrouded in a subdued silence.

'You are so fortunate, *commissario*...Beppe,' was about all Giorgia said.

'I'm so sorry, Giorgia.'

Beppe resisted the temptation to come out with meaningless platitudes. Inside, he simply vowed to ensure that Giulio Spanò would remain behind bars for the remainder of his time on earth. He would be praying that Giorgia would find a new partner, worthy of her, next time he was on a car journey of any length on his own. Beppe's belief in an invisible 'force' outside his sphere of comprehension was deep-rooted – and had been given a blessing by his great friend and supporter, Don Emanuele, the Archbishop of Pescara, during some deep discussion they had had a few months previously.

'It's why I stop short of being an atheist,' Beppe had once confided to his friend.

'I believe that yours is a perfectly sound starting-point, *commissario*,' had been the simple but ironic reply.

And so, what occurred next was a shock to Beppe's system. He and Giorgia were walking into the village church in the company of her own parents, her brother and Daniele Capriotti's whole family following close behind them. Some of the women-folk were dabbing at tearful eyes with brilliant-white linen handkerchiefs, whilst the male contingent was visibly attempting to suppress their emotions by dint of sheer will-power. But Beppe was staring at the old parish priest, Don Pietro, who was in the company of a much taller priest who had his back turned towards the approaching group.

'It can't be him!' he said just loud enough for Giorgia to turn a questioning face towards him.

But it was not only possible but a reality! The Archbishop, Don Emanuele, turned round at a sign from the parish priest.

'One ray of light in the darkness, Giorgia. Don Emanuele, our archbishop, will be here to help you cope with your great loss.'

'But…I'm not really *religious* you know, Beppe,' said Giorgia in a fierce, apologetic whisper.

'Neither is Don Emanuele – at least not in the accepted sense of the word.'

It was too late for further explanations. They had drawn level with the archbishop.

Out of courtesy – or habit – Giorgia Scarpa held out her hand to be shaken by this imposing cleric. She was shocked that the 'normal' expression on the archbishop's face on seeing her arrive was transformed in an instant to one of exaltant, inner intensity. She had the sensation that he was looking at her from another dimension altogether – almost as if he had seen an apparition. The hand which she had proffered was ignored – not out of lack of manners, she realised, but because he had not noticed her gesture. She found herself mesmerised by his steely grey eyes. Then, to her consternation, he spoke in a voice that seemed to be an echo which resonated from somewhere deep inside her.

'Do not be afraid, Giorgia. You will not be alone for long. And you will have your Daniele's blessing.'

And the moment was over. The archbishop was smiling again and was shaking hands with the newcomers.

'Shall we get on with the service?' he said in a practical tone of voice to the parish priest.

Beppe took a shaken Giorgia by the arm and led her to an aisle seat next to the simply-draped coffin.

'You have just had your first contact with the most remarkable man I have ever known, Giorgia.'

'But didn't you hear what he said to me, Beppe?' asked Giorgia.

'No, did he speak to you?' asked Beppe, looking puzzled.

Giorgia merely shook her head from side to side, too mystified to respond.

The ceremony around the coffin was carried out by Don Emanuele. In the end, he turned to face the small congregation, which included the whole family from the Olive Press and the old archivist and his sister; Don Pietro had played his part in rallying the troops. The archbishop was looking drained, as if some invisible mass of energy had gone out of him.

'May God bless you all. Daniele did not die in vain,' he stated simply as the six coffin-bearers stood up and shouldered the coffin, carrying it out of the church and up the hill to the centuries-old cemetery.

Don Pietro, with Don Emanuele by his side, was solemnly pronouncing the final words as the coffin was lowered into the ground.

Such was the height of the hill that Beppe, briefly looking away towards the mountains rising in the distance as Giorgia was scattering a handful of soil on top of the coffin, realised that he could see The Vendetta Tree, standing alone in all its gnarled and tranquil old age. It looked serenely indifferent to the sordid affairs of mankind. He escorted Giorgia downhill again. She was looking solemn but deeply engrossed in her own thoughts.

* * *

There had been no talk of holding a post-funeral get-together, simply because nobody knew how many people – or indeed which people – were likely to turn up to bid farewell to Daniele Capriotti. There was no other venue available, so the instinctive impulse was to gravitate towards the one-and-only bar in town.

Thus, the little community who had welded together outside the church simply followed Adelina Russo, the bar-owner, down to *L'Olivo Nero* and filed into the bar behind her.

The *commissario* looked at his watch. It was half-past eight and he was due to meet the *Questore* and the finance police outside the church at nine o'clock. He never felt relaxed whilst strutting around dressed to kill in his 'official' uniform. He wanted simply to disappear. But he became painfully aware that all eyes were upon him. The news of this *commissario's* trick with the mirror in the coffin, which had, in the eyes of the locals, finally and publicly unmasked the Smiling Man for what he really was, had captured the imagination of the whole village. He inwardly shrugged his shoulders and entered the bar with everybody else – caught up in the general feeling of a release from suffering which his intervention and the reverent burial of the man who had died in their cause seemed to have engendered.

147

Within minutes, the *frantoista,* Davide Di Sabatino, had clapped his hands together to catch everybody's attention and had proceeded to deliver a eulogy about the policeman who had 'saved their village' from the grip of the mafia.

'Parola al commissario!' [68] called out someone as soon as the *frantoista* had finished speaking.

The whole assembly was applauding whilst looking expectantly in Beppe's direction.

'No escape,' thought Beppe, giving way with a good grace. He prayed inwardly that the right words would emerge from his lips. He thought of Sonia and his kids looking at him with that stare which always seemed to express their secret admiration of him - not always fully deserved, he felt. He could not let his 'family' down.

Beppe smiled at his audience - his heart warmed by their somewhat premature optimism.

'It is all of you here today who deserve the award for bravery. **You** *are the ones who have suffered – often in silence. You all have to thank Don Pietro. He was the one who plucked up the courage to notify the police of what was happening under our very noses. Without him, the incursion of the mafia into your lives might never have come to light.*

In a few minutes' time, the Questore – Mariastella Martellini – will be arriving in Picciano in the company of the

---

[68] Speech! – lit: 'Word to the commissario'

Guardia. They will spend the next few days picking apart all the contracts that you have been constrained to sign. From that point of view, your troubles are over.

But that is only half the story, I am sorry to say. We still have the task of proving –unequivocally – that Giulio Spanò was responsible for the murder of Giorgia's husband. The Vendetta Tree killing must be completely watertight before an arrest can be made – on the charge of murder. The mafia are always far too clever to leave traces of their crimes – as I know from bitter experience.

But I am a patient man. This is a matter for the police. You are all free to live your normal lives again. Don Giulio is under house arrest. But please do not hesitate to contact the police if you suspect that this mafioso is trying to re-establish his influence over you in any way. Just phone the Questura in Pescara – your Don Pietro has the number!

The parish priest was blushing as if he was guilty of some misdemeanour.

It just remains for me to wish you all 'buona fortuna' and a happy and prosperous future. And now, I really must leave you and meet the Questore and the Guardia – who will be arriving within the next few minutes.

Beppe was tempted to add: '*Your* troubles are over, whereas *mine* are about to begin. But he left the words unsaid. In any event, the outburst of spontaneous applause and the cheers of *'Bravo, commissario!'* would have drowned out his coda completely.

Beppe tried to catch the attention of Giorgia Scarpa before he left the bar. But she was engaged in deep conversation with a man who, if he was not mistaken, looked remarkably like a living version of the only photo he had seen of Daniele Capriotti. A brother? A cousin? Could be either. Giorgia was totally engrossed in her conversation and more relaxed than he had ever seen her during their brief acquaintance.

Beppe caught a few words of their conversation as he walked past the couple on his way to the door. The man looked briefly at Beppe as he walked by with a vague nod of recognition in Beppe's direction. Giorgia did not notice his presence at all.

'You must come and stay with me, Giorgia,' the man was saying. 'Just until you feel more at peace with yourself.'

The *commissario* was still racking his brains as to the nature of the archbishop's intervention back in the church.

What secret words had Don Emanuele uttered to Giorgia? he wondered. The archbishop had excused himself to Beppe before being whisked away by a waiting taxi immediately after the burial without any explanation as to his unexpected presence at the funeral. It must have been Don Pietro who had contacted Don Emanuele, Beppe assumed. He would make it his business to find out what had transpired between Giorgia and Don Emanuele – by whatever means necessary. He even had a vision of himself arresting Don Emanuele and extracting the information on the grounds that the archbishop had been withholding vital evidence. He found this extravagant fantasy very appealing.

* * *

Beppe needed an introduction only to the senior *Guardia di Finanza* officer – the other three officers were from Pescara. He knew them well. They knew *him* equally as well. He was greeted by the three local finance police with a wry smile on their faces, whose message was clear – a *mélange* of 'Thanks a bunch for the extra work you have given us' and a more subtle 'Thank you for doing our job for us'. But the handshaking was entirely amicable.

The senior *Finanza* officer from Rome introduced himself as *Commandante* Proietti, who shook Beppe's hand firmly. He looked hard at Beppe and said:

'My colleagues have been telling me all about you, *commissario* - how you keep them fully employed.'

Only the gleam in his eyes told Beppe that he had a sense of humour.

'*È un grande piacere conoscerLa, commandante,*' [69] replied Beppe.

The *Guardia* officers, with Mariastella Martellini for once in the back seat, followed Beppe's car over the bridge to the double gates which shielded the mafioso's house from public view.

Beppe was not surprised to see his own three officers on guard outside the gates, which had begun ominously to swing open of their own accord, symbolising in Beppe's imagination the overture of the monumental opus that the four *Guardia* officers and his own *Questore* were about to perform.

'I'll talk to you tomorrow – or perhaps this evening - *commissario,* to let you know how things are going.'

These were Mariastella's final words before their car was driven into the grounds of Giulio Spanò's fortress – his home in name only for another few days.

Beppe lingered for another ten minutes or so, chatting to his officers.

'I'll make sure you get relieved soon Luigi, Pippo, Cristina. You must be exhausted by now. I thank you *di cuore*[70] for your devotion to duty…'

'No need to worry, *capo.* Mariastella…the *Questore,'* Pippo Cafarelli corrected himself automatically, 'told us to tell you not to worry about that side of things. She's got a roster

---

[69] It's a great pleasure to meet you
[70] From the heart

organised – which includes an officer called Flavia Evangelista, from Collecorvini.'

'She volunteered her services free of charge,' added Officer Cristina Cardinale with a broad grin on her face.

Beppe was secretly delighted by his two 'personal' recruits, Emma Campione and Cristina Cardinale. But he felt it incumbent on himself to treat Officer Cardinale's flippant comment with a hard look.

She merely returned his stare with an engaging smile. The two 'girls' knew exactly where they stood vis-à-vis their *capo*. He was the 'hero' whose exploits had determined their decision to become police officers.

Beppe took his leave with a strange feeling that matters were out of his hands. He was at a loss to know what to do next. He paid a brief visit to the parish priest and an even briefer visit to the old archivist and his sister before heading home.

His feeling that he had become a mere accessory in this investigation was destined to be very short-lived.

* * *

Sonia flew into his welcoming arms for a long-overdue hug. It was the first time in ages, or so it seemed, that they had both sat down to lunch together. Normally, Sonia was content to eat a salad and something quick for Lorenzo who, to his evident frustration, still had a few days to wait until he could begin attending his *scuola materna* on a full-time basis. [71] Today, to celebrate Beppe's early return, Sonia had prepared a dish of *fusilli al ragù* [72] which Lorenzo shared with them, looking in wonder at his father, trying to understand why it required his dad's presence to warrant his first man-sized lunch for ages. His rapidly developing powers of speech were as yet unable to articulate the necessary words to get an answer to this mystery.

Veronica could not contain her joy at being picked up outside her *scuola elementare* [73] by her *papà*. As far as she could recall, this had *never* ever happened at any stage in her past life so far. She, unlike her more thoughtful brother, chatted endlessly about every little detail of her day whilst skipping along with her hand in his. It was brought home forcibly to Beppe's mind how work interfered with the more important things in life. He would have to devise some devious scheme which would guarantee his suspension from duty – as he had managed unwittingly to achieve under the auspices of his old *Questore,* who had been 'obliged' to suspend him for a period of three whole months.[74]

After the family's supper, he had put his kids to bed and told them a potted version of his day in lieu of a bedtime story.

---

[71] A nursery school
[72] A pasta dish with lamb sauce from Abruzzo
[73] A primary school
[74] See The Vanishing Physicist

Lorenzo fell asleep before he had finished, but Veronica kept on asking him searching questions.

'What has happened to Giorgia?' she asked. 'I thought she was supposed to come and stay with us tonight?'

Beppe did not know how to answer that question accurately.

'I think she has made friends with one of Daniele's cousins, *tesoro*. She was looking very pleased with herself when I left her.'

Beppe planted a kiss on both his children's foreheads, which caused Lorenzo to stir in his sleep and Veronica, who insisted on returning the kiss on her father's cheek.

Now, he felt like taking Sonia to bed as darkness fell. But, she reminded him forcibly, there was one more matter to attend to before he could relax. Beppe sighed. He could not think of anything else to justify putting off the task in hand.

'Stay with me, *amore,*' he pleaded. It often fell to Sonia to sooth her mother-in-law's ruffled feathers.

Reluctantly, Beppe selected his mother's number whilst remembering to put the device on to loudspeaker mode for Sonia's benefit. More often than not, Sonia was reduced to a state of suppressed giggles during Beppe's conversations with his doting but wilful maternal parent. This phone call would, initially at least, not break that mould.

- Ciao mamma! Sono io!

There was an unaccustomedly long silence on the other end of the line.

- Mamma? Ci sei? [75]

- *Ma tu – chi sei?*

- It's me, mamma. Your son.

- *Do you know? I had almost forgotten I had a son.*

- Mamma, you know I phoned you less than a week ago. Where are you?

- *I'm at home, of course. Where else would I be?*

- I was hoping you might have moved up to friends or relatives further north, mamma. As I suggested, last time I spoke to you.

- *Giuseppe, I have lived here for over seventy years. You do not seriously believe that I am going to move somewhere foreign, do you? Just because you have very carelessly upset some locals. I am simply not going anywhere. You can be quite sure of that…*

- But mamma, as I tried to explain to you, you and papà might be in danger if…'

- *Giuseppe. I am not afraid of those people. I have despised them since I was a teenager. I am certainly not afraid of them now. What can they do? Shoot me? I'm quite ready for that and it will save funeral costs.*

---

[75] Are you still there?

Beppe looked up despairingly at Sonia. But, as usual, she was desperately trying to suppress her mirth.

- *Besides which, Giuseppe, a couple of that mob have already been round here. I shooed them away with a broom. They asked about your father, of course, so I spun them a long story about how your father lived somewhere up north as a bus driver. I even lied about his name. I said he was called Gabriele – instead of Corrado. I'm not stupid you know!*

Beppe had turned pale, but it was impossible to stop the flow of words – even more so than usual.

- But mamma…

- *Niente 'ma'![76] Giuseppe. My mind is made up. I'm staying here. So there!*

Beppe was used to his mother's stubborn determination never to admit that any other way of life was possible except the one she had always been used to. But this was a different set of circumstances.

- I would like to speak to my father, *mamma*.

- *Your father is not here, Giuseppe. He said he was going visiting after lunch. He didn't tell me where he was going and he's not back yet. It's most unlike him.*

---

[76] No 'buts'

Beppe's heart missed a beat. His father had, he knew, given up having a mobile phone, simply because he had grown weary of Beppe's mother pestering him whenever he went out - even to the local minimart, or to sit with his fishing-rod on the rocks near the harbour.

- Please, mamma, tell him to phone me as soon as he gets back.

- *If I remember, Giuseppe...'* said his mother and hung up.

Beppe looked at Sonia – who wiped away the tears of suppressed laughter. She was looking solemn by the time the eccentric phone conversation had come to an end.

She made no attempt to tell Beppe not to be concerned. Instead, she led him to the bedroom and got undressed.

'I've been thinking about a third child, *amore.* It would be what we've always wanted, wouldn't it? I hate even numbers...'

Beppe looked at her intensely. It was like coming back to the real world after talking to his mother. It reminded him forcibly what life was really all about. Besides which, he reasoned, his father always knew what to do in every situation. He should have more faith in his father's survival instincts.

They lay in bed talking about everything that had transpired in Picciano on that eventful day – before other priorities led them down a different path.

13: The Smiling Man digs his own grave...

By the end of the first day in the company of that sexy-looking *Questore* and those pompous, interfering *Guardia di Finanza* goons, who had dismantled every contract that he had ever made in this pathetic little town, it had become obvious that he would have to take steps to cover his back.

He was already in secret dread of punishment and derision from his own family back in Catanzaro. At least he had succeeded in ensuring that his 'brothers' in the Spanò clan had managed to identify that bastard *commissario's* family. It was the only thing that he had managed to get right since his arrest.

That female *Questore* from Pescara had spent hours interviewing and probing into the life of his 'woman', Monica. *She* wouldn't betray him – she was too stupid to know what was going on anyway. As long as she had her hair and nails done on a weekly basis, she was happy. And she was good in bed, it had to be admitted and not a bad cook – even if she *was* from Milan! But when he had looked out of the window and seen that *Questore* woman walking side-by-side with his daughter, Aurora, he began to seethe inside. He could even see the policewoman patting and talking familiarly to his daughter's horse. Who knows what Aurora would tell her – even though she adored her *papà,* he never really understood what was going on inside her head. Whatever she said, he could deny it point blank in court. He couldn't remember the medical word for his lovely daughter's affliction. Usually, she just lived her sweet young life in her own dream world – or so it seemed to him.

It was well beyond five in the evening before those cops had left him in peace.

'We'll be back tomorrow morning at ten o'clock, *Signor* Spanò,' the one from Rome had promised him. 'Stay in your own house and grounds. If you attempt to evade us, it will be a full-scale manhunt that you will be inviting. And you will, if necessary, be shot on sight.'

Left to himself and his two 'women', he had eaten a hurried meal and had drunk enough wine to put himself in the mood for what he had to do. He had quizzed Aurora as to what she had talked about to that police lady. 'Horses, mainly *papà,'* she had replied. 'She was *simpatica*[77] to me, but not quite as *simpatica* as that other one.'

The Smiling Man had not really taken in his daughter's closing words. He was already plotting his covert night time activities. He knew just how much he would take a malicious, sadistic pleasure in what he was intending to do. His overriding aim was to ensure he would never be accused of the murder of that treacherous little bitch's husband – what was his name? Capriotti, that was it. He had let his sadistic pleasure in killing get the better of him, on that occasion. He had shot the man in

---

[77] Kind, friendly, nice

the back of his brainless head with his own gun – with his two stooges as witnesses.

* * *

Aurora Spanò could not sleep that night. She felt too confused by the day's events to fall into her usual untroubled slumber – when her dreams would be peopled by stallions ridden by other girls – sometimes young men - slightly older than she was. But when they went racing through the woods it was always her Barone who finished first. She sighed and gave up the idea of trying to fall asleep.

It was by no means the first time she had decided to go riding in the woods after dark. The moon was shining and the stars were bright in the heavens. She could pretend she was taking some of her dream friends for a night time ride through the woods on her *papà's* estate. They would love that, wouldn't they!

So, she got dressed in her riding jacket and jodhpurs. She wouldn't bother with the helmet. Her 'mother', who was not her real mum anyway, wouldn't be there to fuss over her and nag her to put her hat on 'just in case you fall off, *tesoro*.'

Monica wouldn't have cared all that much even if she did come off her horse, thought Aurora. Besides which, Barone would never allow that to happen.

And so, Aurora went silently downstairs, and out of the back door. The dogs growled at her in the back of their throats from somewhere in the shadows.

'*Calma, Argo! Calma, Milo! Sono io...*'

The two German Shepherd dogs did not even bother to get up from where they were lying.

In the stables, her father's horse and their pet pony did not stir. Barone sensed Aurora's presence and whinnied in anticipation of her silent arrival. Tonight, thought Aurora, she would do what she was never allowed to do with adults present. She would ride Barone bare-back. Even her *papà's* grubby ruffians used to threaten to tell her dad if ever they caught her trying to ride her horse without the usual accoutrements.

Tonight felt different! Something in the air had changed. Maybe it was all those strangers who had suddenly invaded the house...and that kind police lady who had talked to her about her pony – just as if she already knew all about horses. Aurora had even offered to let the lady mount Barone. What was the name she had given? It was a long name, beginning with M. But the police lady had smiled at her and put an arm round her shoulder.

'Next time, Aurora. I should really be back with those policemen...and your dad.'

Aurora had wanted to ask why those policemen were talking to her *papà*. But she had a strange feeling that she did not really want to know the reason for their visit.

Aurora bent over and whispered something in her horse's ear. Barone set off at a steady walking pace up the hill towards the darkling woods which ran along the ridge. He had sensed the change in habit of his mount, who was holding on to his mane for support. He had to adjust his normal behaviour, aware of an altered sense of balance in his precious human cargo. As they mounted the hillside and entered the forest, Aurora heard the sound of voices somewhere below her. She looked downhill and could make out three figures. She recognised her father's voice, but there was something discordant about it. She had never heard him talking like this before. It made her feel strange inside. She whispered in Barone's ear again:

'Sta' fermo, Barone. Non ti muovere.'[78]

The horse came to an obedient halt. Aurora was craning her ears to listen to what was being said. The other two figures, she realised, were Mimo and Antò. They looked as if they were digging a hole. Was that a pistol in her *papà's* hand? She felt a chill of shock running up and down her spine. Barone gave a nervous shudder which, for a brief second, Aurora felt down the length of his body.

---

[78] Stay still... Don't move

164

His two underlings, Antò and Mimo had been woken up from a wine-induced sleep hardly aware of what was happening when their *capo* shook them roughly awake.

'Intruders up there, *ragazzi*. Take your pistols and grab a couple of spades. We may have a couple of bodies to dispose of by the end of the night – who knows?'

Antò and Mimo looked at each other covertly as The Smiling Man began the ascent up towards the ridge. They might not have been blessed with a very high IQ, but they knew the signs. They could both see the fear in each other's eyes. Mimo, slightly brighter than his counterpart, indicated the pistol in his holster and gave Antò a quizzical look which – without a word being spoken – clearly said: 'Why would he tell us to take guns with us if he was intending to eliminate us?' Then a deeper, much blacker thought came into his mind. They would have to be very wary of their *capo*. He had once boasted to them that he had killed a total of six people in Catanzaro. 'Three of them with my bare hands,' he had added with sadistic pleasure.

They had been ordered to start digging a deep hole as soon as they had stopped below the summit of the forested ridge above them.

'Where are these intruders, *capo?*' asked Mimo suspiciously.

'Up there in the forest somewhere. Aurora told me she had seen two strangers walking along with rifles over their shoulders. We'll find them easily enough.'

'So why didn't you bring the dogs with us, *capo?*' asked Antò, whose wine-muddled suspicions were beginning to become clearer by the second.

'The dogs make too much noise,' snapped The Smiling Man. 'Just finish the digging!'

The impatience in his voice was matched by the expression of sadistic anticipation he felt building up inside.

The two diggers simultaneously threw down their tools. Enough was enough! Their hands instinctively felt for their pistols. But one glance at the mafioso was enough. He had a leer on his face which was unmistakable. His pistol, Mimo noticed in terror, was equipped with a silencer.

'Look at this from my perspective, *ragazzi.* We killed that wimp of a man and you were the ones who hung him out to dry. I cannot run the risk of hoping that one day, under pressure from that *commissario,* you won't grass me up to save your miserable skins. You do see what I'm getting at don't you?'

It was Antò who first began babbling in fear for his life, pleading pitifully to be spared.

'Save your breath, Antò,' shouted Mimo. 'He's going to kill us both.'

Mimo's words floated on the night air up to the top of the ridge where Aurora was looking on in petrified silence.

Mimo did the only thing he could in the circumstances. Old habits always die hard. He took out his pistol and shot Antò in the head. His body fell neatly into the hole they had been digging.

'Now you are safe, *capo*. You know you can trust me not to blab.'

Don Giulio Spanò was smiling at Mimo.

'*Bravo,* Mimo! I knew I could count on you. Let's get this body covered up. I'll give you a hand.'

He climbed down inside the hole and reached for Antò's gun, turned it on Mimo and shot him dead at point blank range.

Ah, that sweet feeling of revenge for his days of suffering. Killing could be so gratifying...

Don Giulio left the two pistols lying next to their one-time owners. He threw the earth over the two bodies and patted down the soil – before removing the thin surgical gloves he had worn and chucking them nonchalantly into the hole before covering them with the remaining soil. Without really thinking, he had chucked his own pistol into the hole where the bodies lay. With all these cops around, you couldn't be too safe. It was the only proof left that he had silenced that Capriotti man for ever. Best to play safe.

Of the two young police officers, who had been drafted in from nearby Penne to carry out the night time vigil, one was asleep and the second was composing text messages on his mobile phone. He heard what sounded like two muffled shots in the darkness – and then a complete silence. He debated whether he should wake up his companion but decided it was not worth the trouble. They had received specific instructions from that formidable lady *Questore* to ensure that nobody left the premises through the main gates – which remained firmly closed, to the officer's great relief.

* * *

Aurora sat there unable to move. Barone had been startled by the two shots but had not made any noise that would give away their presence. The girl was numb, shivering from the shock of witnessing murder for the first time in her life. She was shaking with a nervous reaction even beneath the heavy riding jacket she was wearing. Her father had completed whatever it was he had done and had begun to walk back down the hill.

On one level, Aurora was already trying to reinterpret what she had seen her father do. She must have made a mistake. Her *papà* would never have done that. He was a kind man – towards her, at least.

168

But on a deeper level she was subconsciously aware that her life had altered forever. She felt alone...oh so alone! She would need to talk to somebody. But who?

She brought her shaking knees together to nudge Barone into a walk. But Barone, driven by some secret equine instinct, had understood that his precious passenger was no longer herself. He turned round and ambled slowly downhill towards the stables of his own accord. Aurora did not countermand his decision.

Aurora dismounted and stroked the horse's muzzle. Then she simply lay down in the warm straw and slept fitfully until dawn. She dreamt she was Joan of Arc – her childhood heroine - fighting off her enemies in a dark forest but finally being carried home to safety by her beloved mount. And yet, when she had finally returned to her room, ignoring Monica's daily inanities in the kitchen, she had but one simple thought running through the shattered perception of her life. There *was* someone she could turn to. But how on earth would she ever manage to find her again?

14: The truth of the matter...

'I will be needing to interview your two...helpers, *Signor* Spanò. Where might I find them?' had been the first question that Mariastella Martellini had shot at the mafioso the following morning. 'Your daughter – I take it she really *is* your daughter – was talking to me about them yesterday. Mimo and Antò, she told me...'

Mariastella had arrived early for day two of the face-to-face encounter, along with the *Guardia di Finanza* team. She had requested the presence of her second-in-command, who had been glad to have something useful to do to take his mind off the so-far unexplained disappearance of his father. Beppe had had no news from his mother as to his reappearance – or otherwise. He had felt reluctant to phone her and ask the key question: 'Is my father back home with you?' He knew only too well that pinning his mother down in any sense of the word was as unpredictable as the eruptions of Mount Etna. It wouldn't cross her mind that her 'neglectful' son might be worried stiff about the safety of his own father.

On hearing the unexpected question, the Smiling Man had looked indifferently at the lady *Questore,* shrugging a casual shoulder by way of response.

He was inwardly cursing the fact that the disappearance of his stooges would be detected so soon. He would have to maintain his *sang-froid*. The sweet smell of blood shed was still lingering about his person. A killing usually took a couple days to fade away and be absorbed into the past – a thing forgotten.

'They'll be around the grounds somewhere, *Signora Questore,*' replied the mafioso, insensitive to the irony of his statement. 'They live in a sort of lodge just behind the stables. Go and have a look for yourself. They are probably still sleeping off another few bottles of cheap red wine,' he had replied scornfully.

Mariastella had left Beppe outside the gate chatting to the three officers on guard duty for that day. It was the turn of *Agenti* Gino Martelli and Danilo Simone to stand on guard outside the gates of the Spanò residence, in the company of Officer Flavia Evangelista, who had volunteered to be available every day, if necessary.

'I only live just up the road in Collecorvini, *Signora Questore,*' she had almost pleaded. 'This is the first time in years that I've had something useful to do!'

Mariastella Martellini briefly re-emerged through the gates and asked Beppe to track down the mafioso's sidekicks.

'I could stay on guard with *Agente* Evangelista, *Dotoressa.* [79] Why don't we give Gino and Danilo a break from the monotony of guard duty and send them in to track down Don Giulio's henchmen?' Beppe suggested to his *capo*.

---

[79] A common and respectful form of address, not just for doctors!

The *Questore* had nodded her consent and excused herself, saying she really ought to be following the interview between the mafioso and the *Guardia*.

'And keep an eye out for Spanò's daughter too, *ragazzi,*' she had added, addressing Gino and Danilo. 'Her name is Aurora. Reassure her, please. She's a very vulnerable young lady. You can't miss her. She's a very pretty teenager with flowing black hair – and a horse!'

The two officers strolled into the grounds, a little overwhelmed by the size of the house. A smart-looking, shapely blond woman was hanging out some washing on a carousel behind the house, seemingly unaffected by the presence of a houseful of police officers.

'Maybe she doesn't have anything to hide,' said Gino.

'Maybe she doesn't know what is really going on,' suggested his companion.

She looked at them indifferently but managed a cursory wave of the hand in their direction.

They found the living quarters of the two henchmen – and an ancient FIAT Tipo parked haphazardly on the grass. It was unlocked and the keys were still in the ignition. They knocked needlessly on the open door before going in.

Apart from the stale smell of old wine and unwashed bodies, there was nothing untoward to be seen. Walking into the sleeping quarters, they were struck by the fact that the beds had apparently not been slept in.

The two officers were relieved to escape back into the open air. They walked round to the other side of the out-buildings where the stables were situated.

They wandered into the stables and surprised a dark-skinned girl of about fifteen or sixteen patiently grooming a horse. Gino looked at Danilo. They had found the daughter – and nodded at each other in recognition of the accuracy of the description which their *Questore* had provided.

'Ciao,' said Danilo. 'You must be Aurora.'

'Che bello cavallo che c'hai!'[80] said Gino. *'Come si chiama?'*

Aurora was looking at these two handsome, young policemen with a wary look in her eyes.

'His name is *Barone,'* she replied. She stopped the grooming and placed the saddle and stirrups on to the animal's back, seemingly anxious to ride off. She didn't feel particularly scared of the two men. In fact, she registered somewhere inside her mind that they were really very *simpatici.* But it wasn't these two strangers she wanted to confide in. She was sure they must be about to ask her the one question she was dreading. She simply could not tell *them* what she had witnessed. Only the

---

[80] What a beautiful horse you have!

173

other one would do! If only she could remember her name. Was it Silvia? She was almost certain it had begun with the letter 'S'.

'Will you accompany us up the hillside, *Signorina* Aurora?' asked one of the officers. What could she do? You don't say 'no' to the police – and they were being very sweet and kind towards her. She nodded as she led Barone out of the stable. She could take them up *that* path and walk past where…**it** had happened. Now it was daylight, she was beginning to doubt what she had seen. Maybe it *was* a dream, she thought, clutching at the one straw which remained. If it *was* a dream, she would not be betraying her father in any way by walking up the hill to that spot.

She accompanied the two officers as they climbed up the steep slope. They chatted to her about her horse, and how long she had known him. She was happy to tell them that she had had him as a foal – 'back home' in Catanzaro, she had let slip.

'Never mind,' she thought. 'I haven't given away any secrets, have I?'

The little group had nearly reached the summit. The patch of earth looked so innocent to her. Surely, she must have been imagining things. Gino and Danilo were looking at each other. Gino frowned at his friend. Danilo was scraping the surface of the soil with his shoe.

They were both astonished at the alacrity with which Aurora had mounted the horse. She rode off at a gallop without a word to either of them.

'It was as if she wanted to escape from us,' said Gino quietly.

Danilo was still automatically displacing the loose soil with the toe of his boot. He thought he had spotted something blue just beneath the surface. Another prod with his toe confirmed he was right. There was a pair of surgical gloves covered with soil.

Was he beginning to think like his *capo,* the *commissario?* Something of their *capo* must surely have rubbed off by now!

'You don't happen to have a plastic evidence bag on you, Gino?'

'Why, do you think it might be important?' asked Gino.

'If we have learnt anything from the *commissario,* it is that one should begin to think laterally. I don't know, Gino. But I am suspicious. And look! there are brown patches on one of the gloves which look as if they might be…'

'I'll go back and get an evidence bag from the car, Danilo,' said Gino. 'You wait here.'

Danilo was assuming that the two gangsters whom they were out searching for had been busy burying something – or digging something up - equally as likely.

Those two stooges, Mimo and Antò, could be almost anywhere in this forest of trees. They could end up searching for them all day. It would make more sense to wait for them in their makeshift home, he reckoned. He should have removed the keys from the ignition to prevent any attempt at evasion. He walked briskly back down the hill, pinching the sleeves of the gloves between thumb and forefinger. It would save Gino having to walk back up the hill again, he thought as he pocketed the car keys from the dented Tipo before heading towards the main gates.

Gino was not sure how to unlock the main gates. There must be a box somewhere nearby. He was reduced to calling out to Beppe through the bars. Beppe had his back to Gino. He was leaning against the bonnet of the police car in deep conversation with *Agente* Evangelista.

'How do I open the gates, *capo?*' Gino called out.

The *commissario* waved a remote-control handset at the gates.

'I purloined this off the Smiling Man. I pointed out to him he would never be needing it again. If looks could kill! What's up, Gino?'

When his colleague explained why he needed an evidence bag from the car, his chief looked very intensely at him, demanding a fuller explanation of what they had discovered.

'It was strange, *capo*. It was the daughter, Aurora, who walked us up the hill – with her horse…'

'They are inseparable, it seems.'

'She almost led us beyond the patch where the soil was bare. And when Danilo began to scrape the loose soil away, she just mounted the horse nimbly and shot off into the woods without a word. It was as if…'

He left the sentence unfinished because he was not sure what he meant to say.

'She knew what was buried there?'

Beppe completed the sentence for him.

Gino sighed out loud. The *commissario* was, as ever, at least one step ahead of everyone else, admitted Gino to himself. Danilo arrived still pinching the gloves between finger and thumb before dropping them into the evidence bag.

'I'll get Mariastella to take this back to Pescara to have it analysed,' said Beppe. 'So, no sign of the two thugs, anywhere?'

'None, *capo,* and their beds had not been slept in as far as we could tell,' added Danilo. There is obviously *something* buried at the top of the hill…'

* * *

Aurora stroked her horse's neck, quietly repeating the words *'Bravo Barone – bravissimo!'* as they slowed down from a gallop to a canter. The horse seemed to know which direction to take with a greater surety than Aurora herself. She had only taken this route twice on previous occasions – both times with her father's horse taking the lead.

Aurora knew where she ultimately wanted to get to – only she could not recall the exact route to follow. But there was no hurry, was there? She did not want to go back home. She spent all afternoon wandering through unchartered territory, with no sense of the passing time. She began to have a sense of freedom which she could not remember experiencing since she had arrived in this foreign part of Italy - which was nothing like her native Calabria.

She was heading into an unknown world in which her father had no place. She patted the horse's neck and trusted that he knew where she wanted to go. Warm tears suddenly welled up in her eyes – and she wept out loud for the first time since she had watched her father last night. She noticed that the light was beginning to fade. 'Where are we, Barone? I need to find that house where I met that policewoman. Take me there, please…'

The horse turned round and trotted for quite some distance back along the route which they had previously taken. Out of the blue, Aurora had the sensation she knew where she was. She recognised the house they were approaching as darkness fell. She began to cry, out of sheer relief.

It was Tommaso Di Sabatino, the *frantoista's* son who heard the clip-clop of a horse's hooves arriving in the spacious courtyard of the olive press. He had been reading a novel in his bedroom, having grown tired of watching some drama called *La Sposa* [81] on Rai 1, which his parents were obviously hooked on. It was a period drama – set in an era when his parents were still children. He took one look at the horse and its rider. He could barely believe his eyes. Without hesitation, he ran downstairs, calling for his parents to tear themselves away from the television.

'We have an unexpected guest, *papà, mamma!*'

Only in his early twenties, Tommaso took one look at Aurora's tear-stained face and felt an overwhelming desire to treat her as he treated his own younger sisters. He held the horse's halter as she dismounted.

'*Ma non c'è tuo padre?*' [82] asked Tommaso, puzzled yet anxious in the same breath. Aurora burst into tears again, sobbing pitifully. Tommaso put his arm round her shoulder, fearing that this familiar gesture would be rejected. But she seemed to find comfort in it. Davide Di Sabatino came out at a run with his wife, Gaetana in close pursuit.

---

[81] The Wife
[82] But isn't your father with you?

It was the mother who took control immediately, leading Aurora indoors to their living quarters and telling Tommaso to take her horse to the paddock – unused by the family for several years.

'Make sure the horse gets water and a bit of oats, or something,' she ordered. 'I'll take care of…Aurora, isn't it?' Go and turn that television off, Davide,' she told her husband. 'It's deafening!'

It was difficult to make a lot of sense out of Aurora's words, but she gathered that her father was being interrogated by the police. But that did not seem to be the matter which was uppermost in the girl's mind. Tommaso had returned from leaving the horse in the paddock.

'Tommaso,' said his mother, 'go and fetch a nice glass of water for Aurora, will you please?'

Even without Tommaso there, the girl still could not seem to explain why she had ridden all that way – in the gathering darkness.

When Tommaso reappeared, she looked appealingly at him, thanking him for his kindness to her as she took sips from the glass.

The gesture seemed to help her concentrate on some inner thought. Tommaso was almost embarrassed that this girl seemed to be addressing him, rather than his mother.

'I need to talk to that nice policewoman who was here last time,' she managed to say. 'I have something so important to tell her that it can't wait. I shall go mad if I cannot tell her. Please could you get her to come back here?' pleaded Aurora. 'I don't know who else to tell.'

It appeared that those few words were all she had wanted to say. But she made no move to leave the house – or its occupants.

Gaetana made a decision.

'We will get in touch with your friend, the policewoman tomorrow morning, Aurora. I seem to remember her name was Sonia, wasn't it?'

A glimmer of light appeared on Aurora's face. She nodded with the brief hint of a smile of relief on her face.

'But I think she lives quite a long way from here – and she has children to look after. So, Aurora, you can stay with us for the night. You – and your horse – will be safe with us.'

Aurora looked at the mother in a strange way, as if she did not quite understand how this had all happened. Gaetana understood perfectly. This girl was in need of a mother – even if she did not realise it yet.

The only made-up bed was in Tommaso's sisters' bedroom. It was Tommaso who took her upstairs to the top floor under the sloping roof. His sisters stirred in their sleep and muttered a *buona notte* simply because they were aware of someone else in the room. Aurora just lay gratefully on the bed and fell asleep immediately with her riding clothes on.

Ten o'clock or not, Davide Di Sabatino made a call to the *Questura* in Pescara. Somebody must be missing this strange but lovely girl. 'They damn-well ought to be!' he said out loud to his non-existent audience. Tommaso and Gaetana had disappeared to their respective bedrooms - the TV drama forgotten in the midst of the real-life drama taking place in their own home.

* * *

The following morning, just as the night watch team were heading home, Beppe arrived outside the mafioso's house, waiting for Danilo, Gino – and the ever-dependable Flavia Evangelista to return for the daytime vigil.

Mariastella arrived in her yellow Alfa Romeo Spider and went into the house after a brief chat with Beppe and his team. The Guardia team had, by that time, got tired of the commute to and from Pescara and had purloined spare rooms in the mafioso's mansion – without asking his permission.

'We should be able to dispense with your night duty team for the couple of days we shall still be here, *commissario*,' they had suggested. 'You all deserve a break.'

It had been the *commandante* from Rome who had ordained the changes.

Beppe, left alone with his team, could see that Danilo and Gino were dying for a bit of action.

'What should we do about the hole, *capo?*' asked Gino, half way through the morning. 'Should Danilo and I go and dig up…whatever's been buried in the ground?'

Gino had waited patiently until Beppe had told *Agente* Evangelista to go and take a break or have a coffee at *L'olivo nero* before he brought up the subject of digging.

Beppe was frowning without answering. The two officers were used to their chief's long silences before he gave an answer.

It took much longer than usual for him to mull over the situation. Gino had almost forgotten that he had asked the question.

'No, *ragazzi,*' he said firmly. 'It will have to be done by the forensic team, in any case. Naturally, I shall tell the *Questore* today about your important discovery, but I have a distinct feeling we may have to play the long game from now on.'

The team, who had remained outside the gates, had no knowledge about Aurora's night time journey. They simply assumed she was in the house – or in the stables.

Officer Flavia Evangelista returned dutifully after her one-hour break.

'Why don't you two go off and get some lunch in the village, *ragazzi?* Agente Evangelista – Flavia – and I will stay here.'

'It's very busy in the bar,' she said hurriedly, in an attempt to cover up her shock at being called by her first name. This *commissario* did not comply to any pre-conceptions she had nurtured about higher-ranking officers' behaviour towards those of inferior grade. It could not be a bad thing, she concluded, and even felt emboldened to ask Beppe what was likely to happen to her and the police station in Collecorvini.

'Do you think I shall simply continue to be the sole officer there, *commissario?'*

'That will be up to our *Questore* to decide, *Agente Flavia.* But knowing her, I would imagine she will promote you up one grade and find a replacement for **you**!'

Officer Evangelista smiled – not for the promotion, but for the acceptable compromise which Beppe had used in addressing her. The prospect of having some real authority in the town of Collecorvini was daunting.

Beppe and Officer Evangelista talked at some length about their respective families, before Beppe's mobile phone rang. To his surprise, he saw Sonia's number on the screen. It must be important, thought Beppe. Sonia would never ring him when on duty. He apologised to Officer Flavia and walked a few steps away to take the call. He felt a stab of fear in his gut. Maybe she had had news of his father! It was thus with a mixture of relief and astonishment that he listened to what Sonia began telling him.

'I'm sure you know this already, Beppe – you are always one step ahead of the rest of us. But. I've just been given a message by Officer Giacomo D'Amico, who's on duty this morning.'

'Go on Sonia,' said Beppe. She had not sounded as if she was about to impart any terrifying news about his father.

'Apparently, Davide Di Sabatino, the *frantoista,* telephoned the *Questura* at about 10 o'clock yesterday evening. He left a message asking for me. Giulio Spanò's daughter had just arrived at the olive press on horseback. It appears the only person who she would talk to about what was upsetting her is *me,* Beppe. The family just put her to bed in their home, fully dressed in her riding gear. They were sure she must have endured some terrible shock. But she simply insisted that I was the only person she could reveal her secret to...'

Beppe remained thoughtful for what seemed ages. Sonia knew from experience that he was mulling over the complex implications of what she had just told him. In the end, he simply said:

185

'It seems you are still on the case, *amore mio*. I will drop in to speak to the family on my way home – just so they will know that Aurora's request has not been ignored.'

'*A presto, amore,*' [83] said Sonia. She went about her daily chores trying to imagine what it was that this confused-sounding teenage girl wanted to tell her. Was it something real? Or was it - more likely - something generated by her own introspective perception of life?

Sonia was soon to change her mind radically about how this seemingly detached girl's mind really worked.

---

[83] See you soon

15: The gloves are off…

'This is pure conjecture, Mariastella, but I suspect that our mafioso friend has assassinated his two side-kicks. Gino and Danilo have discovered a patch where the earth has been recently dug up and then put back again. Danilo began to scrape away the top layer of soil with his foot and he discovered this just beneath the surface,'

Beppe thrust the evidence bag containing the blue gloves into the lady *Questore's* hand.

'I was wondering if you could give them to our forensic experts when you go back to the *Questura* this evening?'

Mariastella gave her second-in-command a resentful look.

'I had been intending to go straight home, *commissario*. But I suppose I could make a detour.'

'I apologise, Mariastella. I suppose we should get the forensic team up here in full regalia. But equally, we could postpone it until the *Guardia* have completed the legal formalities with *Signor* Spanò. What do you think, *capo?*'

Mariastella was looking weary. He felt sorry for her – guilty almost - that the speed with which the process of this investigation was progressing had left her mentally and emotionally stretched to her limits.

'Let's see what evidence these gloves provide us with. Then we will decide when to excavate that patch of land. But I have to say, Beppe, that I fear you may be right about what we shall find. I detected something odd in Spanò's attitude today. He seemed unnaturally sure of himself. Maybe it was more than sheer bravado?'

'From *his* point of view, it would be the natural thing to do. It is unlikely that he strung Daniele Capriotti up on that olive tree with his own bare hands.'

'You have done brilliantly, *commissario*. I am truly impressed by the progress you have made. You leave me breathless!'

'It is our team effort, Mariastella. I cannot take the credit alone.'

'Is there anything else I ought to know, Beppe?' she asked him with weary irony.

'Well, as it happens, yes. There has been another quite extraordinary development today…'

'May we sit in my car, *caro commissario?* I have been on my feet all day – and these boots I am wearing are killing my feet. I have some soft shoes in my car.'

Beppe ended up pulling the boots off her feet. He was glad there was nobody else in the vicinity to witness this almost intimate act.

Mariastella found the episode amusing. At least she was smiling again.

'So, what is it you have to tell me, *commissario?* Has Officer Evangelista fallen in love with you? The way she was looking at you this morning…!'

How is it that women always seem to notice these inconsequential details, Beppe was wondering. He graced her comment with an eyebrow raised in mild surprise and simply said:

'If only it was as simple as that, *dotoressa,* it would be easier to come to terms with.'

Then he told her about the phone call he had received from Sonia. Her tiredness vanished in a trice. She was looking alertly at her second-in-command.

'*Santo cielo,* Beppe![84] That is the last thing I was expecting you to say. Aurora gave me the impression of being scared of the outside world. What do you think is behind such a desperate move? It seems quite out of character.'

'Your guess is as good as mine, Mariastella.'

Beppe had become very thoughtful.

'Just maybe…she saw something which frightened her so much that escape was the only way out.'

The lady *Questore* could think of only one explanation – and only one solution to it.

---

[84] Good heavens! Lit: holy sky!

Beppe could read what was going through her mind, but said nothing.

'Don't worry, Beppe. We'll do it tomorrow – but very discreetly!'

The surveillance team had been sent home. The night-watch had been cancelled because of the presence of the three *Guardia* officers, remaining within the Spanò household.

'You may well be reassigned to a different location tomorrow, *Agente* Flavia,' Beppe informed the officer from Collecorvini. 'Someone will contact you tomorrow morning – probably myself or the *Questore.*'

Agente Evangelista looked puzzled – but there was no explanation forthcoming.

* * *

Beppe arrived at the *frantoio* and found the whole family sitting round the large, rectangular wooden table in the kitchen. It was 'family reunion' time, Beppe supposed. He smiled at everyone and introduced himself as *Commissario* Stancato from Pescara – just in case they had forgotten who he really was after his charade with The Smiling Man.

Davide, Tommaso and Gaetana made as if to stand up and shake Beppe's hand. He made a sign for them not to trouble to stand up, as he walked round the table shaking their hands.

Tommaso's two sisters relaxed and smiled at Beppe. Aurora was looking fearfully at Beppe.

'*Tutto bene,* Aurora,' he reassured her. 'Your *papà* doesn't know where you are. How is Barone?'

The mention of the horse's name altered her facial expression in an instant. But she still did not utter a word nor did she smile at this 'stranger'.

'We've spent all day making a makeshift stable behind the house to make Aurora's horse comfortable,' explained Tommaso. 'I think Aurora is feeling a bit tired, aren't you, *tesoro*?'[85]

Aurora nodded, contentedly. It had been years since anybody had called her their 'sweetie'. It was obvious to her that everybody in the room trusted this stranger. She had not really taken in this policeman from the time when he – not dressed as a policeman and speaking with a funny accent – had appeared at the *frantoio* in the company of…Sonia!

Beppe smiled warmly at this silent teenage girl.

'I have just come to tell you that Sonia will be here tomorrow morning to meet you again. She remembers you very well, Aurora.'

Now the girl was smiling.

'Oh, do you know Sonia…*Signor commiss…?*'

---

[85] Treasure : sweetie – a familiar term of endearment.

Beppe was struck by the fact that this girl, probably a recluse for years, had never come across the word before. She had mistaken his title for his name. Aurora blushed when the three adults laughed quietly at the innocence of her question.

'I should say so, Aurora. I'm married to her and she is the mother of my two children. (Why had he nearly said 'three'?) I hope you will meet them all one day. But Sonia is going to come specially to see you tomorrow morning. I believe you have something vital to tell her?'

Aurora nodded solemnly at Beppe. Her face had clouded over with anxiety. But she managed to say *'Grazie, signore.'*

'Call me Beppe, Aurora. It's easier than saying *commissario,'* he added kindly.

Aurora looked at him intently, not smiling – but there was an undercurrent of silent gratitude in those big brown eyes. The *commissario* did the round of handshakes again, waving cheerfully at Aurora and Tommaso's two younger sisters.

'A domani, ragazzi. At about half past nine. No later, I promise.'

* * *

There seemed to be a festive atmosphere upstairs when Beppe arrived back home in Atri.

He had stopped to chat to Roberto and Irene, Sonia's parents, who occupied the ground and first floors. Veronica and Lorenzo's voices could be heard even from two floors up.

'They are excited because their mother, it seems, is going back to being a policewoman for one day. And tomorrow being a Saturday, I think your children are pestering Sonia to be allowed to accompany you,' explained Roberto.

'We are going to visit one of our sons tomorrow, Beppe,' explained Irene. 'As you know, Marco lives in Teramo. Veronica and Lorenzo are welcome to come with us, of course. But I think they are trying to persuade their mother to let them go with her instead. Veronica has been claiming that Sonia will need protecting because it sounds like a dangerous mission. You know what a vivid imagination our granddaughter has, Beppe.'

'Well, I had better go up and settle matters. Sonia doesn't seem to have made much headway. It sounds as if she's needing a bit of moral support,' suggested Beppe, taking his leave of his amused parents-in-law.

'*In bocca al lupo,* Beppe,' said Roberto ironically.

Beppe thought it advisable to put on his stern paternal look as he walked into the living room. His severe stare always succeeded in unnerving his team – or even hardened criminals, if he was lucky. It did not seem to have any effect on Veronica, who appeared to believe that her presence the following day was already a *fait accompli.*

'I'm going to meet a real-life horse, *papà,*' she declared. Lorenzo nodded obediently at a stern look from his sister.

'Your mother and I will discuss the matter together, *ragazzi,*' stated Beppe quietly. 'Go and wash your hands before dinner.'

With an all too precocious adolescent pout on her face, Veronica led her brother to the floor above, trying to look appealingly at her mother at the same time. Sonia and Beppe both smiled at the expression on her face. Veronica knew that she could never be sure of victory when both her parents ganged up on her.

'We've got to act cool, Lori,' she said in a conspiratorial voice. Lorenzo's vocabulary was not yet quite up to the task of putting his sister in her place. But the resentful expression on his face clearly informed his sister that he considered *he* had been acting cool all along.

Sonia and Beppe took one look at each other and shrugged in resignation. It certainly could not do any harm - and it might even have a positive effect.

'But we will have to go in two cars, *amore,*' Beppe pointed out. 'Tomorrow is going to be a very challenging day *chez* Giulio Spanò, I suspect.'

'Does he know that his daughter has gone missing, Beppe?'

'That is a very interesting question, Sonia. If he hadn't realised Aurora is not in the house when I left this afternoon, he will certainly have found out by tomorrow morning,' concluded Beppe.

'She must have a mobile phone on her,' said Sonia. 'What will happen if that bastard calls her tonight? She might well lose her nerve.'

Beppe was looking hard at Sonia. Why in the name of all the saints had he not foreseen *that* problem?

'Why don't you phone up the *frantoista* and talk to him – while I finish getting dinner ready?' suggested Sonia.

Beppe did just that, with his heart pounding.

'Che stronzo che sei, Beppe Stancato!' [86] he swore under his breath.

'I'll pass you on to Tommaso,' said the mother, who had answered the phone. He seems to have taken Aurora under his wing, *commissario.'*

'Don't worry, *commissario,'* were Tommaso's calm and reassuring words. 'I took care of that eventuality. I have switched her phone off and I'm keeping it in a safe place. Aurora understands the risk involved. *A domani, commissario!'*

Beppe returned to the kitchen where Sonia was serving up her favourite local lamb dish with Rosemary and scrambled egg.[87]

---

[86] What a fool, you are...
[87] Agnello Cacio e Uova, it's called. See recipe by Valentina Harris

'Thank you, *amore*. I never gave phones a single thought,' he explained shame-facedly.

'You can't be expected to think of everything, my *commissario.*'

Veronica was astounded at the ease with which her desire to accompany her mother the next day had been achieved. Lorenzo simply smiled happily.

'Should I wear a uniform – or just ordinary clothes?' asked Sonia as they were eating.

Dai, mamma! [88] You look great in your uniform!' said Veronica.

'I am sure that you must have told Aurora you were a police officer when you first met her – even if you were dressed normally on that famous occasion. Maybe a light summer uniform might reassure her,' suggested Beppe.

'Can I wear my cowboy outfit?' asked Lorenzo, who had reached that stage when kids love to dress up to enhance their image in the eyes of the world.

'What, Lori? You want to scare this girl to death all over again!' stated Veronica teasingly.

Sonia smiled at her daughter's verbal attack but told Lorenzo he could wear what he liked. 'That young lady's been

---

[88] Go on! Lit: 'Give' An expression used to urge someone to take a particular course of action.

eavesdropping,' she said to herself. 'How on earth does she seem to know about Aurora?'

There was no point in probing more deeply, she considered.

'Maybe, just maybe you will be allowed to sit on her horse,' she said. 'So, you will really look the part with your cowboy outfit on, Lori.'

'I'm going to wear my jeans, *mamma* – especially if I'm going to have to climb up on to a horse!' Veronica decided, already self-conscious when it came to her seven-year-old body being exposed in public.

The matter of their dress code was settled.

* * *

The little convoy of two cars arrived just after nine o'clock in the courtyard of the *frantoio.* Lorenzo had travelled in his mother's car because, to his obvious humiliation, he still had to use a child's seat. Veronica had wanted to share the journey with her *papà* – whom she rarely had the chance to monopolise on normal days. She had even said sorry to her *mamma* for her act of desertion.

Veronica kept up a running commentary throughout the forty-five-minute journey. At one point, after a rare pause lasting all of one minute, she gave her father a sideways glance and asked out of the blue:

'When is *mamma* going to have another baby?'

'What makes you think we haven't got our hands full already just looking after you two?' stated Beppe with mock severity. He wanted to test her reaction. All Veronica did was giggle merrily.

'Would you like another brother or sister, Vero?' he asked.

'I think so, yes – because we are such a happy family, aren't we? It would be a pity if there was never anyone else to share it with us – *non è vero, papà?*' [89]

Beppe put out a hand and ruffled his daughter's hair affectionately. She thrust her head away from the gesture, but was secretly content that she had succeeded in formulating her thoughts so accurately.

'Brava, tesoro!' he said simply. Inside he was wondering if his daughter had had some premonition.

'Both hands on the steering wheel please, *papà!*' she said, echoing the admonishing words she had so often heard her mother use while Beppe was driving.

They completed the last lap of the journey in relative silence, Veronica becoming excited as she sensed their destination was nearby.

There were already a couple of customers stocking up with olive oil. Word had quickly spread that the threat from the

---

[89] Isn't that so? Isn't that true?

local mafioso had been removed and business had magically picked up again.

It was Tommaso who was there to greet his visitors.

'Aurora is still upstairs with my little sisters,' he explained. 'I get the impression she is a bit reluctant to meet you, *Signora Sonia* – now that the moment of truth has arrived.'

'It is just as I expected, Tommaso,' replied Sonia. 'Don't worry. I'll go and talk to her in private, as long as someone can look after Veronica and Lorenzo.'

Beppe was already being called on his mobile by an anxious Officer Danilo Simone.

'There's only myself, Gino and *Agente* Evangelista here, *commissario*. The *Questore* got us to stay on guard today so that we can take the forensic team up to where the earth has been disturbed. And the *Questore* is getting a bit rattled because you are not here yet. She wants you to create some distraction so that the forensic people can do their job unnoticed.'

'I have to go to the Spanò house,' Beppe explained to Sonia and Tommaso. 'It seems that a whole army of technicians from the forensic team has arrived and is waiting out of sight under Mariastella's orders.'

'Don't worry. I'll look after your children, *commissario,*' Tommaso reassured the parents. 'Come on you two. We'll go and make the acquaintance of a horse called Barone.'

Beppe shot off at speed and Sonia, after receiving simple directions, went upstairs in search of Aurora. She would have to rely completely on her natural instincts over the next fifteen minutes or so. After all, she reasoned, it is not every day that a vulnerable teenage girl has to denounce her father for cold-bloodied murder – assuming that this was the burden which Aurora was bearing.

'La poverina!' [90] muttered Sonia to herself as she climbed the wooden staircase, guided by the sound of girly voices coming from a room somewhere above her.

Aurora's reaction when Sonia entered the bedroom was predictable. It took her an age of ticking seconds before she made the connection between the uniformed woman who had just entered the bedroom and the policewoman whom she had begun to confide in during an encounter belonging to a previous, long-ago life, which had since been dashed on the rocks.

'Ciao, Aurora. Yes, it's me – Sonia,' said Sonia holding her arms partly open in a welcoming gesture.

Aurora ran towards Sonia with a guilty smile on her face. She had rashly initiated a course of action which she was no longer sure she wanted to face up to.

Sonia took one look at Aurora's face as she held the girl in a brief embrace. She knew instinctively that she would be

---

[90] The poor little thing

spelling the end of trust if she so much as mentioned why she was present.

'Aurora, *tesoro mio,* I know I should have asked you first but I had to bring my son and daughter with me. They only agreed to come at all because I promised them a ride on Barone...I do hope you'll forgive me...'

There was no need to complete the sentence. Aurora was practically dragging Sonia out of the room, filled with joy that she could forget why she had brought this policewoman all the way to this place.

'Aren't you going to introduce me to your new friends, Aurora? They might want to come too.'

'Caterina and....'

'Lucia,' said the elder of Tommaso's sisters, supplying her own name.

Aurora happily resaddled her horse and led him out into the paddock. It was Veronica who assumed the right to be given the first ride – barely a second after she had been introduced to a smiling Aurora – who took one look at Veronica and adjusted the stirrups accordingly.

'Don't look so anxious, Sonia,' said Aurora. 'Barone is quite used to children – and I shall walk with him all the time.

Veronica looked nervous for the first three circuits.

'I'm so much taller than you, *mamma,*' she proclaimed from on high after the fourth circuit. She looked in her element, thought her mother. It was only after the twelfth circuit that vociferous protests from Lorenzo brought his sister's solo ride round paradise to an end.

'Lorenzo is a bit too small to ride on his own, Sonia,' said Aurora. 'Despite being dressed up as a cowboy,' she said admiring Lorenzo's outfit.

Under protest, Veronica agreed to hold on to her brother. It was that or having to dismount and allow Aurora to take over, she realised.

The group had spent almost two hours riding around the paddock. Even Sonia had a go – keeping quiet about the fact that she had been a horse-rider in her younger days. But Aurora, who had spotted the way Sonia hitched herself up and sat in the saddle recognised that she was no amateur. To Sonia's alarm, Aurora let go of the reigns and whispered something in the horse's ear. Barone set off at a trot and did three circuits of the paddock until Sonia herself reigned the horse in.

'I love the way your *culetto*[91] bounces up and down as you ride, *mamma!*' announced her daughter, cheekily.

Sonia felt too exhausted from the effort required to remain upright in the saddle to chide her daughter. Besides which, everyone – including Aurora – had burst out laughing at Veronica's cheerful appraisal of her mother's alluring physical attributes.

---

[91] Nice little bum – in common parlance!

Sonia took one look at Aurora's relaxed face and decided this was the right moment. Tommaso had re-emerged from the house and announced it was nearly lunchtime. There had been no invitation; it was just assumed the visitors would stay and share the simple family lunch.

Sonia led Aurora to one side saying quietly:

'If it helps you, *tesoro mio,* I think *I* can tell *you* what it is you feel so reluctant to talk about…'

Aurora looked shocked but nodded in acquiescence. One minute later, the floodgates opened and Aurora managed to complete the details herself between the therapeutic outburst of tears. By the time Aurora and Sonia walked back inside the house, a rather silent gathering had already finished eating. This suited Aurora, who could not hide her tear-stained face. She sat with Sonia and ate the first homely meal she had had in years.

'I love it here, Sonia,' she confided. 'Davide has already said I can stay here for as long as I like. They even want to send me to school one day…'

Mission accomplished, thought Sonia joyfully. She would call Beppe as soon as she could. It took an effort to remind herself that she was acting out a minor role in a complex police operation initiated by her own husband – who had been the first one to seriously question the supposed suicide of a man found hanging lifeless from the branch of an ancient olive tree.

What an age seemed to have passed since that gruesome discovery had been reported.

* * *

It was the first time that Beppe had seen the *Questore* on edge. As he drove up to the gates of the Spanò mansion, Mariastella was anxiously looking at her watch and fingering her mobile phone as if undecided as to whether she should make a call or not. She was standing a metre or so apart from the usual team of police officers – Danilo Simone, Gino Martelli and *Agente* Flavia Evangelista from Collecorvini.

The relief on Mariastella's face on seeing her second-in-command arrive was patently clear.

'I'm sorry, Mariastella. I had to drop Sonia and our two children off at the *frantoio*. I didn't realise…'

Mariastella Martellini dismissed Beppe's apology with a wave of her hand.

'It's OK, Beppe. You're here now. That's all that matters. I feel that everything is happening at once today. I've got the forensics team waiting down by the *Olivo Nero*. I suspect they might well be inside the bar by now.'

'So, we're sending in the troops straight away, are we *capo?*' Beppe asked calmly.

'I reckon we should bring matters to a head, Beppe. There seems no point in playing cat and mouse with that bastard. Let's nail him with suspected murder, at least – while we tie up the loose ends…'

'I entirely agree with you, Mariastella,' replied Beppe quietly, thinking that the 'loose ends' were going to trigger off a whole new set of problems as yet unforeseen. 'Did forensics find anything interesting on those gloves?'

'Oh yes, they've taken blood samples and they found traces of DNA inside the gloves. But one of the things we are going to do this morning is take samples of his DNA and blood to see if they match those on the gloves. That will give him something to think about. At this stage, I do not really care if he spots the forensics team going up the hillside…'

'It's going to work out fine, Mariastella,' Beppe reassured his chief.

'I would like you to be present with me while we interview the mafioso today, Beppe.'

'Of course, Mariastella. It was what I was expecting to do.'

'Come inside as soon as you've welcomed the forensics team, Beppe. Officers Gino and Danilo can show them where the site is which they will be digging up. Bruno Esposito, the chief toxicologist, has come with the team. He says he wants to get involved in this case again. He's still worried about those Xylella-infected plants he discovered on the first day of this investigation.'

Beppe always felt reassured by the toxicologist's presence. His expertise went well beyond the boundaries of his official job title.

The *Questore* made a rapid phone call to summon the forensics team – well aware she would be interrupting their *cappuccini* and *cornetti*. [92]

She nodded at Beppe and walked back into the house, ready to do battle with the Smiling Man. She had intuited that this final day – marking the end of the formal interviews - would be turbulent.

* * *

By late afternoon, the three senior *Guardia* officers had taken their leave, carrying a pile of folders and documents which they were sequestering. It had been Bruno Esposito himself, dressed in a white coat and wearing a mask, who had appeared on the scene and carried out a simple swab test for DNA and taken a sample of Giulio Spanò's blood.

The *commandante* from Rome took Beppe to one side before leaving and complimented him unreservedly on his handling of the case.

'Your very personable-looking *Questore* has been filling me in on your achievements over the last few days, *commissario.*'

---

[92] croissants

'Kind of her!' said Beppe with quiet irony.

'This scam has been quite obviously one of the many money-laundering schemes set up by the *'ndrangheta* all over our beloved peninsula,' stated the *commandante,* sadly. 'This one was, mercifully, relatively easy to unravel. But if you are wanting to nail that man for the original murder of – what was his name? – Scarpetti?'

'Capriotti,' corrected Beppe.

'Thank you, *commissario*... I'm sure you will quite easily manage to pin the killing on him. He's brutal, but relatively naïve, I have the impression. You just need to find his Achilles Heel.'

'Oh, I think we've already found his *punto debole,*[93]*com mandante,'* said Beppe maliciously.

To Beppe's surprise, the *commandante* had shaken Beppe's hand in both of his before departing with a warm smile on his face.

The mafioso, had tolerated Bruno Esposito's medical ministrations with feigned indifference while he continued to smile mockingly in Beppe's direction. He might have been less cocky had he known how the session was to unfurl as the late afternoon progressed into early evening.

The first sign of cracks appearing in Don Giulio Spanò's armour of amused indifference was quick to make itself

---

[93] Weak point

apparent soon after the departure of the *Guardia di Finanza* team.

Beppe and the *Questore,* Mariastella Martellini, were left alone with The Smiling Man. A quick call to Officers Gino and Danilo brought them indoors to the room where the interviews had taken place. Bruno Esposito joined the group unexpectedly a few minutes later. He looked at Beppe and nodded meaningfully.

Was it at that point when Don Giulio spotted the departure of the minibus containing the forensics team, closely followed by an anonymous-looking unmarked van?

'What the hell is THAT doing on my land?' he asked with the first note of panic in his voice.

Beppe looked quizzically at his boss. Mariastella Martellini merely nodded curtly at her second-in-command.

'That van contains the bodies of your two murdered henchmen, *Signor* Spanò.'

The shock on the mafioso's face was short-lived. He shot a leering smile in Beppe's direction.

'They had a stupid argument about which one of them was the more important,' Spanò explained coolly. 'They managed to shoot each other – it happened days ago, officers. I didn't report it because I didn't want to bother the police with two low-life scum like that. That's all that happened, *agenti!'*

His words were greeted with a silent stare of utter disbelief on the five faces.

'I want my lawyer present!'

Spanò had unconsciously raised his voice as he uttered the clichéd words.

'And so you shall, *Signor* Spanò. As soon as the time is ripe. No doubt she will come running up from Catanzaro as soon as you have contacted your…family members.'

It had been the lady *Questore* who had spoken these words with icy precision.

'How the hell did you…? began the mafioso before he could check himself. His family employed two lawyers on a permanent basis. The male lawyer dealt with the serious cases while the younger and less experienced female lawyer 'practised' on the less important cases.

Spanò glared at this high-ranking woman police officer with hatred. He had been humiliated just by the assumption that his guilt – or otherwise – was considered to be of such minor importance that he would be defended by the family's woman lawyer.

'Brava, Signora Questore!' Beppe said to himself.

'You won't be able to prove I had anything to do with the deaths of those two idiots!'

Giulio Spanò was back on the attack.

Silence had fallen. All but the chief toxicologist knew who would speak next. Beppe, despite himself, was taking a sadistic pleasure at the prospect of demolishing the mafioso's futile attempt at defending himself. He really is totally unaware of the deep hole he has dug for himself, thought Beppe.

'Unfortunately for you, Don Giulio, you are quite wrong in your assumption. We have a witness to your crime.'

Inside, the mafioso had turned to ice. He summoned all his resentment to sneer whilst staring straight into the *commissario's* eyes.

'Oh yes? And who might that be? That doddery old parish priest? The Holy Spirit?'

Beppe counted up to ten, savouring the last few seconds before he knew that he would be kindling the fires of Hell.

'Your own daughter, Aurora, Don Giulio!'

The mafioso had turned as white as a sheet. For the first time in their acquaintance, any hint of a smirk had vanished forever. Only then did Spanò realise that he had not set eyes on his daughter for the last forty-eight hours.

He had murder in his eyes – directed exclusively at Beppe.

'You've taken MY DAUGHTER into custody? You bastard policeman!' he shouted, losing all self-control.

'No, Don Giulio. She left of her own accord after witnessing the murderous activities of her own father.'

The inevitable response was instantly forthcoming.

'Well, *commissaaario,*' he said with pure evil in his eyes. 'We've got your father!'

There was a gasp of horror from all those present – with the exception of Beppe himself.

'Please leave us alone for a few minutes, *Signora Questore, ragazzi...*'

Mariastella was too nonplussed to object to Beppe's highly irregular request. She merely muttered to the others:

'*Dai, ragazzi,* we shall wait in the corridor.'

* * *

Beppe had outwardly remained totally passive whilst the mafioso was still glaring at him with a look of evil triumph in his eyes.

'Well, *commissario,* it's a life for a life, I would say,' hissed Don Giulio.

'*You* may say so, Don Giulio. Personally, I would say that we have saved your daughter from a life of unadulterated subservience and enforced loneliness. Thus, only YOU will be guilty of murder!'

Giulio Spanò had been skillfully out-manoeuvred yet again by this bastard policeman who had ruined his life and his reputation within his clan. He closed the distance between himself and this hated figure with remarkable alacrity – only coming to a sudden halt at the sight of a police pistol pointing directly at his forehead.

But it was the look in the policeman's eyes which told him clearly what would happen if ever his father was found dead.

16: *L'angoscia della mamma di Beppe...*
(Beppe's mother in distress)

'Potete entrare, signori,'[94] Beppe called out to his companions, who had been standing as close to the door as possible, hoping to overhear the exchange of words between Beppe and the mafioso. But it was a very short-lived event. Beppe, with one swift movement, had returned his pistol to its holster before his companions had time to register the gesture.

'Cuff him, Danilo. *Signora Questore,* will you do the honours?'

'Giulio Spanò, I declare you under arrest for the murder of... *(At this juncture, Mariastella had to look at a piece of paper which she had been clutching in her hand)* Antonio Norabito and Domenico Laganà. You are also being charged for your involvement in the murder of Daniele Capriotti. Officers Martelli and Simone will accompany you to fetch items of clothing that you may require over the next few days. You will be able to call your lawyer, *Avvocato* Federica Greco, under our supervision.'

It was over. The 'easy part' of this investigation had been completed, Beppe was thinking.

Mariastella Martellini took one look at her second-in-command and said simply:

---

[94] You can enter / come back in

'Thank you for all you have done to get us this far, Beppe. Now please go home and be with your family.'

Despite his inner torment concerning the fate of his father in distant Calabria, Beppe had a quizzical look on his face – wanting to probe into Mariastella's seemingly miraculous knowledge about the Spanò clan's personal lawyers. But his *capo* merely smiled mischievously and repeated her injunction that Beppe should go home.

'You are not the only person in our team capable of delivering surprises, *commissario!* I shall fill you in with the mundane details next time we talk.'

There was another matter which was troubling Beppe, too urgent to be shelved. But he could not bring himself to formulate it into solid words.

'And yes, *caro collega,* we shall also be discussing your desire to return to Catanzaro. First of all, go home and find out if Spanò's threat has been put into effect. We'll decide what to do in the light of what you discover.'

To his alarm, Beppe was feeling a profound affection towards his leader. He had a brief image in his mind of holding her legs and pulling off her boots. It had been such an intimate gesture. But on this occasion, he limited himself to solemnly shaking Mariastella's proffered hand.

Officers Gino and Danilo had already gone upstairs to supervise their prisoner packing a hold-all.

Beppe waved a hand in Bruno Esposito's direction and headed for his car without another word.

Mariastella had one last task to perform. She took a bewildered Monica into a quiet corner – not difficult to find in the now empty house – and explained to her that she would have to find somewhere else to live.

The blond lady shrugged her shoulders and said simply to the *Questore:* 'That's OK. I knew it couldn't last. It's the story of my life…'

* * *

Beppe drove off into the encroaching darkness. He had contemplated phoning Sonia before he left in order to ask her to call his mother before he reached home. But he admitted to himself that this was simply dictated by cowardice. He set off at a dangerously fast pace – to lessen the distance between him and the truth which he knew he would have to face up to before the evening was out.

Sonia was quick to notice his distress and did her best to persuade Veronica and Lorenzo to go to bed as soon as supper was finished. But Beppe was obliged to maintain his loving, fatherly role whilst his two children related their horse-riding adventure of that morning.

'Did you know that *mamma* knows how to bounce up and down so sexily on horseback, *papà?'* asked Veronica delightedly. It appeared that this was the image which had cancelled out all the others in their daughter's mind.

It was well past eight o'clock before Beppe could unburden himself to Sonia as to what had transpired that afternoon.

'It might have been a lie meant to unsettle me and to avenge himself for me finally trapping him,' explained Beppe. 'But his words had the ring of truth to them – as if it was a secret which he was not supposed to reveal...'

'Come on Beppe. I'll phone your mother on my mobile – and put it in loudspeaker mode. It's better to know the truth than to remain in agonising suspense.'

The 'truth' emerged in one long, breathless and tearful out-pouring of words.

The conversation had begun with a brief exchange of the usual protests on Imelda's part that her son never remembered that she still existed on Planet Earth.

'Of course, he remembers you, Imelda,' said Sonia. 'He talks about you every day. But he has been exceptionally busy over the past few days. He is here with me now and wants to talk to you. He is anxious to know if his father is back home *sano e salvo...* ' [95]

That was as far as Sonia got before Beppe's mother began to pour out her soul.

_____

[95] Safe and sound

'*È colpa mia...tutto colpa mia!* [96] I went and blurted it all out in the chemist's shop the evening before your father never came back from his walk. I had to tell somebody that you told us to flee from Catanzaro and that I didn't want to leave. But I forgot that 'those people' own the chemist shop... that's why the prices are so high and they don't have to pay a pizzo [97] like most of the other shops... But Maria in the chemist's shop is so kind. She just works there but she probably got scared and went and repeated what I said to someone else who ran to those crooks in the Spanò family. They've got Corrado [98] and now they'll kill him. They've probably killed him already and it's all my stupid fault. I should have listened to you Beppe and taken him away. What have you done to annoy those people, Beppe? You should have known you can't cross swords with them and get away with it...'

Imelda seemed to have forgotten that she was talking to Sonia. She became hysterical and was wailing like a lost soul in Hades. Beppe took pity on her and took the phone off Sonia.

'*Mamma. Mamma!* It's your son speaking to you now. Please calm down.'

The pitiful wailing stopped instantly.

'So, who was I talking to just now?' she asked quite crossly.

---

[96] It's all my fault
[97] 'Protection money' exacted by the mafia clans.
[98] Beppe's father's first name

'That was Sonia, *mamma*. Now it's me.'

'You mean I have to tell you all over again, Giuseppe?'

'No, *mamma*, I heard every word.'

'But how come...?'

She was permanently confused by the notion that two people could simultaneously hear what was being said over a phone.

'These silly modern gadgets!' she declared and began all over again with her tirade.

'It's all my fault, Giuseppe. All my stupid fault!'

'*Basta, mamma!* [99] It is not your fault at all. You are not responsible for the evil deeds of the *'ndrangheta*. You are a good person, a perfect mother, and you deserve to go straight to heaven...'

The kindness in his voice must have struck the right chord. Imelda burst into tears of relief as she uttered an endless number of *grazie Giuseppes* before she began to calm down.

'*Mamma*, I have to ask my superior officer's permission. But I shall do my best to come down to Catanzaro as soon as possible to be with you...'

'But what if he says 'no', Beppe. Policemen have no idea about the needs of dotty elderly mothers like me!'

My senior officer is a woman, *mamma.*'

---

[99] That's enough!

This snippet of information was followed by a protracted silence as his mother tried to digest such an alien concept. Beppe took advantage of the silence to assure his mother he would let her know the next day. He closed the call quickly. He saw Sonia looking at him with a hint of fear in her eyes. She always dreaded the moment when Beppe was forced to leave home as the crisis point of an investigation was reached. She would need to be consoled in as many ways as he could think of. Throughout his lengthy career in this 'foreign' part of Italy, he had always dreaded that the ever-present danger of his local mafia would force him to return to Catanzaro. He hugged Sonia tightly, until he felt the tension in her body ebbing away. He did not offer her any empty reassurances. They simply went to bed where Beppe held her tight and tried to console her by convincing her that he would not be in any particular danger.

'I'll be going with someone in my team, *amore*. And there will be all the local police force and the *Carabinieri* backing us up. Mariastella won't let me take any risks – you know that, don't you?'

'It's just so far away this time, Beppe,' she said in a little voice. They fell asleep still intertwined in each other's arms.

* * *

For the first time in what seemed like ages, Beppe had driven down to the police headquarters in Pescara instead of heading inland to the little commune of Picciano. He was sitting opposite his *capo* who was being exceptionally sympathetic towards him.

'I made the mistake of asking for a volunteer to accompany you down to Catanzaro, Beppe.'

'Why a mistake, Mariastella?' he asked.

'Because everyone – even *Agente* Lina Rapino – offered to go with you.'

As much as he respected the redoubtable officer Rapino, he looked at his chief with a silent appeal which spoke volumes.

'Don't worry,' smiled the lady *Questore*. 'I decided you would be safer with Officer Pippo Cafarelli. You are, after all, practically bosom pals, aren't you? He was most insistent that it should be him. I can only allow you one officer - but I've been in touch with your former chief, who should contact the *Carabinieri*. As yet, they have had no reports of anyone by the name of Corrado Stancato being abducted.'

'And yet he has gone missing, Mariastella.'

'I'm sorry, Beppe. I *can* only spare you Pippo to keep you company on your pilgrimage to save your father. I'm under pressure to send someone to Collecorvini to be with Officer Flavia Evangelista. She is insisting that Picciano needs someone to keep an eye out for trouble. – even though the mafioso's household has been reduced to one lady called Monica.'

'Beppe sighed. This investigation had become very untidy, he felt.

'*Agente* Evangelista would be very gainfully employed, Mariastella, if she was to keep an eye on the Hanging Man's wife – Giorgia Scarpa. I am quite sure that this elusive – if abused - young lady has played some part in this drama, which we are still unaware of.'

'*Davvero, Beppe?*' [100] 'What makes you think that?'

Beppe shook his head. 'Call it intuition. I have a feeling that she still has not given us some vital piece of information which will enable us to pin Daniele Capriotti's murder on Giulio Spanò…'

It was Mariastella's turn to let out a long sigh.

'This *has* become an immensely complex business,' she admitted.

'How is our mafioso faring, Mariastella?' asked Beppe – merely out of duty.

'Accusing us of kidnapping his daughter during his waking hours – and awaiting the arrival of his lawyer from Catanzaro. I get the impression that his clan has washed their hands of him. His lady lawyer, *Signorina* Federica Greco, does not appear to be in any great hurry to make an appearance…'

---

[100] Really?

The two brought their conversation to an end.

'Go home now. Beppe. Pippo will come and pick you up tomorrow morning...not too early, he says.'

Beppe stood up to leave. Was his chief going to come round to his side of the desk to shake him by the hand? She did, but for only the third – or was it the fourth - time in their acquaintance, she gave him an affectionate hug.

'*Stammi bene, commissario,*' [101]

* * *

'*Zio,*' [102] said Don Giulio Spanò to the *boss* of his clan. '*I'm sorry to trouble you again. I just want to ask you to make sure that a certain person who we are entertaining does not come to any harm – not just yet, anyway. I think the police will be all over the place soon.*'

'*Che sarà sarà. You cocked up your assignment – so you will have to accept the consequences. We'll keep him alive only so long as it suits us. Capito, stronzo?*' [103]

His uncle cut him off abruptly. Giulio Spanò switched off the mobile phone he had smuggled into his cell. If he tried to make another call, it might be detected. He felt abandoned to his fate. He did not care whether that cop's father lived or died. He

---

[101] Take care : look after yourself
[102] Uncle
[103] Imbecile! Bloody fool!

was only concerned about preserving his own life. He had understood perfectly the look in the eyes of that *sbirro* pointing the pistol at his temple. If his father died too soon, that cop would get to him somehow.

Unbeknown to the mafioso, the call he had made had been intercepted by the technical team in the basement of the *Questura* in Pescara. They had deliberately planted his phone in such a way that he had imported his own *cellulare* into his cell – making it look like a careless oversight on the part of the police or the prison guards. The ploy had been worked out by Beppe with the help and ingenuity of the two technicians who worked in the basement of the *Questura,* Marco Pollutri and the ebullient Bianca Bomba – who always lived up to her name.

Bianca Bomba sent the phone number of the mafia boss in Catanzaro to her favourite *commissario* with a cheeky message saying that she hoped Beppe would put the knowledge to proper use.

* * *

For the first time in his life as a policeman – or even as a tourist - *Agente* Pippo Cafarelli found himself in Calabria after a relentlessly speedy car journey down towards the Ionian Sea, with Beppe doing most of the driving.

'I know the way like I know my own pockets,' [104] was his excuse to Pippo for hogging the driver's seat.

Catanzaro rose from the marina up the steeply sloping streets of the town with its cathedral and *campanile* [105] sitting nobly on the summit of the hill – so that the Church could at least pretend to be more powerful than the darker forces which held sway on the lower levels of the town. Pippo drew in his breath in admiration of the scene before him.

'I guess I was expecting Catanzaro to be flat – like Puglia,' he explained to Beppe.

'Well, you are about to have your concept of Calabria shaken even more in the next few minutes, Pippo – you are about to make the acquaintance of my mother once again – but on *her* home territory this time. I am quite sure she will not recognise you from the day of our wedding all those years ago.'

As it turned out, Beppe's prognostication turned out to be accurate. On being introduced to Beppe's mother, a smiling and compliant Pippo Cafarelli was treated to a hard stare.

'I assumed you would come down with that other lady policeman who I know so well, Beppe! What's her name…?'

Beppe sighed in mock despair. But in light of his mother's old age and current source of suffering, he said patiently:

---

[104] 'Conosco la strada come le mie tasche' – Like the back of my hand.
[105] Bell tower

'*No, mamma.* You are thinking of Sonia. She is my wife and mother of two of your grandchildren. This is my colleague and friend, Pippo. He saved my life a few years ago…'

'How do you expect me to remember all this, Beppe, when you keep me in the dark about everything you do?' she protested. Pippo, who was poignantly reminded of his own mother from Foggia, planted a *bacio* on each of Imelda's cheeks. The gesture immediately softened the severe stance of Beppe's mother.

'Well, I suppose you had better join us for supper, *giovanotto,'* [106] she declared, going into the kitchen and producing a dish of meat *lasagne* copious enough to feed the whole of Beppe's team back in Pescara.

'Tomorrow, *mamma,'* Beppe explained, 'we must all go together to the police station and make an official 'missing person's' declaration about my father. Then we can start searching for him in earnest.'

The tears gathered in the corner of Imelda's eyes, but she looked reassured by the presence of her son – and his 'junior' colleague, whom she mildly chided for not waiting for grace to have been said before he tucked hungrily into his food. Beppe smirked at Pippo and waggled an admonishing finger in his direction. Pippo grinned - he felt at home.

---

[106] Young man – Pippo is well into his thirties or early forties

* * *

The following morning, Beppe and Pippo escorted Imelda to the police station – Pippo, in uniform, on her right and Beppe on his mother's left. She was quite content to be the centre of attention as she walked along the familiar route in full view of everybody from shopkeepers to neighbours – most of them greeting her as if she was a local celebrity on parade for all to see. Her very own son had deigned to visit her in the hour of her need. The Blessed Virgin would have a special place in her prayers - along with several tours of the rosary beads. Then the reason for her son's visit reminded her that she should be in mourning. Her daughter, Valentina, had taken Giuseppe's warning seriously and had spirited herself away to somewhere in Molise with her two children in tow.

'What a sensible, well-balanced daughter I gave birth to,' considered Imelda. 'Not like my wayward son…'

They arrived at the police station where Beppe's former chief was waiting for them. A mere formality – she simply had to admit to this weary-looking chief of police that her husband had disappeared into thin air. She signed the declaration with an illegible signature and her legal duty was done.

'Beppe – can we have a quiet word together?' said Alberto Sordi – the *Commissario Capo* of the Catanzaro police force.

'Your mother has just made your father's disappearance official,' said Alberto. 'But what in the name of all the saints do we do next, Beppe?'

'I am as much in the dark as you, *capo.* I think we should make my father's disappearance public knowledge by reporting it in the press – and maybe on the local television too. What about contacting the *Carabinieri?*' suggested Beppe.

'The media report I can deal with, Beppe. I would advise you against involving the *Carabinieri* unless we really have to. The outcome may turn out to be unpredictable,' added a cynical Alberto Sordi. 'The *Carabinieri* have their own methods of dealing with the mafia.'

'I don't suppose we have any idea where they might have taken my father, do we, *capo?* Word has it – this from my lady *Questore* in Pescara – that my *papà* is still alive. Our 'junior' mafioso in prison has had his phone tapped without his knowledge…'

'I have heard that the Spanò mob have a hideaway somewhere in the vicinity of Catanzaro, Beppe. But it could be anywhere up in those mountains…'

Beppe had spent years of his life as a simple *ispettore* trying to bolster up his chief's morale. It appeared that in the intervening years of his absence that very little had changed in that respect. Beppe was having a distant memory of a threat he had once received from the clan that they would take him up the mountains and feed him to the wild boar. There must be some place up there above Catanzaro where the clan had a hideaway.

'Don't worry yourself, *capo,*' Beppe consoled his former chief. 'Something will turn up soon. It nearly always does. But do you absolutely trust your team? I need to ask…'

'Well, on the whole, Beppe, yes I do.'

'I feel there is about to be a 'but'…'

'It's just this young female officer who joined us recently. I don't know… I have a feeling she may have some connection with the mob. I cannot be precise.'

'Can you give me a name, Alberto?' he asked his former chief. 'I could get my colleague Pippo Cafarelli to do a search for us. He's far in advance of us oldies in his internet skills.'

'She's called Luisa Pugliese, Beppe.'

There was nothing to be added. He would get Pippo to spend the morning researching to see what he came up with.

'It's just that looking for my *papà* is such a sensitive issue. It could be fatal if our manoeuvres were revealed to the mob – but useful if we found out there *was* a connection between her and the clan.'

'You have no idea how I have missed you over these years,' said Alberto Sordi, who, Beppe noticed, was looking at him with eyes that had moistened with impending tears. He gave his former chief a hug of consolation. It should be the other way round, thought Beppe ironically.

'Something will come up, *capo,*' he repeated.

In point of fact, he had just had an idea. It was such a long shot as to be little short of a pipe-dream. But there was no reason not to tap into this unlikely source – one never knew until it had been put to the test.

He would phone Sonia as soon as he was on his own. Right now, he would have to rescue Pippo from the ordeal of looking after his mother in the neighbouring bar.

He was relieved to discover that his friend and colleague was showing a hidden and invaluable skill – that of knowing how to deal with elderly ladies.

'Bravo, Pippo!' he muttered to himself as he drew near the table on the *terrazzo* where they were sitting under a colourful sun-shade. A look of pure relief came over Pippo's face on spotting Beppe's approach.

17: *Aurora Spanò reveals a remarkable talent...*

Sonia listened intently to what Beppe was telling her. He had instinctively explained his devious scheme to Sonia in the most convoluted language possible – as if there was a risk that *his* call might be intercepted. Nowadays, one could never be sure who might be eavesdropping in on one's private thoughts and words.

'I know it's a long shot, but Aurora lived most of her young life down here in and around Catanzaro. I know she seems very withdrawn but...'

'I think your idea is brilliant, Beppe. And judging by Aurora's recent reaction to her father, she has shown a hidden streak of courage and determination. I will phone her and drive back to Picciano just as soon as I have taken the kids to school tomorrow. It sounds as if there is no time to lose. Leave it all to me, *amore...* and please don't take any risks – or I shall report you to Mariastella!'

Beppe smiled at the thinly veiled threat. One of them at a time, he could cope with – just about. But a combined team effort would be invincible.

The second day spent in Catanzaro dawned with the promise of warm sunshine and a fresh northerly breeze to cool the air. How different the air felt and smelt to that in Pescara! Even the sounds of people going about their daily business struck a different note. In the deep south, you could still hear the street vendors in their clapped-out vans calling out an endless list of their wares in the hope of stimulating a bit of income. Beppe even questioned whether the emotions that he was experiencing bordered on homesickness. He and Pippo were sitting having their espressos and custard cream-filled pastry cakes – both thinking that life in southern Italy had its advantages. Pippo had had the forethought to buy a copy of the local newspaper. Beppe's former boss had carried out his promise of ensuring that Beppe's father's disappearance would be made public knowledge. No doubt the local radio and TV stations would be reporting the abduction of one Corrado Stancato – purportedly by the local *'ndrangheta* clan – to a resigned local population throughout the neighbourhood.

'The father of a much-loved and respected police officer,' stated the newspaper article.

'Do you think that this will produce any helpful results, *capo?*'

Beppe shrugged his shoulders.

'Not really, but the whole scenario is all about making the mafia feel uncomfortable. They are more likely to show their hand if they think the police are seriously investigating an abduction. And that will make them think twice before they...go too far. It will give us a bit more time. The local population will simply clam up and shrug their shoulders – you know from your experience with the *Sacra Corona Unita* [107] in Puglia what it's like, Pippo.'

Pippo merely nodded in agreement.

'We'll make a show of going round as many houses as possible today. You never know – somebody might have seen something. It might jog a memory. But someone in the Spanò clan will get to hear about it by lunchtime at the latest.'

Pippo let out a sigh and concentrated on his second espresso coffee.

'I phoned Sonia last night,' said Beppe. 'We will try getting to the Spanò clan through their back door, so to speak...'

Pippo looked at his chief. He had that mischievous gleam in his eye which told him that his chief had some devious scheme in his head.

'Ah, I see! *Ho capito, commissario!*' [108]

* * *

Sonia arrived at the *frantoio* at just after nine o'clock to be greeted by Tommaso, the owner's son.

'*Ciao,* Sonia! A pleasure to see you again so soon! I understand from Aurora that you have some deep dark secret to share with her? She is intrigued – in her own special way.'

---

[107] The mafia in Puglia – particularly strong in Foggia – Pippo's home town
[108] I have understood : Got you!

'Well, I want to enlist her aid in our investigation.'

'I thought the case was already solved, Sonia.'

Sonia debated whether to tell Tommaso why she was there – just to satisfy his amiable curiosity – but decided against it for now.

'It's just a loose end, really,' she said.

The expression on the young man's face indicated clearly that he was not convinced.

'Let me talk to Aurora first, Tommaso. It may well be that she will not be able to help us, in which case, there will be nothing to relate.'

Tommaso smiled. He had been right. There *was* an unknown factor behind this visit.

'Well, Sonia – Aurora is where you would expect her to be,' he said, nodding in the direction of the makeshift stable round the side of the farmhouse. 'Lucky you came this week, though, she is going to start private lessons next week. The elderly gentleman who runs the town's *archivio* – Leonardo Scafa – has offered to give her Italian and maths lessons free of charge. I gather you have met him and his sister already?'

'That is wonderful news, Tommaso. I suppose she can go to school at some stage?'

'We're working on that, Sonia. But she has never been to school in her life, so she will have to be with children in the local school who are much younger than she is. Fortunately, she is happy with that arrangement. She says she loves younger children.'

Sonia found Aurora in intimate conversation with Barone – as if she was discussing some deep philosophical matter with her horse. She smiled disarmingly at Sonia, displaying a faultless set of front teeth. She looked like any well-formed teenage girl – with her jet-black hair and gleaming brown eyes. She is beautiful, thought Sonia.

She was struck by the total innocence of this girl, who had led too sheltered a life. At least, the Smiling Man had spared his daughter the unwanted attention of predatory male eyes devouring her body with lustful looks. Aurora was unspoilt – as innocent on the inside as she was alluring on the outside.

'I am sorry to involve you in all this again, Aurora. But there is something that has happened to my husband's father. He lives in Catanzaro.'

Sonia told the girl about the disappearance of Corrado Stancato.

'We just wondered if you could help us, Aurora...' asked Sonia with her heart in her mouth.

Aurora fell silent. Her face was devoid of all expression. She did not look puzzled nor frightened – just deep in thought. She finally turned to her horse and whispered words which Sonia could hardly hear. It sounded as if she had said: *You were right, Barone. It isn't finished yet, is it?'*

To Sonia, she said simply:

'We must go somewhere quiet. I shall need to concentrate, Sonia. Come with me...'

She led Sonia indoors and upstairs to a bedroom all of her own. Sonia was struck by the totally adult way in which Aurora was acting. There was a whole person under the skin whom she, Sonia, had hitherto underestimated. Aurora sat on the double bed and patted the duvet to invite Sonia to sit down beside her.

'May I record what you are going to say on my mobile, Aurora? I think it's going to save someone's life.'

A simple nod of her head. Then, as if in a dream or a trance, Aurora began to speak in an even, unhesitant voice.

'Yes, Sonia, I know where they would have taken him. I've spent so many weeks in that place with my mum and my sister. It was our mountain retreat.'

She fell silent for a few minutes, as if deciding where she should begin the journey. Sonia was mesmerised by the account which followed – delivered in a smooth, almost uninflected voice.

Yes, I remember the journey. O.K, I'm leaving Catanzaro now. You go up on the map. To the left side, not the right. I remember following the road on a map with my finger-tip. You first go to a town called MMMMMM...No, I'm getting it wrong. It begins

235

with a G, not an M, but there's an M in the middle. I can see it standing up tall in the middle of the word. GAM...No... GIMI...GIMIGLIANO! That's it! Va bene...You have to go up the hill to the top past the school. I remember the sound of children's voices on the right. And then past the church where the bells are ringing. There's a funny shoe-mender who sits outside a shop, polishing people's shoes on a machine with a brush that goes round and round without stopping. Then you have to go left up a road that's suddenly bumpy. Don't go right there because the proper road just goes round and downhill again. Oh yes, there's a sign by the road which says 'Pericolo – cinghiali in libertà' [109] *with a silhouette of a wild boar on it. I remember being so scared that I had bad dreams at night time with those animals snuffling at my feet with their nasty little tusks sticking out of the side of their cheeks! Wait a minute...Yes, you take the left turning not the right after that. The right turning just goes up the mountain side. You go along a scary road where it just drops down into a canyon on your left for a hundred metres or so. I was so afraid we would fall into the river at the bottom. I always had my eyes closed at that point. Then you come across another fork in the road. Go left...always left. There's a skull-and-crossbones sign there – to put people off going up to our house, my papà always said. And there you are...That beautiful house in the middle of nowhere,*

---

[109] Danger – wild boar roaming free

where you can pick the fruit and nuts off the trees...and where my cousin keeps wild boar in a huge pen. And where the stars shine at night like candles in the sky...

Oh yes, now I remember! There was just one 'bad' place us little ones were afraid of. A sort of cellar beneath the ground floor. There was a trapdoor hidden under a kind of wicker carpet in the main kitchen. My great-uncle – when he got annoyed by the misbehaviour of some of the older boys – nearly every day, it happened – used to make one of them sleep in the cellar on the one-and-only wooden bed down there. No lights – and only one window which was almost below ground level... You had to climb down by a ladder. They kept the wine down there because it was so cool...could be really cold at night. The boys took it in turns to annoy my great-uncle – who is the real boss of the clan. They turned it into a sort of 'I-dare-you' competition – to see who could get Zio Albano riled up so he would send them down below. (Aurora gave a merry little giggle at the memory) The winner was allowed to be the gang leader – and told them which shops to visit in the town. My great-uncle gave them pocket money for giving grief to certain shopkeepers if they got difficult about paying their 'pizzo'. I never found that side of things funny at all. I felt the gelataio, [110] who was always kind and smiley to me, only did it 'cos he was scared of us...

---

[110] Ice-cream maker

There, Sonia, if there's a safe, secret hiding place, I guess it would be here…'

Aurora had stopped talking, Sonia realised. Mesmerised by the girl's voice, Sonia finally removed her finger from the 'hold' key and stopped recording the silence that had followed this extraordinary monologue. Aurora took several long seconds before she looked at Sonia and smiled a beaming smile.

'Funny how I can remember things from my childhood but I do my best to forget more recent things,' she said. 'I do so hope I've helped you, Sonia. I'm so sorry about Beppe's *papà*. I don't understand why my family does such awful things to other people all the time. I'm so glad I've broken free from them now…'

Aurora fell into a reverie for so long that Sonia felt she had to do something to bring this beautiful girl back to normal life. She couldn't just get up and go home as if nothing had happened – even though she was dying to send the recorded message off to Beppe immediately. She looked at her watch and was amazed to see it was only ten o'clock. It felt to Sonia as if she had been listening to Aurora's story for hours – as if she had travelled back in time and place and only just come back down to earth in some future age.

'What shall we do now, Sonia?' asked Aurora.

'What a pity we don't have two horses, isn't it, Aurora?' she said – intending it to be a joke.

Aurora giggled again.

'I hoped you would say that, Sonia! Barone can take two riders on his back easily. You can sit in the saddle and use the stirrups and reins. I'll ride bareback behind you.'

It had not been what Sonia had in mind before she drove back to Atri to pick up her kids from school just before lunchtime. As soon as they went back to the ground floor, they met Tommaso coming out of the olive press.

'Of course, you will stay and have lunch with us at midday, won't you?' he asked Sonia.

Sonia demurred and began to make excuses.

'*Dai* Sonia! Stay for lunch, *ti prego!*' [111] begged Aurora. 'We can go for a proper ride this time.'

How could she refuse Aurora at this point? A quick call to her parents who were always more than willing to go and fetch Lorenzo and Veronica from school and give them lunch. The children did not always feel the same way – but took it with a good grace. Today was no exception when Irene told them that *mamma* was being a police officer again.

To Sonia's astonishment, Aurora asked her a question:

'You're sure that my father is not at the house in Picciano, aren't you?'

---

[111] Go on! I beg you!

'Your father is locked up in a cell, Aurora. I'm so sorry…'

'I'm not, Sonia. He deserves to be. But I am worried about his horse – and the pony.'

Sonia was astounded. She was not sure whether *anybody* in Beppe's team had thought about the plight of these animals during the course of recent events.

'You're not seriously suggesting we both ride all the way back to Picciano on one horse, are you Aurora? I could easily go by car and meet you there,' she suggested hopefully.

Apparently, one horse for both of them was precisely what this young lady had in mind.

'You'll love the ride, Sonia. If we go straight back to the house it will only take thirty minutes each way. We'll easily be back here in time for lunch. *Dai, dai, dai!*'

She is learning to be quite assertive, thought Sonia. I suppose I should be pleased.

Before parting company, Sonia had promised Aurora that Giulio Spanò's neglected steed would be found a home by the Pescara police.

'Maybe, he could become a police horse?' suggested Aurora. 'Although he does become a bit skittish when the mood takes him.'

'That's not a bad idea, Aurora. I can see him joining the *Guardia Forestale.*

'I didn't even know they existed, Sonia. That would be brilliant. *Grazie, grazie, grazie!'*

'And I'm sure we can find a home for the pony in Picciano.'

'The two dogs must have wandered off, Sonia. They were never tied up.'

'Just two more stray dogs wandering around loose in the Italian countryside,' thought Sonia with philosophical resignation.

* * *

It was much later in the day, when she had arrived back – saddle-sore – to their home in Atri that Sonia found the time to send the voicemail to Beppe's mobile. She had had to relate the whole story to Veronica at her daughter's insistence. Veronica bombarded her mother with questions whilst Lorenzo simply listened in silence with his mouth open, entirely enthralled by his mother's account.

'But this must be our family secret for now,' she had told her children. 'No telling ANYBODY at school until *Nonno* Corrado is safe – swear to it!'

'Giurin giurello, mamma,' [112] they announced solemnly in chorus.

---

[112] The equivalent of 'Cross my heart and hope to die!'

For the first time during this protracted and complex investigation, *Commissario* Beppe Stancato was grinning broadly. It was a positive step forward in the search for his missing father. Aurora's account had the ring of truth to it. His father would not have been taken any further afield than was strictly necessary for the quick assassination of a little-known local. He listened and relistened to Aurora's recording, spellbound at every turn – before allowing his friend Pippo to pass judgement on it.

'Bravo, commissario! That clinches the matter, *vero?* And I've got news for you about that policewoman, Luisa Pugliese. Your chief was right. She's been unofficially engaged to one of the nephews of the *boss* of the Spanò clan for five years. Poor girl, she's probably just being used by the clan and being kept on a string with the prospect of marriage.'

Beppe nodded in agreement, adding only:

'Let's take my mother out to eat this evening, Pippo. I don't think I can face a third dose of her lasagne!'

18: Papà Corrado's rescue does not go quite to plan...

Beppe fell asleep that night and did not wake up until dawn. He had had a dream. It was so vivid that as soon as he returned to consciousness, he realised it had not been so much a dream as a vision. It was one of those rare moments in his life – which were commonplace as far as his spiritual hero, the Archbishop of Pescara was concerned – when it seemed that some exterior power had implanted the images and sounds in his brain. Had he told Don Emanuele about it, this holy man would have smiled and said something like: 'Why should you be astonished, Beppe? The Holy Spirit is simply giving you a helping hand.'

Converting the 'dream' into reality would, he realised, take up at least thirty-six of the twenty-four hours available to him. He would have to hire a band of musicians and also hire a coach. The musicians, he was sure, were available. It was one of the truly remarkable phenomena in the south of his beloved homeland that musicians who could play a variety of musical instruments could be summoned out of thin air as if by magic. They were usually employed in towns all over the south to walk through the streets leading a procession towards the local cemetery. But they also came from out of nowhere to enliven the local *feste*.

Beppe got dressed and shaved well before breakfast time and only woke Pippo up when he had outlined in his mind what tasks lay ahead of them that day.

Beppe's version of divine providence did not stop with his dream. As soon as the two officers stepped through the doors of the police station, *Commissario-Capo* Alberto Sordi greeted them with the words:

'Our *sindaco*, [113] Carlo Quarta, wishes to meet you, Beppe. At your earliest convenience. You are to go alone, he requested.'

Beppe's former chief had a mischievous glint in his eyes.

'I said you would go and see him as soon as you arrived,' added Alberto.

The prospect of being slowed up by some fussy old public official with ribbons attached promised to be the first of many frustrations during this vital day.

His ex-chief read the expression of mild irritation on Beppe's face.

'I think you are in for a surprise, Beppe,' he said smugly. 'Carlo Quarta has very pronounced views on the local mafia clan.'

---

[113] Mayor

The major surprise, apart from the fact that the mayor was considerably younger than Beppe himself, was heightened by his opening words.

'I was talking on the phone to a lady called Mariastella Martellini yesterday afternoon. 'She seemed to think you might need a helping hand when dealing with the local mob.'

The mayor's *closing* words were even more astonishing.

'I've been waiting for a chance to strike a blow which will dent their complacent belief that they can go on sucking the life out of this town with impunity. I suspect I might end up a victim of their anger before I am much older, Beppe. But at least I would like to go out with the knowledge that I have fought against this evil which besets our land.'

The intervening conversation had taken just under one hour as Beppe had outlined his plan to rescue his father. The young mayor had undertaken to organise practically everything which Beppe had envisaged.

'I love your plan, Beppe! It smacks of genius! It will really give those bastards something to think about. With all that going on, they simply would not dare to finish off your father. I'm sorry to have to confess that news of his abduction had simply not come to my attention. We shall change all that, won't we, *commissario!*'

Beppe even found time to phone Sonia but thought it more expedient not to go into too fine a detail as to what his scheme involved. She would almost certainly worry unduly about him. But he was able to tell her, without stretching the truth, that so many people would be present that there could not possibly be any risk to his own person.

Beppe had requested that his chief should assign *Agente* Luisa Pugliese the task of staying with his mother until the 'show' was over.

'That way she won't be in a position to know exactly what is going on - nor report it to the *boss* until it is too late.'

'*Ottima idea,*[114] Beppe! I like it!' said Alberto Sordi, who looked half fearful but at the same time excited by the transformation which his former friend and colleague had wrought in the space of forty-eight hours.

* * *

Some of the three thousand inhabitants of Gimigliano – minus the children, who were already at school – were astounded to see a coach arrive in their *piazza,* followed closely by a number of private cars whose drivers and passengers had not been able to find room on the coach.

The first to disembark were the musicians wearing their purple uniforms and carrying their various musical instruments with them. The rest seemed to be ordinary citizens – until, that

---

[114] Great idea!

is, they began to unfurl makeshift banners with a variety of messages on them saying things like: *'Free Corrado'* and even heartfelt proclamations such as *'No more mafia'* and *'Refuse to pay the pizzo'*.

It was just as if an unexpected *festa* was about to take place in their little township. The amazing thing was, considered the villagers, the sight of six uniformed *poliziotti* led by a man in his forties who was organising the procession with quiet efficiency. In no time at all, the police were heading off uphill towards the school followed by the musicians who had begun to play *Fratelli d'Italia* [115] with great gusto. The inhabitants of what the villagers assumed to be people from Catanzaro tagged on behind the band.

Emboldened by the sheer numbers of people, the curious inhabitants mingled in with the visitors. As they drew level with the school, the children ran out into the school yard – ignoring the orders from their teachers. They clamoured up to the locked school gates but, to their frustration, could get no further. Instead, they started cheering the procession on whilst the handful of puzzled teaching staff looked on, realising that it would take at least half an hour before any semblance of discipline would be restored.

Commissario Beppe Stancato was secretly thrilled to notice that an ancient, bearded cobbler was standing holding a

---

[115] The Italian national anthem

pair of shoes behind a foot-operated revolving polisher. He sent a prayer of gratitude to a young lady called Aurora – whom he hardly knew at all. He led the procession along the route, picking out the various signposts indicated by Aurora, including the sign with the wild boar on it. She was right about the road which dropped off sharply to a river gorge below. The road was only wide enough for one car to pass safely. The procession had to proceed almost in single file for about five-hundred metres. The musicians had to interrupt their rendition of 'O sole mio' and concentrate on the narrow road.

They started up again with an aria from Aida as soon as the procession began walking up a forested path towards a clearing. Beppe spotted the house just a couple of hundred metres further on. His heart was beating fast. It was 'that' moment in time during an investigation that he felt at his most vulnerable. He alone was responsible for mustering some one hundred and fifty people on a mission which could end in total failure. Why was he always driven to be so unconventional? It was too late to draw back now. He heard Sonia's voice inside his head encouraging him to continue.

You know your instincts are always right, amore,' she was saying.

'Not necessarily on this occasion,' he feared.

The time for reconsidering his rash act was at an end.

On the raised veranda surrounding the mafioso's country house, had appeared two burly country bumpkins waving some sophisticated repeater rifles in the air. A tough but diminutive looking woman in her fifties emerged from inside the house and stood defiantly between the two brothers – or so Beppe assumed.

The mafia thugs did not know what to do. They could hardly start firing at so many people – especially as the row of policemen were aiming their pistols menacingly in their direction.

The procession came to a halt at about fifty metres from the house.

Only one man continued walking towards the house, followed after a thirty-second-long pause by the uniformed police who were holding their weapons in both hands as they advanced with legs bent to present as low a profile as possible.

'Do not move,' called out the advancing figure – who was, inexplicably to the mobsters, totally unarmed. 'And do not use that mobile phone, *signora!*' called out the man. 'Put your weapons down, *signori* – *SUBITO*' [116] We have not come to arrest you – yet. We have come to collect the man you are holding prisoner. That is our sole business.'

It was the moment of truth. The two gangsters did not react to the words or attempt to laugh out loud. They were

---

[116] At once!

simply bewildered that this man seemed to have such an accurate knowledge about what was supposed to be a secret according to their *boss* Don Albano.

Beppe felt an enormous sense of relief flood through his body. They were holding his father prisoner. The thugs laid down the rifles. As if by sheer instinct, the band and the 'banner-waving' crowd of civilians began to edge forward, not wanting to miss out on what was to follow.

The policemen arrived at the house and mounted the steps onto the veranda. They collected the two automatic rifles.

'Are these what you use to shoot the wild boar, *signori?*' asked Pippo sarcastically. 'It doesn't give the poor beasts much chance, does it?

The two thugs did not react to the jibe. They were too shocked by the laid-back attitude of these policemen, speaking to them in 'real Italian' and laughing at them as if they counted for nothing.

Beppe led the woman into the big rustic kitchen. She muttered something aggressively in dialect.

'You won't find nobody 'ere, Mr Policeman. You just wait till Don Albano hears about this…'

Commissario Stancato, at your service, *signora,'* said Beppe, speaking in dialect. 'That name mean anything to you?'

The woman turned one shade paler – a pallor that quickly became whiter still as this unfamiliar policeman with the most disconcerting stare she had ever encountered began calmly to remove the rug from the floor which led to the cellar.

'Aurora, you are a shining star!' thought Beppe as he pulled on the handles which lifted the trapdoor to the cellar.

There arose a stench of sweat, urine – and worse, from the darkness below. Beppe's heart sank.

He turned to the woman and growled at her.

'Get me a torch – or put a light on down there. How dare you keep anyone imprisoned in this inhumane manner! I've changed my mind. I shall arrest all three of you and to hell with the bunch of crooks you associate with!'

He peered again down into the cellar. His eyes grew more accustomed to the gloom. There was some light seeping through a window. He could make out a crude bed in one corner and then a pale, skeletal face peering out from under a bed cover. A tray containing some half-eaten food lay on the floor by the bed.

He was handed a torch by one of the police officers who had come into the kitchen from outside.

He shone it on the face that was still staring in fear at him. Beppe felt a choking sensation in his throat.

'But you're not my father! What's your name, *signore?'*

'Corrado Stancato,' came the feeble reply.

'Those stronzi have abducted the wrong man!' Beppe snarled to the people in the kitchen.

'Just be patient, *signor* Stancato,' said Beppe in a gentler voice. 'We are the police. We have come to take you home.'

The pallid face was transformed by a smile of gratitude. The man struggled from the bed and stood up shakily, still grinning.

19: The smiling man with the suitcase...

Beppe was torn between disappointment and a rare feeling of elation that he had carried out an act of kindness. Moments such as this always made police work rewarding.

He had arrested the two 'brothers' – who were probably two cousins at the very least – on the grounds of abducting and detaining the other Corrado Stancato - as well as threatening a crowd of nigh-on one hundred citizens with automatic rifles. That would do for now! As to the woman, he relented and told her she could stay where she was for now. He tartly suggested she might want to clean up the cellar before any other guests arrived.

Pippo attempted to console Beppe by pointing out what he, Beppe, already knew:

'You told me years ago, *capo,* that 'Stancato' is quite a common surname in and around Catanzaro...'

'It's OK, Pippo. It is a disappointment not to have found my father, but I'm looking on the bright side. He has every chance of still being alive somewhere. In the light of our just having rescued Corrado Number Two, it occurs to me that we might need to look for my *papà* a bit closer to home,' Beppe suggested enigmatically.

Pippo looked at his friend and nodded. He was thinking along the same lines as his chief.

'Hai capito, Pippo, vero?'[117]

The little group of policemen with their two prisoners and the rescued man rejoined the crowd of followers who had been waiting in the clearing at the edge of the forest. They cheered and clapped as Beppe drew level with them.

Beppe turned to the two policemen who were handcuffed to one of each of the prisoners. They were two of the Catanzaro officers.

'OK *ragazzi,'* said Beppe. 'Take the cuffs off your own wrists and release the right wrist of the prisoners. The two local cops did as they were told, but were looking puzzled.

'Now keep one cuff on their left wrist and hang on to the other closed handcuff tightly in your right hand. We don't want them to escape, do we…?'

The two local policemen were looking nonplussed at their temporary chief.

'Just do as he says, *ragazzi!'* Pippo advised them.

The procession continued to descend towards the village of Gimigliano. Beppe and the other Corrado led the procession at a leisurely pace. The rescued man had grown a bit steadier on his feet and had finally woken up to the strange circumstances of his miraculous escape.

'But why did you think I was your father?' he asked Beppe.

---

[117] You understand what I'm saying, don't you?

'Ah, that's a long story, *Signor* Corrado. Let's just say it was a case of mistaken identity for now, shall we? *Tutto bene ciò che finisce bene.'[118]*

The two local cops looked at each other as they crossed the narrow path above the sheer drop to the river below. Now they understood why this unusual *commissario* had not wanted to have them attached to their prisoners. Their respect for him increased tenfold. Jumping to their deaths would probably have been an easier way out for the two crooks than to face the wrath of their mafioso *boss.*

The band had decided to celebrate the rescue of this elderly man and played the procession triumphantly into the village. The citizens of Catanzaro came to the spontaneous decision to wave their banners and chant *Abbasso la mafia!* [119] feeling secure in the company of so many of their fellow citizens. As far as they could tell, they had helped to deal a small blow to their local clan.

The procession was met by photographers and TV cameras as planned. The young mayor of Catanzaro was present, dressed in full regalia. He was smiling triumphantly at the reporter who was interviewing him. The TV report would go out to viewers throughout the region well before the day was out.

---

[118] All's well that ends well
[119] Down with the mafia

Beppe made a formal speech thanking the people of Catanzaro for their company and assuring them they had played a vital part in rescuing an innocent man from the jaws of death. He was cheered by all and sundry. Some of those present seemed to remember him as a junior officer in their town many years previously.

Back in Catanzaro, Beppe and his former chief accompanied the 'wrong' Corrado Stancato back home to a tearful but happy wife.

The rescued man had excused himself and gone upstairs to shower and change his clothes.

'Why did you not report your husband's disappearance to us, *cara signora?'* asked *Commissario* Alberto Sordi.

The predictable answer was whispered in a timid voice.

'THEY told me my husband would be shot if I went to the police, *commissario.'*

'But why would they think you have a son who is a policeman?' Beppe asked her.

'Our son *is* a policeman, *commissario.* He belongs to the *Carabinieri* up north in Milano.'

Beppe supposed that was how they had abducted the wrong man. Maybe his own mother telling the mafia mob that he was a bus driver – or whatever she had invented on the spur of the moment - had spared his own father from the ordeal suffered by this lady's husband.

* * *

Beppe and Pippo went out to 'celebrate' in the local bar before returning home to break the news to Imelda. They knew she would have cooked a special lunch to celebrate the return of her husband. Both men needed a dose of Dutch courage before they could face her inevitable heart-rending wails of grief.

It happened just as they feared – only much worse! Imelda had unceremoniously thrown a whole lamb stew down the toilet and flushed it away with a single gesture.

Hours later, after a myriad number of attempts, Beppe had managed to calm her down, while Pippo prepared salami sandwiches in the kitchen – as a substitute lunch.

'*Mamma,* we must be positive. *Papà* must be alive somewhere or we would have heard about it if he had had an accident.'

Pippo was present when Beppe finally managed to calm his mother down sufficiently to ask her a simple question.

'*Mamma* – try to think back to the moment when *papà* left you. Did he take anything with him? Was he carrying anything?'

Returning to her normal self, Imelda retorted in her habitual manner:

'Yes, of course, Giuseppe! He had a little suitcase with him! He never left the house empty-handed.'

'Did he say anything to you, *mamma?* What were his final words?'

'How can I be expected to remember that, Giuseppe? He said something like *See you soon,* I suppose.'

Beppe let out a frustrated sigh. Pippo had a mischievous gleam in his eyes. The police forces of two towns in Italy had been mobilised and a massive search had been instigated – on the simple say-so of Beppe's mother.

'Well, it's a good job we went through with it all, *capo.* After all, we did manage to save the life of an innocent man!' Pippo pointed out.

* * *

It was quite early the following morning as Beppe, Pippo and a subdued Imelda were having their breakfast round the kitchen table that there was a knock on the front door. Beppe went to see who it was.

He found his sister Valentina's husband, Bruno, standing there with a broad grin on his face.

'I've got your *papà* with me in the car, Beppe. He saw a report yesterday evening on the local TV. He just wanted to make sure it was safe to come home again. Since Valentina took the kids to Molise, we've been hiding out in our summer house up in the hills.'

Beppe laughed out loud – a mixture of joy and a feeling of pure relief after the unnecessary suffering caused by his own mother's muddled way of going through her life. Corrado got out of the car with a contented smile on his face at being greeted by his son. He was carrying a modest-sized suitcase.

Beppe hugged his father tightly, patting him on his back repeatedly to reassure himself of the solidity of his father's presence before marching him triumphantly into the kitchen.

'Oh, there you are Corrado!' said Imelda crossly. 'Why did you go away without telling me where you were going?'

Corrado looked at his beloved son and shrugged his shoulders in mock despair.

'So good to be back home again, *carissima!*' he said to his wife.

'Now I've got to go out and buy another shoulder of lamb, Corrado. Just because you couldn't tell me a simple thing like where you were off to.'

Did Pippo detect an undercurrent of affection in her voice? He was thinking fondly of how similar Imelda and his own mother sounded when addressing those whom they secretly loved – expressed in the most acerbic tone of voice possible.

* * *

After a late lunch, Beppe and his father decided to walk together down to the marina – something they had not done for ages. Pippo was left to be spoilt by Imelda – who insisted on feeding him the cakes that she had bought from the local *pasticceria* [120] the previous day – to celebrate the return of her husband. By the end of lunch, nobody had felt hungry enough to face the cream filled *cannoli*. [121]

Pippo managed to escape for a few minutes, saying he should phone his wife back in Pescara – but only after he had been subjected to a barrage of personal questions about Mariangela, when they intended to start a family and why they had never considered spending a holiday in Catanzaro.

Beppe and his father linked arms and walked side by side to the quayside where Corrado regularly went fishing with his rod in the hope of catching a sea bass or a sea bream which he would grill over a barbecue. His principal motive was, however, to buy himself a couple of hours' peace and quiet – not being overly concerned whether he caught a fish or not.

On this occasion, however, he was happy to listen to his son's account of his tussle with the mafioso in the village of Picciano and the fascinating tale of a teenage girl and her horse.

'I guess you didn't tell *mamma* where you were going that day?' asked Beppe at some stage of their conversation.

---

[120] Cake shop
[121] Originally a Sicilian delicacy

'No, I didn't dare. I did my uttermost to persuade her to leave Catanzaro with me, but I suspected she would dig her heels in. So, I called Bruno and he came and picked me up from the port after dark. I didn't want to cause *you* problems with the local mob and I knew there was a risk that your mother would blurt something out which might have compromised your situation, Beppe…'

'I believe *mamma* managed to throw the mob off the scent only too well, *papà*. Did you know there is another Corrado Stancato in Catanzaro?'

'I know of at least two other men with the same surname, Beppe. Stancato is a peculiarly local surname, even if the 'Corrado' versions are limited to a few oldies from the mid-twentieth century!'

Beppe regaled his father with the drama that had been enacted the previous day. It was the first time in years that he had heard his father chuckle with mirth at the description of the other Corrado's rescue. The two sat in comfortable silence for a long time, listening to the sound of the sea lapping against the harbour wall.

'Do you ever miss Calabria, Beppe?' asked his father out of the blue.

'This time, yes, I feel nostalgic for life in the deep south – probably just because life is so less predictable. But mainly I miss being nearer to the family. I'm just so sorry I can't see you more often, *papà.*'

'That's how life is, Beppe. Maybe I will come up and visit you in Pescara – Valentina would love that. She has tried to convince your mother to come too. But…well, you know only too well how unlikely that is.'

'I shall have to return to Pescara tomorrow – or the day after. There is one loose end in the case of the Smiling Man that is niggling me, *papà.* Then there's the trial…'

'I understand, Beppe. It is good that we have spent so much time together today. You can have no idea what it means to me…'

'I think I do,' said Beppe as they walked back to the house where Imelda was already preparing a copious dinner.

Only when he had retreated to the bedroom did Beppe phone Sonia to tell her about his father's safe return.

What the *commissario* omitted to tell Pippo – or anyone else come to that – was about the phone call he had made to the local *boss,* using the number he had been supplied with by the Pescara technicians. He only just succeeded in convincing the mafioso boss that a face-to-face encounter was unnecessary. He was needed urgently back in Pescara, he had claimed.

There had been no doubt in the mafioso's mind that his *faux pas* in abducting the wrong Corrado Stancato would be made common knowledge in Catanzaro if there was ever any attempt to interfere with the lives of his – Beppe's – own family. Albano Spanò – being a 'gentleman' – told Beppe that he considered him to be a worthy rival. He had gone so far as to undertake that he would ensure the safe passage of Beppe's family members into the indefinite future. Beppe had feigned a sense of mutual respect for the mafioso – stifling his desire to crow over his victorious *coup*.

20: On the road to Damascus?

The drive back to Pescara was executed at a steadier rate of kilometres per hour compared to the outward journey. Beppe deigned to allow Pippo to do most of the driving and even suggested they should stop for lunch. Pippo had opted to take a more easterly route and had headed for the Adriatic coast along roads which were more familiar to him. He took the ring road round his native Foggia despite Beppe's amiable suggestion that they should drop in and visit *his* mother.

'It only seems fair, Pippo, that I should get to meet *your* mother in her native surroundings.'

'Only if we have a day to spare, *commissario,*' replied Pippo. 'She talks non-stop – even when she's eating. I would not recommend that course of action.'

Pippo drove up the coast and stopped in a breath-takingly beautiful seaside town called Termoli.'

'Are we still in Puglia?' asked Beppe, whose sense of geography of this part of their peninsula was vague.

'No, Beppe – we are now in Molise – which is the smallest region in the whole of Italy – as everybody knows! But Termoli is a little gem on the Adriatic coast – as you can see for yourself.'

Beppe – despite himself – felt the usual twinge of irritation at those cursed words *'as everybody knows'*. He had a very poor knowledge of certain aspects of his own homeland and resented it when other people knew more than he did.

But Pippo was right, admitted Beppe, as he admired the ancient fortifications of this picturesque little town with its view across the expanse of sparkling water where the distant mountains of Bosnia and Montenegro raised their shoulders above the Adriatic Sea.

'Besides,' added Pippo, 'after two days of your mother's cooking, I thought we should eat some simple fish dish – whilst admiring the scenery.'

Beppe entirely concurred.

'A nice fresh piece of skate or sea bass sounds ideal. Bravo Pippo!'

* * *

They were back in Via Pesaro by four o'clock in the afternoon. Beppe wanted to discuss his next move with Mariastella before Pippo drove him north on the short journey back to Atri – and his family.

'But surely, all we have to do now is wait for the trial, Beppe?'

Her intonation made the statement sound like a question.

'We should be able to put him away for years, Mariastella - that is quite true. But I would like to make sure that he is convicted for *omicidio colposo* [122] by proving that he was directly responsible for the killing of Daniele Capriotti. I just *know* that his widow, Giorgia Scarpa, has played some part in Daniele's misadventure which she is not sharing with us.'

'You mean she is partly responsible for his death, *mio caro commissario?*'

'I wouldn't go as far as that, no. It is as if she is concealing a guilty secret behind her genuine grief. If we knew what she was hiding, we should be able to pin Daniele Capriotti's murder fairly and squarely on Giulio Spanò – giving him and his lawyer no room to wriggle out of it,' Beppe concluded.

The lady *Questore* let out a resigned sigh. She had learnt, since the time she had been appointed to the *Questura* in Pescara, that her second-in-command was never wrong when he had one of his intuitive insights.

'And how do you intend to set about this undertaking, dare I ask?'

'With your permission, Mariastella, I would like to enlist Sonia's help again – just for a day. Assuming Giorgia hasn't vanished in the meantime.'

'Vanished? I hope not. She will most definitely be needed as a prime witness during the trial.

---

[122] Premeditated murder

'Precisely, and it is just such a public exposure I sense she would like to avoid,' explained Beppe.

'Well, I did as you requested, *mio commissario.* I asked *Agente* Flavia Evangelista to go round to Giorgia's home and keep a friendly eye on her. I haven't heard back from her so far. I'll give her a call, Beppe, and phone you – or text you - later on. So, are you heading home now?'

Well, almost, Mariastella. I also want to find out what it was that the archbishop, Don Emanuele, said to Giorgia Scarpa at her husband's funeral service – the real one, that is. He said something which changed her grief to hope – in the space of five seconds…'

'And how do you intend to find that out, Beppe?'

'A visit to the presbytery on our way back to Atri in a few minutes' time – if Pippo will allow me,' smiled Beppe sweetly.

'*In bocca al lupo, commissario!* Let me know the outcome – as soon as you have one, that is,' concluded Mariastella. 'And welcome back! I am so happy that you found your *papà.'*

'It was more a case of *him* finding *me,* to tell you the truth, Mariastella.'

'Oh, I think it is more than that, Beppe. I received a very detailed account of your intervention in Catanzaro just before you came upstairs to see me,' said the lady *Questore.* 'Your former *capo* was waxing eloquent over the phone about your achievements. I wish I had been present to witness it all first-hand…'

They merely shook hands this time as Beppe took his leave.

Mariastella was praying that she was not going to regret giving her second-in-command a free hand for the second time running during the present investigation. So far, it had paid off, she had to admit.

* * *

A woman whom they instantly recognised opened the presbytery door to them. Beppe and Pippo stood on the threshold open-mouthed.

'*Buona sera, Pippo. Buona sera, commissario'* said the familiar figure of Eugenia Mancini – whom they both knew in connection with a previous investigation in a town called Pazzoli.

'Ex-mayoress,' explained Eugenia. 'I stood down after my first four-year term of office – just because I felt like a break from being the *sindaco* [123] And my daughter, Alice, is already in her second year at the *Liceo Scientifico* here in Pescara. So now

---

[123] Mayor : mayoress. Eugenia appears in the fourth novel in the series – Death Is Buried.

I have the happy task of looking after the Archbishop – and my two-year old son, Leo, who is asleep at the moment.'

'It is good to see you looking so well and happy, Eugenia,' said the *commissario,* to dispel the two men's shock at meeting her again in such unexpected circumstances.

In Pazzoli, it had been common gossip that the Archbishop was the natural father of her second child. Beppe wondered if her move to Pescara had been to escape the rumours.

Officially, this scurrilous report was neither denied nor admitted by Eugenia. Don Emanuele himself merely smiled on the rare occasions when some reporter or an over-inquisitive parishioner dared to raise the issue – as if such an accusation was risible in the eyes of God.

'Well, don't just stand there!' exclaimed Eugenia in a tone of mock severity. 'Come in. Don Emanuele is expecting you.'

'How can he be...?' began Beppe. But he knew that, where this enigmatic priest was concerned, anything was possible. His gift of prescience had been amply demonstrated to the *commissario* in the past.

'He's in the cathedral, hearing someone's confession,' explained Eugenia in the same tone of voice she would have used if she had been explaining that he was putting on a change of socks.

Beppe smiled at Eugenia.

'I'm so glad *you* haven't changed at all, *mia cara!*' [124]

Two minutes later, Don Emanuele walked into the kitchen where Beppe and Pippo were sitting at a family-sized wooden table.

Don Emanuele beamed at both men.

'So how can I help you, my friends?'

'Well, as you were expecting us, Don Emanuele, I was hoping you would know already why we are here,' said Beppe.

Don Emanuele laughed – it was impossible to offend this godly man, as Beppe knew full well.

'Ah, is that what Eugenia told you? She has a very sharp sense of humour, doesn't she?' said Don Emanuele.

'Well, just in case you *really* didn't know, I need your help with the case we are investigating at present, Don Emanuele.'

'Ah yes – so you want me to tell you what happened between me and Giorgia in church, just before we buried Daniele.'

It wasn't a question, so Beppe – based on his past experiences of Don Emanuele's intuitive grasp of the world around him – simply continued, stifling his astonishment:

---

[124] My dear

'Could you tell me what it was you said to Giorgia, Don Emanuele? It seemed to change her grief into something resembling hope in the twinkling of an eye.'

The Archbishop looked solemnly at Beppe and Pippo before replying.

'I am not trying to be unhelpful, *signori,* but I cannot remember what, if anything, I said. The Holy Spirit did the talking inside her head, I imagine.'

This response was frustrating for Beppe – but he was not surprised. In one sense, it did not matter what had been said – or who had said it. Beppe was painfully aware that he had simply wished to satisfy his own curiosity.

Don Emanuele looked sympathetically at his friend – not wishing to send him away with the impression that the visit had been a fruitless one.

'All I can say, Beppe, is that I am sure that Giorgia had some deeply-buried sense of shame – a memory that she is trying to cancel out because it is too painful to face up to. That was the vivid impression I had when I was standing near her.'

Beppe stood up without a word. He had a look on his face which was close to adoration.

'*Grazie mille,* Don Emanuele. Now I can finally bring this distressing investigation to its conclusion,' he said, as they prepared to leave the spacious kitchen.

Instead of kissing the Archbishop's ring – as is the custom - Beppe bestowed a kiss on Eugenia's forehead before she accompanied Pippo and Beppe to the front door of the *canonica*.

* * *

'Well, *capo,*' said Pippo, driving northwards towards Atri with his foot pressed down hard on the accelerator, 'I guess Don Emanuele confirmed a conclusion which you had already arrived at of your own accord?'

'*Appunto*, Pippo. But now my vague musings have the stamp of spiritual authority.'

The presence of the ex-mayoress of Pazzoli as Don Emanuele's housekeeper was not considered to be a subject worthy of detailed debate, in the light of the gravity of Don Emanuele's revelation.

'Eugenia looks content with life,' was all Pippo had to say on the subject.

Beppe made no comment for several seconds.

'I am sure those two know what they are doing, Pippo. Whatever their relationship is, it must be a good one. And more importantly, Don Emanuele has not lost his magical powers as a result of their union.'

Pippo laughed at his chief's choice of wording.

'Ah! You believe Don Emanuele is a sort of *mago*,[125] do you, *commissario?*'

'No comment, *Agente* Cafarelli…and slow down a bit. I would like to be in one piece by the time I arrive home.'

---

[125] Conjurer : magician : I tre maghi = The Three Wise Men (of biblical fame)

21:   Inside the mind of Giorgia Scarpa...

Veronica was of an age where she could appreciate the humorous side to her *papà's* account of the rescue of the old man – who was not her *nonno*. She interjected numerous questions and comments as the thrilling story unfolded. Lorenzo, on the other hand, sat enthralled by the whole saga of the procession up the mountain side and the discovery of the old man hidden in the cellar beneath the kitchen – added to the threat of innocent people being shot with automatic rifles.

Beppe noticed that Lorenzo could not find the words to tell his over-excitable sister that this tale constituted a life-threatening situation for his very own and unique *papà*. Lorenzo was reduced to scowling at Veronica every time she interrupted the narrative.

Sonia was simply fascinated by the events Beppe was describing. She sat on the wide sofa with her arms round the shoulders of her two children – sometimes pulling her daughter towards her with a brief gesture which was intended to stop her interrupting all the time.

It was nearly eleven o'clock before Beppe and Sonia were alone. Beppe began to explain to Sonia how he would need her to don her uniform once again to help him winkle out the secrets which he suspected Giorgia Scarpa had been too traumatised to reveal in public.

They were in bed when they were interrupted by a phone call from Mariastella Martellini. She apologised for the lateness of her call and then informed Beppe that Giorgia Scarpa was absent from her house in Picciano.

'Officer Flavia Evangelista has been round three times to the house near the Vendetta Tree. But there is no sign of her – nor her beat-up old Peugeot.' explained the lady *Questore* with some alarm.

'Do not be concerned, Mariastella,' said Beppe. 'I think I know roughly where to find her. And Sonia has her mobile number. We shall work out a strategy to get the lady concerned to open up.'

The *Questore* sounded tired. She bid the couple 'goodnight' and wished them *sogni d'oro* [126] before bringing the call to an end.

'Have you noticed, *amore,* how different the personalities of our two children have become?' asked Sonia.

'Thank heaven for that! The laws of nature are at work.'

'But it makes you wonder, doesn't it, what number three will be like.'

There was a silence from Beppe's side of the bed. He had fallen asleep out of sheer exhaustion.

'Well, maybe we shall soon know,' Sonia said for her own benefit.

---

[126] Sweet dreams – dreams of gold

'You mean we are going to play a kind of 'good cop' versus 'bad cop' game?' asked an astonished Sonia at the breakfast table the following morning.

'You could put it that way, Sonia.'

'Which begs the question, Beppe. Which one of us is going to play the bad cop?'

Sonia knew the answer already, but was curious as to how Beppe would explain it.

'You would need to exercise a degree of ruthlessness which you would be reluctant to inflict on Giorgia,' was Beppe's response. 'After all, you and she are already on very good terms. So I guess it will have to be me who plays the *poliziotto cattivo.*'

'Do you really believe that it is going to be so problematic to get her to talk openly, Beppe?'

'If I am right, Sonia, it will be like breaking down an outer shell to reach this secret place that she has created for her own emotional survival.'

'But what led you to this conclusion, Beppe? It all seemed so black and white when we first met Giorgia.'

'Yes, but real life is rarely so simple. It is only recently that I have come to realise that it was what Giorgia did *NOT* tell us at the time that set me off on this train of thought.'

'I still find it hard to believe that a young woman like Giorgia…'

'Don Emanuele thinks as I do, *amore*. I went to see him before I came home yesterday evening. He sensed she had buried some dark secret in her soul.'

'But Don Emanuele was only with Giorgia for about ten seconds at Daniel Capriotti's funeral.'

'As you know, Sonia, with Don Emanuele, that is as long as it takes sometimes.'

Sonia nodded silently.

'*Va bene,* Beppe. But I'm relieved that it will be me acting as the good cop.'

'The first step is to find her and get her to return to Picciano. She will need to get used to the notion that she will have to appear at Giulio Spanò's trial.'

'Let me go and get dressed – in my police gear. I can't play even the 'good cop' if I am still wearing my pyjamas!'

Sonia took Veronica to her school and Lorenzo to his *scuola materna* [127] - both children thrilled by the unexpected treat of being accompanied to school by their 'policewoman' mother, revelling in the effect this would have on their classmates. Lorenzo simply looked engagingly smug. But it was Veronica who wove the fantastic tale to her inquisitive classmates that her mother was off to track down a woman who

---

[127] Nursery school

277

had vanished into thin air while she and her friend were sitting having a picnic on a beach.

'Veronica!' her teacher said kindly but firmly. 'I think you might be letting your imagination run away with you, don't you?'

'Well, this lady really has vanished *somewhere!*' stated Veronica defiantly - in a convincing enough manner to save most of her face in front of her classmates.

* * *

'Try sending her a text message, Sonia,' suggested Beppe after three attempts to get an answer from Giorgia had failed.

We urgently need your help, Giorgia! Please talk to me as soon as possible.

There was no reply forthcoming.

'I must answer her, Filippo!'

'Only if you want to give your position away, Giorgia.'

'But it's Sonia. She has been really kind to me. I can't suddenly not speak to her.'

'She's from the police, tesoro. Don't forget that simple fact.'

'But she won't hurt me. Why don't I just see what she wants? Maybe it's a problem with my house – or with the olive trees...'

The man she was with shrugged his shoulders.

'It's up to you, Giorgia. But you are safe with me here. Don't say later that I didn't warn you. Why not leave it a while and see if she keeps calling? That way you will know if it's really urgent.'

Beppe was ready to play the waiting game.

'She will be mulling over whether she should reply or not. There might well be someone with her who thinks they are protecting her. Give it another fifteen minutes, Sonia.'

Beppe had that strong, patient look on his face that Sonia knew so well. The wearing-down 'game' had begun.

After precisely fifteen long minutes, Beppe nodded at Sonia again, making a telephone shape with his hand to his ears to mean she should make a call rather than sending a text message. Sonia did so twice with no result. Beppe urged her to try again after thirty seconds had elapsed. This time, she heard a desperate little voice saying 'Son...' before the call was cut off.

The *commissario* had a knowing look on his face.

'Now send her a text message, Sonia.'

'What shall I say in the message?'

'Ciao Giorgia. Please talk to me – it's urgent. If you don't, we shall have to send out the police in Ascoli Picena [128]to look for you. I promise it's nothing bad.'

Beppe had dictated the message to Sonia in short bursts. Sonia, like so many Italian women he knew, could type out a complex message in seconds as their nimble fingers danced over the tiny keys. It was an impressive feminine trait, considered the *commissario*.

Beppe held up the fingers of both hands, closed them into a fist shape and repeated the gesture in silence two more times.

'Minutes or seconds?' Sonia mouthed the words.

Beppe merely gave Sonia a hard look to imply what a silly question that had been. After twenty-five seconds, Sonia's mobile sprang into life. Sonia put the device into loudspeaker mode, giving her husband a scathing look – irritated yet impressed that he always seemed to know more about human behaviour than she did.

'Giorgia, finally! You don't need to worry, *mia cara*. You aren't in any trouble, you know. But we really do need your help. So much has happened since you left Picciano and

---

[128] Ascoli Picena is a town just over the border with Abruzzo – in the region called Le Marche. About 90 kilometres north of Atri.

went to Ascoli – you wouldn't believe it! Beppe and I will meet you at your house.'

Giorgia began to formulate a question to Sonia.

'Can I bring...?'

Beppe was nodding his head even before Giorgia could complete the request.

'*Sì, cara* – of course you can bring a friend with you. What's her name?'

But Beppe was shaking his head before the question was even out of Sonia's mouth. Once again, he had that know-it-all smirk on his face. Sonia just had time to prepare herself for Giorgia's answer.

'*Filippo?*' said Sonia, repeating the friend's name whilst scowling at her husband – simply because he had realised in advance that the friend would be a man.

* * *

'How, in the name of all the saints, did you know it was a man – and above all, that she is in Ascoli Picena?' Sonia asked crossly.

For the umpteenth time in their shared life, she had become aware that her husband seemed to have the answer to everything well before anyone else had even posed the question. However, his reply to her question was modest in the extreme.

'The answer is, I didn't know. I was taking a bit of a gamble, *amore mio*. After the funeral – the real one - I joined the 'congregation' in the *Olivo Nero* for a few minutes. Giorgia was in deep conversation with a man who looked very similar to Daniele Capriotti – a relative of his, I supposed. Giorgia had eyes only for this man. I barely had time to talk to Daniele's parents before I left. They told me they lived in Ascoli Picena. It seemed logical to assume the whole family live in that town. You know how Italian families in the South always live on each other's doorstep. It's not too hard to imagine that people in the centre of our country are equally attached to their family members. There! You see? Elementary, *mia cara* Sonia.'

Sonia sighed.

'Bravo, Beppe,' she said with admiration in her eyes.

They set off immediately in the direction of Picciano at a brisk pace, to make sure they arrived before Giorgia – and her 'friend', Filippo.

'It didn't take long for her to replace her husband if this Filippo is more than just a friend,' said Sonia thoughtfully.

'No, it does say a lot about the young lady's state of mind, doesn't it, Sonia? In her defence, she might well have got to know this cousin – or whoever he is – before Daniele was murdered. But I still need to know what words she heard in her head after Don Emanuele's intervention in the church. *That* is what has been bugging me over the past few days,' said Beppe enigmatically.

* * *

Giorgia arrived at her house in Picciano in a middle-aged BMW – just old enough not to appear too flashy. The same description applied to Filippo, considered Beppe on seeing Giorgia's companion alighting from his car.

Giorgia looked warily at Beppe whilst smiling nervously at Sonia. They were introduced to her companion as Filippo Capriotti. So far, Beppe's assumption had been confirmed.

Beppe took one look at Giorgia's face and felt deeply sorry for her. If he was still intending to play the role of the *sbirro cattivo* [129] at least he should keep his voice gentle and rely on the steady stare instead. Better still, why not leave it all to Sonia?

'What happened to your old Peugeot, Giorgia?' he asked.

To his surprise, Giorgia looked petrified by this innocent question.

'I...it... I had to have it t... t... towed away, *commissario,*' she stammered. She had turned a bright red.

The man called Filippo ran round to Giorgia's side of the car, scowled at Beppe and put an affectionate arm around her shoulders.

---

[129] The bad cop

So, the Peugeot has something to do with her inner turmoil, thought Beppe. He looked at Sonia to see if she had made the same link. She merely looked at him and nodded. It was not clear if she had made the connection.

Filippo explained, in a fussy, stilted manner, that he was a cousin of the 'deceased'.

'I am a lawyer,' added Giorgia's companion when the introductions had been completed. 'I am here to see that Giorgia is properly represented, if that is acceptable…'

Beppe was instantly certain that this was *not* acceptable in any circumstances. He hoped and prayed that Giorgia had not committed herself to this man in any way – emotionally or professionally. That would have been too rash a move.

Beppe went straight into offensive mode.

Congratulations, *Signor* Capriotti - you sound, and look, exactly like a lawyer! All I have to say to you is that you did absolutely the right thing in bringing Giorgia down here. But she does not need a lawyer, simply because she has not committed a crime…'

'I insist on being with her when you interview her,' said Filippo in a pompous manner.

Beppe fixed the man with his most concentrated and disconcerting stare for all of twenty-one seconds – a record, he calculated - before he felt the need to blink.

'What Giorgia needs most of all in this testing period in her life, Filippo, is a shoulder to cry on. And preferably a woman's shoulder. That is why my wife, Sonia, is with me – and yes, she is not just dressed up as a cop,' Beppe said sharply – he had pre-emptied the question he was sure this finicky individual was about to ask.

'I would advise you to drive back home to Ascoli, *Signor* Capriotti. There is little point in your hanging around here.'

'Giorgia is coming home with me, *commissario*' said the lawyer-friend tersely.

'No, she is not, Filippo! She is coming back home with us. And that is an end to the discussion!'

Beppe's mouth was open in astonishment. It was Sonia who had broken her silence with this curt interjection. Beppe recovered quickly and spoke to Filippo in a jocular manner.

'You see, Filippo? The women have decided for us. There is nothing either of us can do. However, before you leave, I would like to have a few words with you – to help me understand Giorgia's situation better. We shall make our way to the local bar while the girls talk together. The drinks are on me.'

The transformation from the aggressive voice to the amicable invitation had completely thrown the lawyer from Ascoli.

There was an uncertain smile on Giorgia's face at the unexpected invitation to stay with Sonia at *her* home. If anything, Beppe had the impression, she looked relieved.

The *commissario* felt he had won the first round. Without being invited, he opened the passenger door of the BMW and got in.

'Let's take the car, Filippo. It will save a bit of time, won't it? I need to have your point of view on all this as soon as possible.'

The ground had been removed from beneath the lawyer-cum-friend's feet. He got into the driver's seat and reversed the car before remembering to wave a departing hand in Giorgia's direction. She did not return the wave, Beppe noticed. Perhaps simply because her mind had already jumped ahead to the new challenge of talking to Sonia.

Inside the *Olivo Nero,* Beppe enjoyed the status of a saviour and a hero rolled into one. Adelina, her face beaming, ran over to the table near the window where Beppe had sat down with his guest – whom she vaguely recognised from the post-funeral get-together. Other drinkers at the bar turned round and raised their glasses in a gesture of gratitude towards this very out-of-the-ordinary police officer.

'What can I get for you two gentlemen?' asked Adelina. Beppe ordered a simple *espresso,* whereas Filippo requested a cold tea. He had hesitated before placing his order. Beppe had the instinctive feeling that he would have ordered something alcoholic, had it not been for the presence of the law.

'*Dai,* Filippo! I won't arrest you for drunken driving! Have what you want. The order changed from a cold tea to a glass of white wine.

'I apologise for my language when you arrived, Filippo. I am feeling on edge about the trial. Giorgia is in the unfortunate position of being our main ally in the battle to make sure that crook Giulio Spanò remains behind bars for at least twenty-five years. Poor girl, she is crucial in this affair, as I am sure you must be aware...'

'I understand, *commissario.* You have your job to do. I was merely being protective towards my...cousin, you understand.'

Beppe was certain that Filippo had wanted to say '*fidanzata*' rather than 'cousin'. Instead, he went on quite irrelevantly to explain that he and Giorgia were not close cousins.

'He's in love with her,' Beppe realised. 'Not the right match for her at all. He was still wondering what Don Emanuele had said at the time of the fake funeral. He already had an inkling.

'You know Giorgia better than I do,' Beppe continued in a conciliatory tone of voice, 'She seems to be suppressing a lot of complex emotions. Has she said anything to you concerning the capture and death of Daniele?'

'Yes, *commissario,* she did begin to talk more freely about it – but then she clammed up again. As if it was simply too painful to bring it all out into the open…'

'Did you glean *anything?'*

'Very little, *commissario.* She and Daniele had been up to visit relatives in Ascoli. I understand that they had reached the outskirts of Picciano when something happened involving that mafioso crook. But she refused to go into any details. I'm sorry to be so vague.'

Beppe patted Filippo's arm in a reassuring manner.

'On the contrary, Filippo. You have given me more of a lead than you realise. You should go back to Ascoli now and leave the rest to us. We shall look after Giorgia as if she was one of our family. She trusts Sonia as if she has known her for years.'

The would-be-lover got meekly into his car and drove off in the direction of Ascoli. Beppe had even managed to shake Filippo's hand in both of his, adding:

'Di nuovo, [130] grazie Filippo.'

Beppe went back inside the bar to pay for the drinks.

Adelina was still smiling at him.

---

[130] Once again

'We are so glad to see you here, *commissario*. You will always be welcome in our little town. But what brings you back so soon? Isn't your investigation over now?'

'Loose ends, Adelina. Nothing for you to be concerned about, *mia cara*. Your little boy will grow up in a safe environment.'

Adelina looked relieved. How had this policeman understood why she had asked him that question? She hadn't even identified the source of her own anxiety until he had uttered those words.

She gave him a spontaneous *bacio* on each cheek.

'Grazie mille, caro commissario!'

Beppe walked downhill towards Giorgia's house. He should delay his return for a bit longer. He did not want to barge in on Sonia while she was still coaxing the truth out of Giorgia. He was unsure why he made the short detour to the meadow where the 'Vendetta Tree' stood in solitary splendour. Just to have a last look at it? So why did he find himself walking up to this ancient living thing? He found himself thinking about his father again. His quiet wisdom had deeply affected him after his father's calm return from his self-imposed exile. Beppe found himself touching the tree's ancient bark. He wanted to put his arms as far round the trunk as they would reach.

This time, there was no doubt about it. He felt some current running through his body – slow and soothing.

'Ah! Now I understand what happened to Giorgia,' he told himself as he walked slowly back towards the house hidden behind the trees.

* * *

Beppe stepped quietly through the open front door which led directly into the rustic kitchen with the wooden table occupying the centre of the room. He heard the sound of Giorgia sobbing pitifully. Sonia had placed a consoling arm round the younger woman's shoulders. Sonia simply nodded at Beppe and signalled for him to come into the room. He sat down at the table by Giorgia's side – as if he was protecting her other flank.

After a while, her sobbing subsided and Beppe spoke to her in a soft voice.

'You were in the car when Giulio Spanò took your husband away from you, weren't you, Giorgia?'

'How in the name of all the saints did you know *that?*' the expression on Sonia's face was asking.

Beppe felt at peace with himself at last – happy that he had not had to play out his role of the 'hard cop' in order to discover what this vulnerable young woman had been too afraid or guilty to admit to publicly – or even to herself.

It would have to wait until much later that night, after he and Sonia were alone in bed, before he discovered just how traumatic Giorgia's experience had been.

* * *

On the way back home to Atri, with a subdued Giorgia sitting in the back seat, Sonia rested her left hand on Beppe's thigh giving it an affectionate squeeze from time to time.

Much later, in bed, her opening words were predictably cutting.

'So, *caro commissario,* you allowed me to bully that poor young woman into submission for nearly an hour – and you knew all along why she was so reluctant to admit what really happened?'

'No, *amore mio,* I put two and two together just before I arrived at Giorgia's house. I have no idea at all of the details.'

Should he tell Sonia about his hugging the Vendetta Tree? Maybe not until later – if at all, he concluded.

With only a glimmer of light coming into their bedroom from outside, Sonia began to relate what Giorgia had told her that morning.

'I did as you suggested, *amore.* I told her what has happened since the day of her husband's funeral – the real one that took place in the cemetery up the hill. She had gathered nothing about the murder of Spanò's two henchmen at the hands of their boss. I gave her a potted version of everything that happened. She was only vaguely aware of the existence of Aurora – and she loved the bit about her witnessing her own father committing murder and riding away on horseback. I am sure it gave the necessary boost to her courage to tell me about how she was involved in her husband's killing. All I had to do was to convince her she had to get everything off her chest once and for all. I made a recording of what she said – just as you suggested. I *did* tell her beforehand, but I'm not sure she actually took it all in. She just poured out her soul. Are you ready for this, *amore?* '

Beppe nodded in the darkness. What he heard took him so completely by surprise that he found himself listening alertly to every word from the outset to the bitter, tearful ending.

We were coming back from a visit to Daniele's parents. I was driving. He had been drinking – on purpose so that he wouldn't have to drive. We began to argue almost as soon as we were on the main highway to Teramo. I was driving fast like I always do when I'm angry, Sonia. I know I shouldn't but it's my way of letting off steam. Daniele was always telling me off for 'driving dangerously' – as he put it. I was telling him, he shouldn't drink so much wine, then he could drive instead of me. He was a really slow driver. It was maddening being in the car when he was at the wheel... I love him really. I loved him truly... (the first sobs began to be heard on the tape*) We started off really happy, you know – until that bastard arrived in Picciano. He had had his way with most of those landowners with olive trees. Those two brutes – I am so glad they are dead – went round intimidating and threatening everyone relentlessly, day after day, week after week... The only ones who resisted were Davide Di Sabatino and his family. You know, the frantoista. He held out for a time, but they got to him through his kids. They signed the final contract in the end...*

Sonia's voice was heard for the first time.

'No, they didn't, Giorgia. They changed their minds – and then Beppe – my husband – came along and took charge.'

I wish I had known, Sonia. (Giorgia's voice was beginning to break down) *And then there was me and Daniele. He didn't seem scared of Don Spanò. He always told him he was a mafioso crook to his face. I don't think he understood what being a member of a mafia clan really meant. I was afraid of Don Spanò. He said he was really fond of me and didn't want any harm to come to me. I knew in my heart of hearts he just wanted me for my body – but he always said he would look after me... 'if anything ever happened to Daniele' – that's what he said.*

(At this point, Giorgia's voice began to become inarticulate as she neared the end of her 'confession'. Beppe had to listen for key words in her narrative)

I don't know why I told him what time we were coming home. I was just scared of him – like everybody else, I suppose. But he was waiting for us with his two henchmen just on the edge of the village. I had to brake suddenly as Don Spanò stepped into the middle of the road. He was pointing a pistol at the windscreen. He made a sign that I should wind down the driver's window. He said he just wanted a quiet word with Daniele – to sort out the problem of contracts. 'We'll bring him back to you as soon as we've finished. Oh Sonia! I could have just put my foot down and driven off at that point. And saved Daniele's life, don't you see? But I was still feeling angry with him. I thought he might as well find out there was no point in continuing to resist that bastard... I never guessed they would murder him. I never realised...

Giorgia's voice became disconsolate with grief.

È tutto colpa mia! Tutto colpa mia, Sonia... [131]

'I switched the recorder off at that point because I thought she had nothing else to add. But I was wrong, Beppe. When she had calmed down a bit, I consoled her as best I could. I kept on telling her that it was not her fault, that Giulio Spanò was the only guilty one. I know I took on the 'bad cop' role just

---

[131] It's all my fault

for a minute – but you told me to find out if she witnessed the act of killing Daniele.

'So, you didn't actually see anything yourself, Giorgia?' I shot the question at her like a bullet.

She shook her head and then told me this:

But he gave me back the ring he had cut off Daniele's finger before they hung him up on the tree. He was SMILING that ghastly smile which I so loathed, Sonia. He thought it was entertaining. He expected me to be grateful…

Then she broke into a flood of tears again, Beppe. That's when you arrived.'

22:   *The vagaries of human nature…*

A phone call from the lady *Questore* at 7.30 next morning woke Beppe and Sonia up from their deep slumber. They had not heard Giorgia calling out in the night – but Veronica and Lorenzo had.

'Like a voice from someone lost at sea,' Veronica told her mother cheerfully on their way to school.

'Will she be staying with us for long?' asked Lorenzo anxiously. He was evidently more deeply affected than his sister.

'No, tesoro mio. She is going to Pescara with your *papà.'*

'Oh, I don't want her to go, *mamma.* I just need to have some cotton wool to block my ears up tonight,' replied Lorenzo in a practical tone of voice.

Sonia bent down and kissed her son on the top of his head.

'Come sei carino, [132]*Lori!* But don't worry, Giorgia will be alright one day. And Mariastella has found someone who will care for her. She has to help the police put that mafioso permanently in prison.'

---

[132] Sweet : nice : lovely etc

Sonia was not sure how much Lorenzo had already understood. He tended to turn new experiences over in his head and ask questions sometimes days later.

'Why is Giorgia so upset, *mamma?* I need to know so that…' began Veronica.

'You can make up a good story to tell your schoolmates, *amore?*'

'*No, mamma!*' said Veronica indignantly. 'It's just that I want to know what's not right in her life. I want her to be happy like I am!'

Sonia repeated the same gesture as she had bestowed on her son. But without the words.

'*Non sono carina, io, come Lori?*' [133] Veronica asked.

'Of course, you are, *tesoro.* You are the best children in the world…'

'I want a baby brother, *mamma.* Or even another sister, if that's what comes out!' Lorenzo added as an afterthought.

'We shall have to wait and see, won't we?' said Sonia – now positively hoping that it would be so. Before getting married, they had both paid lip-service to the idea of having a large family.

The reality of bringing up children had, until then, caused them to shelve the project. She felt certain that three children

---

[133] Aren't *I* as sweet as Lori is?

nowadays constituted a 'large family' – when too many Italian women had abandoned the notion of having even one child.

* * *

There was a protracted – but not uncomfortable – silence for the first ten or so kilometres of Beppe's steady drive down to Pescara – with Giorgia and suitcase beside him in the passenger seat.

It was Beppe who first broke the silence.

'I'm just being nosey, Giorgia. But I have been wondering for days what it was that you heard Don Emanuele telling you in the church, that day. If it's too personal, just tell me to mind my own business…'

There! He had done it – finally! Asked the question that had been nagging away in his head for days!

To Beppe's great surprise, she giggled. The sound was music to his ears.

'Why didn't you ask *him?*'

'I *did,* Giorgia – and all he said was, whatever words you heard, it must have been the Holy Spirit speaking to you. One becomes used to that sort of response from our Archbishop. So – I was none the wiser.'

Giorgia remained silent for minutes on end before replying – obviously overcome with emotion at the mysterious concept she had just been presented with. Then came her response:

'I heard a voice saying so clearly: *'Fear not, Giorgia. You will not be alone for long.'*

'When I saw you next time, you were in the bar, *L'Olivo Nero,* Giorgia. You were in deep conversation with a man whom I now know to be called Filippo. Does that mean you took the words literally?'

Beppe's question was answered – not by a giggle – but by a tinkling burst of laughter which lasted until she had run out of breath.

'What a lovely person you are, *commissario!* I haven't felt like laughing for…months, if not years! It is so reassuring to be with normal people again.'

Beppe was smiling at her, taken aback by her unexpected reaction to his question.

'I felt so happy after hearing those magic words in church, Beppe. But I never considered taking them quite so literally. I am sure Filippo fancies me – that became uncomfortably obvious after a couple of days. But no, Beppe. I do not think he is remotely the one for me. I'm sorry to disappoint you!'

'In point of fact, Giorgia, I am relieved.'

'*Meno male, commissario!*' [134] she said ironically. 'May I ask why?'

'No, you may not! It was an instinctive reaction not a rational one.'

She simply smiled at his retort and was happy enough to sink back into her own thoughts for the rest of the drive down to the *Questura* in Pescara. She only asked two questions – one after the other.

'Do you know who I am staying with? May I call you Beppe?'

'As long as we are on our own, Giorgia, yes. And the answer to your first question is 'no' – I don't know. But I am sure our *Questore* would not entrust our principal witness to just anybody.'

'Is he open-minded like you are, Beppe, with a pretty wife and two beautiful children? If so, I shall feel comfortable with him.

'The *Questore's* name is Mariastella. And she is relatively young and some might consider very attractive. She was present in the church in Picciano on both of those memorable occasions – but you probably had your mind on other matters, *cara* Giorgia.'

Beppe still enjoyed concealing the fact that his *capo* was a woman – just to see the surprised look on the other person's face.

---

[134] Just as well

But Giorgia quietened down. She turned to Beppe and smiled in relief.

Beppe took a chance and brought up the other two issues that had been bothering him.

'What do you know about those white flowers in pots that were left out by someone in the olive grove just behind your house, Giorgia? The ones you put in your greenhouse. Did you realise they could have infected your trees with the Xylella virus?'

She looked alarmed – and puzzled.

'Daniele mentioned them to me – I don't think *he* knew what they were. It must have been the Spanò mob who put them there. Maybe they thought we would sign their contract without a fuss if the trees got diseased? It could be just another dirty trick on their part. They were quite pitiless, you know…'

'And I hate myself for asking this question, Giorgia. I'm so deeply sorry that I have to know the answer. But do you have that ring with you? It might be needed during the trial.'

She looked at him – about to cry again. But she caught the look of sorrow and embarrassment in the expression on Beppe's face. Thus, she merely patted her handbag and said nothing.

* * *

The day of Don Giulio's trial drew ever nearer. Giorgia had been whisked away by Mariastella Martellini to some undisclosed destination at the end of every day when she, Giorgia, had to be present at the *Questura* with the lawyer for the prosecution. Beppe hardly clapped eyes on her from one visit to the next. But, he noticed, she looked amazingly *tranquilla* and usually gave him a beaming smile if their paths crossed.

Mariastella remained suitably vague on the rare occasions when Beppe had attempted to elicit details of Giorgia's whereabouts, replying merely: 'Somewhere very safe and out-of-the-way in the Abruzzo countryside, *commissario.'*

Beppe himself spent hours with the self-same lawyer – whose name was *Avvocatessa* Federica Fellini. She had been especially chosen for the occasion by the DIA [135] in Rome, Mariastella had informed him.

Beppe was no longer startled by the number of women in professional roles who seemed to have usurped such positions of authority during the still young twenty-first century - his own *capo* being the most prominent. It was a healthy sign that Italy was finally emerging from the Dark Ages, he considered – but seldom stated openly. A secret part of him was still attempting to cling on to the notion that a man was there to protect the

---

[135] Direzione Investigativa Antimafia - The anti-mafia police force.

'weaker' sex. He was almost convinced that many of the women he knew thought so too!

The *avvocatessa* for the prosecution was clever, wily and had a phenomenal memory for details. She reminded Beppe of his headmistress at the *liceo* which he had attended in Catanzaro – whom everyone had been in total awe of.

The lawyer for the defence had arrived belatedly from Catanzaro – apparently against her will and better judgement, judging by her studied casualness. Beppe was informed by a caring prison warder, who never once missed mass on Sundays, that the lawyer from Calabria had had a brief conversation with none other than the Archbishop, Don Emanuele, whilst he was carrying out his regular tour of all the inmates – a mission he undertook tirelessly on a weekly basis. He did the same for the women's prison too, Beppe had discovered.

It was ironic, thought Beppe, that *two* lady lawyers would represent the State and the Spanò clan respectively – and that both of them had the same first name – Federica. As to their physical appearance, however, there was no similarity.

Avvocatessa Federica Greco, the unofficial appointee of the Catanzaro mob, was young, but very sharp, and gave the general impression that her presence in Pescara to defend the Spanò nephew was a mere formality. Beppe had gained the distinct feeling that the Catanzaro clan had washed their hands of the whole matter of the olive oil take-over plot in the village of Picciano. They were taking steps to defend their own - just because that was what the mafia did.

When it came to the trial, Beppe would be astonished that *Avvocatessa* F. Greco put up such a good fight. Obviously, she could not lose face in public if she intended to go on representing the Catanzaro branch of the *'ndrangheta* with impunity.

'Best of luck to her!' thought Beppe. He would have to ask Don Emanuele what had transpired between himself and the mafia lawyer during his prison visit – and ask if he had made any headway as regards the state of The Smiling Man's soul! That would be a very long road indeed, Beppe imagined. There must be some limit even to Don Emanuele's spiritual powers? Deep down inside, Beppe did not really *want* The Smiling Man's soul to be saved. It was a disturbing sensation – and one that he had rarely felt so intensely towards any of the villains he had helped to put behind bars in the past.

* * *

The trial of Giulio Spanò took place in Pescara, presided over by three independent magistrates – and no jury. It is common legal practice in Italy to hold trials for serious crimes without a public jury being involved. The impartiality and competence of the judges is widely taken for granted. In general, the system works well. Since this trial would be lengthy and complex, only salient aspects of the procedures, which are certain to be of interest to you - the readers - will be reported here.

Excerpts from the trial (1)   Giorgia Scarpa's role.
GS – Giorgia Scarpa.   FF – Federica Fellini: lawyer for the prosecution.   FG – Federica Greco: lawyer for the defence.

FG: On reflection, would it not be the case, Signora Scarpa, that you simply made an assumption that your husband was murdered by my client? After all, you drove off as quickly as you could, happily leaving him in the hands of my client and his friends, did you not? Would you have reacted in that manner had you known that your husband's life was at risk?

GS: I did not drive off 'happily' as you put it so eloquently. I was scared stiff of what would happen if I had refused to let him out of the car – to him and to me. No, I never thought Don Giulio Spanò would put a gun to my husband's head and murder him...

FG: But there is precisely no proof that things happened in this way, I would argue to the court. Did the bullet which killed your husband match either of the pistols found buried in the grave where Antò and Mimo were found? No, it is on record that the bullet was fired from a different weapon altogether. My client was never found to have a pistol in his possession. I have that assurance from Don Spanò himself.

There was a burst of cynical laughter from the public gallery. Judge Roberto Renzetti intervened at this point and invited FF to cross-question the witness.

FF: My colleague acting for the defence has made a valid point, *Signora* Scarpa. There seems to be nobody who can actually claim to have witnessed the murder of your husband, Daniele Capriotti. What makes you so certain that it is the accused who is guilty of this heartless crime?

GS: Why else would they have made him get out of the car? We were only half a kilometre from our home. Why would he hold us up at pistol point in the middle of a darkened road? Why would he say he wanted to discuss a contract with my husband? Just because we were the last inhabitants in the town who refused to comply, I would say. We were the only people left standing in his way. That is on record. Twenty-three land-owners had already been forced to sign away their livelihoods to this ghastly Calabrian mob...

FF: But there may still be a handful of people in this hearing who are unconvinced by your harrowing account, Signora Scarpa. What would you say to *them,* Giorgia?

GS: *(Who had finally reached the most painful part of her husband's death. She was on the point of weeping.)*
Because that bastard cut off my husband's finger with the ring on it – because it was too tight to get off. He didn't want my husband's body to be identified when he had him strung up on that olive tree. Daniele never removed it from his finger throughout our four years of marriage. It belonged to his great-grandfather and was passed down to Daniele. Any of his family will identify it, your honours. It even has the family name, Capriotti, engraved on the inside.

FF: I am sorry to put you through this horrible experience again, Signora Scarpa. But the obvious question has to answered. How exactly did you come to be back in possession of your husband's ring?

GS: *(Who no longer attempted to hold back her tears.)*
Because Giulio Spanò came to my house the following morning and handed me the ring he had cut off Daniele's finger. He was SMILING, for God's sake. He said to me: 'Now your troubles are over, *carrissima* Giorgia. You know you always argued that

307

you should hand over your land to me. Now you will be able to have your way. Then he made me have sex with him…'

There was a gasp of horror from the public gallery – many of whom had travelled to Pecscara from Picciano – including Don Pietro, the parish priest and the old archivist, Leonardo Scafa.

FF: I am sorry, Giorgia. Do you happen to have this ring on you to show their lordships?

A tearful Giorgia Scarpa – well briefed throughout the whole procedure by her lawyer, took the ring out of her jacket pocket and handed it to the usher.

Judge Renzetti looked at the ring and passed it onto his two colleagues, Judges Arianna Di Matteo and Paolo d'Incecco.

'Would you like to cross-question the witness, Avvocato Greco?'

The lawyer from Calabria replied simply: 'No, your honour.'

In the dock, Don Giulio Spanò was looking vengefully at the whole court – but especially at Giorgia Scarpa. That was before he saw that 'cop' staring at him. Then he remembered where he was and began smiling again.

Excerpts from the trial (2) Aurora Spanò's role.

AS – Aurora Spanò   FF – Federica Fellini   FG – Federica Greco

Aurora Spanò, looking as white as a sheet, is accompanied to the witness stand for the second time by a uniformed Mariastella Martellini, who has a comforting arm round the young woman's shoulder. The *Questore* remains by her side throughout the interrogation.

FG: Signorina Spanò – Aurora. I am so sorry to have to question you at all about the story you told the court regarding your father. I will not make you repeat it because it must be so painful for you. But do you not think you might have been mistaken about what you saw? It was dark and it must all have happened so quickly. Do you not believe your father when he says that Mimo and Antò shot each other at the same time? You could so easily have been mistaken – and nobody here will blame you for changing your mind.

FF   Objection, your honours. This is a heartless attempt to play on Signorina Spanò's wish to protect her father.

Judge Renzetti lets out a sigh and looks at his two fellow judges. It is the lady judge, Arianna Di Matteo who speaks – almost reluctantly. 'Let Aurora answer the question'.

In the courtroom, nobody was moving. Nobody even whispered to a neighbour. Aurora's face was rigid with tension. Everyone – including her own father – was staring at her pale face, witnessing the internal struggle that must have been raging inside her head. She remained silent for what seemed like an interminable age. Mariastella Martellini simply put out an arm and stroked the back of her head once.

Aurora Spanò breaks down into tears of remorse and shouts out the words:

'My father is a killer. I saw him shoot the man called Mimi with the gun he had taken from Anto. Then I just told Barone to turn round and run into the forest. It all happened just like I said.'

Don Giulio Spanò, despite Federica Greco's warning hand on his arm stands up and shouts out:

'Aurora, *tesoro!* How can you say such things about your *papà* who loves you?'

Judge Renzetti brings him back to order immediately as Aurora, at the limits of her endurance, calls out:

'Perchè è vero, papà!' [136]

---

[136] Because it is true

Mariastella, at a nod from the lady judge, leads a tearful Aurora away and out of the courtroom.

There is an expression on the mafioso's face that nobody – including Beppe Stancato – has ever witnessed before; one of remorse.

'Maybe Don Emanuele will not be wasting his time, after all'

Excerpts from the trial (3) Bruno Esposito – speaking for the forensics team. *BE – Bruno Esposito*

FF: The court would like to hear from you, Dottore, what proof, if any, you have found in support of Aurora Spanò's account of the killing of the two mafiosi – Domenico Laganà and Antonio Morabito – otherwise known as Mimo and Antò.

BE: The account given by Giulio Spanò that his two henchmen shot each other simultaneously does not tally with the forensic evidence. Mimo and Antò had identical pistols. Had they shot each other from opposite sides of the pit – as Signor Spanò claims – the penetration of the small calibre projectiles would have been identical. But with Mimo, the bullet nearly went completely through his head and out the other side. This tallies exactly with Aurora's account of events – that Mimo was shot at point blank range by the accused, using Antò's pistol.

FF:	And is it true that the accused threw his own pistol in the pit before filling it with the soil? An aspect of this brutal scene that Aurora would not have witnessed since she had already ridden off into the forest.

BE:	Yes, Avvocato Fellini. The third pistol belonging to the accused was discovered later on after a second search. He did not even bother to wipe his own fingerprints off the hand-grip. He simply assumed that nobody would ever discover this grave.

FF:	A final question, Dottore Esposito. Could one of the three weapons discovered have been used previously in the murder of Daniele Capriotti?

BE:	Yes, it was Giulio Spanò's pistol, which we dug out of the grave, that had been used to kill Daniele Capriotti.

His honour, Giudice Renzetti, invited the lawyer for the defence to cross-examine Bruno Esposito. To Don Giulio Spanò's humiliation and despair, his lawyer shrugged her shoulders and said:
'No, Vostro Onore. In point of fact, I resign from my position as defence lawyer for Giulio Spanò forthwith. I was lied to by my ex-client as to the third pistol.'

Avvocatessa Federica Greco simply looked relieved that her part in this farce was over – even if she suspected she might be looking for a post elsewhere in Italy – probably in Milano or Torino; any job she could find in a city as far away from Catanzaro as possible.

After a brief consultation with his fellow judges, Giudice Renzetti pronounced the inevitable sentence in one word: 'ERGASTOLO' [137]

---

[137] Life imprisonment - a life sentence   *(Pron: air-**GA** sto-lo)*

23: *Mariastella through the Looking-Glass…*

The rumours circulating around the *Questura* in a side-street near the river Pescara never really took on a definite form. It was more like a game of Chinese Whispers. By the end of day one of the game, nobody was sure who had initiated what Beppe himself, much later in the day, dismissed as *pettegolezzi.* [138]

It was not as if the gossip was malicious – it was more light-hearted speculation.

It was claimed that, some days before the trial, Mariastella Martellini and Giorgia Scarpa had been spotted together in one of the larger stores in Pescara. They had been choosing knickers and bras and trying on girly outfits in the intimacy of the same changing cabin, emerging arm in arm and giggling like a couple of school girls.

Nobody had been particularly cautious about whom they passed on the gossip to – but at some point, *Agente* Lina Rapino must have caught wind of what she alone out of all the team of officers would have construed as 'scurrilous gossip'. Outraged at the hint of scandal, she went up to report what she had heard directly to the lady *Questore*. Mariastella had, disconcertingly from Officer Rapino's perspective, burst into unrestrained laughter. On seeing her frowning reaction, Mariastella had

---

[138] gossip

feigned a serious face and reassured her overly prim colleague that she had absolutely nothing to worry about.

Lina Rapino left the *Questore's* office and returned downstairs to those 'heathens' with whom she had to share her workplace, with a feeling of relief. Nobody could be guilty of such a perversion if they could laugh it off as her chief had just done. She even smiled at the stupid quips that were being made by some of her 'less mature' colleagues – as she considered them to be.

Beppe had kept himself apart from it all, paying no heed to what was being said. But despite himself, he recalled the occasion when, travelling together in Mariastella's yellow Alfa Romeo sports car towards L'Aquila, she had jokingly said something about preferring the company of younger women. She had wanted to reassure Beppe that Sonia's minor fit of jealousy at their being together in the cramped space of her two-seater car did not pose a risk to his fidelity. Beppe had dismissed her declaration as a joke.

He had been summoned upstairs about four o'clock on that day to discuss various matters which arose from the Vendetta Tree investigation.

He found Mariastella Martellini looking serene and relaxed behind her desk.

'I suppose you have heard the gossip going around downstairs about me, haven't you Beppe?' she asked. 'I knew

315

this would happen as soon as I spotted Officers Campione and Cardinale in the Coin [139] department store, a couple of days ago.'

Beppe smiled, shrugged his shoulders and nodded.

'A bit of amicable speculation, I think, Mariastella. Nobody is being underhand. It will all blow over by tomorrow, I suspect.

'Oh, I am not worried at all! But it may be a surprise to you to learn that I do care what *you* think, Beppe!'

'In quale senso, Mariastella?' he asked, genuinely puzzled.

Mariastella Martellini uttered a deep sigh. Her brow had set in a frown.

'Human beings are so strange, aren't they Beppe? We always think that other people should behave in a predictable, easy-to-explain manner – that their thoughts and actions should always be constant and logical. Yet, inside each one of us, there is a constant ebb and flow of ever-changing emotions and chaotic thoughts which we somehow manage to come to terms with. If we don't manage to line them up in some order, we would simply go mad. I think I know myself inside out, but if I began to share my thoughts with someone like you – whom I trust and like completely – you would think I was crazy. I don't

---

[139] Coin – an 'Italianised' version of Cohen – is a nationwide department store.

make a choice between whether I prefer men or women, Beppe. But I do love Giorgia – just as I love my Spanish boy-friend – who is an airline pilot and much younger than I am. Do you understand what I am saying?'

'Yes, I do Mariastella. Of course I do! And I respect you even more than I did five minutes ago. There, what do you say to that?'

His *capo* said nothing but came round to the opposite side of her desk and hugged her second-in-command more warmly than she had ever done in the past.

'I could almost love you too – if you didn't have Sonia,' she laughed cheekily as she drew apart from Beppe and returned to her side of the desk. 'I just wanted to thank you for everything you have done over the past few weeks, *caro commissario*. You are a remarkable man.'

'Do I take it that you have been hiding Giorgia in your own home, Mariastella?' Beppe asked out of genuine curiosity.

It occurred to Beppe that he had no idea where his chief lived. He had barely given it a thought.

'You and your family should come and visit us, Beppe. It's got huge grounds – and I have a swimming pool, dogs, goats and a donkey called, *Stallone*. Your children would love it there.'

'Where *do* you live, Mariastella? I have never thought to ask you.'

'I'll tell you when you accept my invitation, Beppe,' she replied tantalisingly.

Beppe descended back down to ground level in a pleasant daze. There were rare moments in life when Mariastella's *'mobile spirits'* interpretation of the human mind made total sense. In those fleeting seconds, you could sense a weird mental uniformity interacting between members of the human race – until one tried to bring the likes of the Smiling Man into the equation. Perhaps it was *that* which Don Emanuele seemed to understand so well?

But Beppe could not help wondering if Giorgia Scarpa believed that Don Emanuele's words, heard just before her husband's funeral, had come to bear fruit in her daily life – in the shape of Mariastella Martellini.

'Well, it could be a lot worse,' he thought kindly – as he headed for home and his precious family in a happy and tranquil frame of mind. The case of the Vendetta Tree was complete.

Epilogo

More than in any other investigation that Beppe had undertaken in his nearly nine years as *commissario* at the police headquarters in Pescara, he had the impression this was the only case where he felt a debt of gratitude to a whole community of people. Above all, he had become almost obsessed with the welfare of a teenage girl called Aurora. Even though his beloved father had not, as it turned out, been in danger of his life, the vivid – no surreal – account that had emanated from this strange girl's mind had enabled him to rescue the elderly man who shared nothing with his own father except his name.

He was disturbed by the fact that he had felt nostalgia for the deep South of his homeland for the first time in years. On previous occasions, he had been obliged to return to his native Catanzaro following his mother's insistent calls to visit her: *'Before I have to witness how my grandchildren have turned out from up there',* she would say pointing at the ceiling, above which she imagined heaven was situated.

His visit to Catanzaro, on this occasion, had become more like a pilgrimage to his past life. He had felt dangerously homesick for the first time since he had made that lengthy solo sea voyage from Catanzaro to Pescara in his own little boat. Originally, it had been envisaged that he should only remain in Pescara for five years. But then, he had fallen in love with Sonia and they had had two totally engaging children. In practical terms, he knew he would have to remain in Abruzzo – and wait until his children had grown up before even thinking of relocating anywhere else.

'Put it out of your mind, Beppe Stancato!' he told himself.

The one and only element of the Vendetta Tree case which would not go away was the existence of a girl called Aurora Spanò. Beppe was not allowed to go on his own to the *frantoio*. As soon as he had launched the idea of a visit to Picciano 'to see how Aurora is doing', he was besieged by two children who insisted on going too.

'You can't possibly think of going to see Aurora without taking us with you, *papà*. It simply will not be permitted!' declared Veronica.

'Is it Aurora or her horse you really want to see?' asked Sonia.

Veronica understood the concept of a 'diplomatic response' even if the words might still not have been a part of her vocabulary.

'Aurora, of course!' she replied immediately.

'*Bugiarda!*' [140] muttered Lorenzo under his breath.

Thus it was, that the following Saturday, Beppe and family set off for the *frantoio* just outside Picciano. He could

---

[140] liar

satisfy himself that Aurora was slowly but surely putting the memories of that horrific experience behind her.

'They are going to adopt me, Sonia,' Aurora confided while they walked Barone round and round in circles with either Veronica or both her and her brother perched on the horse's back.

'She has long periods where she remains in her room. She is a strange girl in many ways – she can be very withdrawn. But we all love her to bits,' Davide told Beppe.

'Especially Tommaso,' added his wife with a twinkle in her eyes. 'He's pretty smitten, I would say. But she still feels like a little girl in so many ways – even if she already looks like an adult on the outside.'

'She's going to start going to school in September,' added Davide. The old archivist – Leo Scafa – says she is a very quick learner. He had to teach her how to write, would you believe, but she's hopeless at maths, so it seems.'

Beppe took himself off to Picciano before lunch and went to visit Adelina in the *Olivo Nero,* the old archivist and his sister – and finally, Don Pietro, the parish priest.

Beppe satisfied himself that the little community was settling back to its former simple lifestyle. The fate of Don Giulio's mafia-financed mansion was still undecided by the authorities. It had already been sequestered.

There was only one more excursion that Beppe, Sonia and children needed to undertake together. He could not – and did not want to – avoid the visit.

'We are going to go and spend the day with Mariastella in her country house - near Pianella, she tells me.'

Beppe explained in great detail to Sonia under what circumstances the *Questore's* invitation had come about. Sonia laughed uproariously.

'And you believed her, Beppe?' she said. 'You still have a lot to learn about that woman. She has many layers. But a sexual preference for other women is not one of them! She was testing you, Beppe!'

'How would you know that, *amore?*' asked Beppe crossly.

'Because I am a woman, of course.'

Sonia's analysis turned out to be accurate. While Veronica spent hours riding around bare-back on a donkey in the large country estate and Lorenzo spent two hours in the swimming pool with his mother and Giorgia, Mariastella Martellini took Beppe to one side.

'I'm sorry I wound you up, Beppe. I simply could not resist it. I have an awfully wicked side to my character and cannot help exploiting it sometimes – especially on men whom I am fond of. It's as if I have to put their character to the test. The real truth is, I cannot have children. I have known this for ages. As soon as I set eyes on Giorgia Scarpa, she felt just like the daughter I could never have. We simply meld together like magic – like mother and daughter. I felt so envious of you and Sonia with your two extraordinarily loveable children. I guess it was my baser nature at work when I led you to believe I was having an affair with Giorgia. I was putting you to the test ... and you passed with flying colours – as usual!'

He tried out his hard, unblinking stare at his chief – but she merely giggled at the feeble attempt. So he gave up and hugged her instead.

'Stop, Beppe!' she protested, pushing him away. 'I am beginning to expect to be hugged by you, you know?'

Beppe would not allow himself to be taken in again.

'Thank you for inviting us today, Mariastella. You live in the most spectacularly beautiful place...'

'Daddy's money,' she said.

'And the Spanish pilot-boyfriend, Mariastella? Was *he* an invention too?'

'No, I am happy to say. He is a gorgeous man who I am really in love with. You will meet him one day, I am sure. We intend to adopt children soon – before we grow too much older.'

Beppe looked and felt pleased for his chief. But she had not finished talking.

'I have to tell you this, Beppe, because I was approached by the authorities and invited to talk to you about a project you might want to consider.'

'Not another investigation involving the mafia, PLEASE!'

'No, *commissario*. It's worse than that, I'm afraid. They are looking for someone suitable to appoint as *Questore* in Teramo. They would like you to consider applying.'

Beppe felt his stomach falling away from the rest of his body. He became aware that his mouth was open.

'Teramo is actually nearer Atri than Pescara, Beppe. You might like to consider it. There! I have done my duty. Let's go and have lunch – outside in the shade of the oak trees.'

Beppe wanted to accuse Mariastella of winding him up yet again. But he knew the post of *Questore* in Teramo was real.

They met Sonia, Giorgia and Lorenzo emerging from the swimming pool. The donkey had grown weary of walking around the estate with Veronica on its back and dutifully delivered her back at the house, refusing to budge until Veronica had reluctantly dismounted.

Beppe was looking almost lasciviously at Sonia as she climbed out of the pool with her figure-hugging bikini barely concealing her breasts. He had a sudden vision – just like Don Emanuele had had all those years ago outside the Cathedral. She *was* expecting their third child. Maybe he knew it before she did this time?

Something of the Archbishop's mysterious powers must have finally rubbed off on him. Or was he just being fanciful?

* * *

'I have a difficult decision to make, *amore.*'

He told Sonia what Mariastella had said to him a few hours previously.

'No, you don't, Beppe!' she replied ambiguously. 'And I have some news to tell you, *amore…*'

'No, you don't, Sonia!' replied Beppe smugly.

'*Mamma?*' exclaimed Lorenzo from his child seat in the rear of the car. Veronica had dozed off.

Whilst driving home to Atri, Beppe was thinking how ambiguous Don Emanuele's words to Giorgia had been. Beppe had merely assumed that they meant she would quickly find another partner. But, at least, it was true that Giorgia was no longer a solitary soul, he reasoned. For the rest, only time would tell…

About the author

Richard Walmsley's novels reflect his dedication to and love of that extraordinary part of Europe called Italy – especially to Puglia, where he lived, loved and taught English to students of the Università del Salento (Lecce) and to Abruzzo – one of the most unspoilt regions of Europe – where many of his novels are set.

Richard Walmsley decries and utterly rejects the devastating political and cultural alienation of the not very United Kingdom from its European partners, whose history and culture we have shared for centuries.

He believes firmly that our ties with Europe MUST survive the political catastrophe that is commonly nicknamed 'Brexit'.

'The biggest example of political self-harm that has ever been perpetrated in our name!' he is fond of quoting.

He hopes that his novels will revive that feeling of oneness with the European Continent – with his series of colourful, entertaining and humorous stories, inspired by Italy and its remarkable citizens. He wishes to thank all those people who have enjoyed his novels – and especially to those who have helped and encouraged him to write them.

April 2022

Printed in Great Britain
by Amazon

20366826R00190